THE UNDERCOVER HEIRESS OF BROCKTON

ENDURING HOPE
BOOK TWO

KELLY J. GOSHORN

The Undercover Heiress of Brockton ©2025 by Kelly J. Goshorn

Print ISBN 979-8-89151-177-4
Adobe Digital Edition (.epub) 979-8-89151-178-1

All scripture quotations, unless otherwise noted, are taken from the King James Version of the Bible.

This book is a work of fiction. Names, characters, places, and incidents are either products of the author's imagination or used fictitiously. Any similarity to actual people, organizations, and/or events is purely coincidental.

Cover image © Kirk DouPonce, DogEared Design

Published by Barbour Publishing, Inc., 1810 Barbour Drive, Uhrichsville, Ohio 44683, www.barbourbooks.com

Our mission is to inspire the world with the life-changing message of the Bible.

Printed in the United States of America.

Praise for *The Undercover Heiress of Brockton*

"Set against the backdrop of a terrible tragedy, *The Undercover Heiress of Brockton* brings a story that will leave readers in awe of the human spirit, swooning and rooting for love, and deeply moved by the truths God speaks. The story of Etta, Leo, and the town of Brockton will be one that lingers in the mind for a long time, and definitely one to revisit again and again. You're not going to want to miss this moving and delightful read."

–Crystal Caudill, Christy Award-winning
author of *Written in Secret*

"With intrigue, danger, and toe-curling romance, Kelly Goshorn hits all the right notes in this beautifully crafted tale. *The Undercover Heiress of Brockton* snagged my attention from the very beginning and didn't let go. With a dashing fireman as a hero and a woman with a secret identity, what's not to love? A sparkling historical romance!"

–Tara Johnson, Christy and Carol Award
nominee of *Engraved on the Heart*

"Set against the backdrop of the historical Brockton shoe factory explosion, *The Undercover Heiress of Brockton* delivers a gently unfolding romance between a heroic fireman and a spirited heroine with secrets. Goshorn brings history to life with heart, grace, and an honest, authentic faith that never feels forced. With wonderfully drawn characters, an emotionally satisfying plot, and a charming setting, this novel will make you smile and settle in from the very first page. A lovely, hope-filled read for fans of Crystal Caudill and Karen Witemeyer."

–Kimberly Duffy, author of *The Weight of Air*
and *The Meet-Cute Manuscript*

DEDICATION

To my daughter Madeline, whose confident, independent spirit inspired my heroine Henrietta Maxwell.

And to every sweet Jesus-lovin' sister who "marches to the beat of her own drum," may you wholeheartedly embrace the woman God has created you to be.

As every man hath received the gift,
even so minister the same one to another,
as good stewards of the manifold grace of God.
1 Peter 4:10

"From the darkness comes light; from death springs up eternity. . ."
The Brockton Times, March 24, 1905

CHAPTER 1

Brockton, Massachusetts
March 15, 1905

Henrietta Maxwell shoved her spectacles higher on the bridge of her nose and summoned her courage as she stared at the giant silver maple towering above her. She could do this. After all, she'd climbed trees in her grandfather's garden on numerous occasions, much to her grandmother's consternation. At five feet eleven inches, climbing trees was the only advantage she'd discovered for her unusual height.

She tugged the men's leather riding gloves snug to her fingers. Grasping the lower bough, she pulled herself onto the sturdy limb and scaled the maple. The absence of leaves this early in spring aided her ascent but provided scant refuge from discovery. She hoped the tree's location behind Bonner Insurance would assist her efforts in evading detection.

Finding a secure spot in the fork of the branches beneath the second-floor window, she sank low into the split and scratched the factitious mustache she sported above her lip. She smoothed her fingers over her bushy false eyebrows, thankful her fellow boarder, Milton Rhoades, was a retired vaudeville actor who could fashion her a top-notch disguise.

Etta glanced at the gold watch dangling from a chain attached to the band of her knickers. While men's clothing may lack style and sophistication, they cornered the market on comfort and functionality. She plucked her notepad and pencil from the shirt pocket beneath her vest.

Her informant, a fireman from Engine Company No. 3, had told her about a possible meeting between members of the Bonner crime family and the deputy fire commissioner, John Nilsson. After three fires in as many months, the business community was on edge. Reports in the rival *Brockton Times* indicated the fires were random flukes, but scuttlebutt on the street indicated someone wanted downtown businessmen to purchase fire insurance from the Bonner Insurance Company, owned and operated by Lars Bonner, the younger brother of Karl Bonner, a known racketeer.

If her informant was correct, this would be the scoop of the decade—the big story Etta needed to convince her boss at the city desk that she deserved her own byline. She was as good, if not better than, any male journalist at the *Brockton Enterprise*, but a condition of her employment required her to conceal her identity behind the moniker Henry Mason or face termination. Only one thing rankled Etta more than concealing her true identity—unethical government officials who took advantage of the public trust.

The low rumble of voices in the office above triggered Etta's curiosity. Carefully, she raised her head until her eyes were flush with the window sash. Heart racing, she squinted through her glasses and jotted down the names of every man she recognized. The Bonner brothers were the first to enter, followed by Nilsson and a stocky man with blond hair who guarded the door. The latter's left hand sported a white bandage.

From what she could tell, her informant had been spot-on. Seeing Nilsson with the Bonner brothers was suspicious, but it didn't prove anything. The deputy fire commissioner could claim he was purchasing insurance for his private residence. If only she could hear what they were saying.

She stuck the pencil behind her ear, closed the notepad, and wedged it in the pocket of her breeches. Although the branch thinned closer to the building, she ducked low and scooted toward the window.

Just when the assembly looked promising, Nilsson rose and abruptly left the office. Etta tapped her finger against her lips. *Now what?* The Bonner brothers by themselves didn't make a story, let alone a conspiracy. While she pondered whether or not her informant may have sent her chasing a wild hair, the guard stepped aside, and another gentleman, dressed in a fine suit, entered.

Slack-jawed, she stared through the glass. Anders Bergstrom, the ward boss for the Campello District, joined the meeting—and Etta sensed her byline getting closer by the minute.

DEPUTY FIRE COMMISSIONER NILSSON DENIES ARSON TO BLAME

Leo Eriksson scoffed at the headline in the *Brockton Times.* He might not be a deputy fire commissioner, but even he knew the odds were slim that three fires plaguing lucrative downtown businesses since January were unrelated. Word around the firehouse said Nilsson had his sights on the commissioner's job come election time. The last thing he'd want is to let the public think his department couldn't keep his constituents safe.

He shoved the paper aside and swiped his toast in the yolk of his over-easy eggs. A few blocks from both his home and the Campello fire station, the Drake Tavern provided the mainstay of the daily diet for him, his brother Jens, and his father, none of whom could prepare much more than a sandwich for themselves. All three preferred to leave even that simple task to the Drake's cook. Leo's brother Gunnar, on the other hand, had married a delightful woman who often took pity on her husband's bachelor family by preparing a delicious home-cooked meal for them.

"Hey, Leo." Gunnar slid into the booth across from him.

"You're late." Leo shoved the last bite of toast in his mouth. "Got tired of waiting."

Gunnar grabbed Leo's cup and swigged the last of his lukewarm coffee. "You see the paper this morning?"

"Only the *Times.*" Leo shook his head and pointed to the front-page article. "The reporters for that rag couldn't find a story if you wrote the column and hand-delivered it."

"Someone's on the take."

Another one of his brother's conspiracy theories. Leo rolled his eyes. "What are you talking about?"

"Dad got a look at the official report for the second fire."

"The one at Brockton Hardware?"

He nodded, then scanned the diner. "It was doctored."

Leo leaned closer. "Dad's positive?"

"Yeah, it made no mention of the match we found in the waste receptacle or the narrow *V* on the wall above it that proved the fire's origin and how fast it burned."

Leo leaned against the booth. "What's he gonna do?"

"He's not sure." Gunnar's gaze darted to the aisle. "Dora Clark's coming this way."

"Good morning, fellas." A smile stretched the width of Dora's face. "I got the job at Grover's Shoes. I start on Monday."

Leo wiped his mouth with the cloth napkin then congratulated his childhood friend. The Clarks were struggling to pay the medical bills following their daughter's emergency surgery a few months back, and Leo had been happy to put in a good word for Dora with one of the plant managers.

Her eyes glistened as she clasped Leo's forearm. "I couldn't have done it without your reference. We'll be able to keep the house. Can't thank you enough."

"Always happy to help, Dora. Give my best to your husband."

"Will do, Leo." She turned away, heels clacking in rhythm with the soft hum of conversations floating in the diner.

Leo rose from the table and pulled a dime from his pocket. "I'd better go. I like to be *on time*, little brother."

He glanced at their waitress behind the counter. "Thanks for breakfast. Excellent as always."

Eva cocked her head, blue eyes sparkling. "You've always been my favorite customer, Leo."

Was Eva Torberg flirting with him?

Probably not. Who'd want a worn-out old man like him?

At thirty, he'd spent the better part of his youth fighting fires and rescuing cats from trees. He loved the job. It was in his blood. Not only was his father the captain of Engine Company No. 1 in downtown Brockton, his brothers were firefighters too. They were the first ones called to render aid to those in need. From accidents involving automobiles to a child trapped in a well to the sad work of dredging the lake for old Mr. Maxwell, who'd wandered off and fallen through the thin ice a few winters back, the community counted on the men of Engine Company No. 1.

Mayor Keith waved Leo over. "Just the Eriksson I wanted to see. Take a seat, young man."

Leo glanced at his watch. "I need to report in at nine sharp."

"Fine. Fine." The mayor folded his newspaper. "This will only take a minute. That leaves you eight to walk less than a block."

Leo sighed. He hated being late. But there was no use arguing. That would only eat up more time. He tugged the chair from beneath the table and seated himself across from the mayor. "How can I help you, sir?"

"I want to know your thoughts about the fires downtown. The reporter from the *Times* seems to think they're all just a coincidence. Has your department found any evidence otherwise?"

"You should speak to Pops about that, sir. He's running the inquest."

"So you do suspect arson?"

"I didn't say that, sir. We're still investigating."

The mayor's dark eyes bore into him, and Leo tensed. "If you want to know more, ask my father to brief you." He stood and touched the brim of his cap. "Good day to you, Mayor."

Bells jingled when Leo exited the Drake. According to Gunnar, someone had deliberately tampered with the report Pops submitted. But who? And how did the reporter from *The Brockton Times* learn the fire commissioner ruled out arson when the department hadn't been informed yet? Was someone feeding false information to the press to keep the businessmen in town from panicking until the commissioner identified a motive and a suspect? Or was something more nefarious going on?

"Hey, what are you doing up there?"

Startled, Etta jerked upright. The branch bowed, knocking her off balance. Her notepad careened into the alley below. She gasped and scrambled to keep her opossum-like hold to the underside of the flapping limb. *Don't look down, Etta. Whatever you do, don't look down.*

"I'm fine." Her voice warbled. She cleared her throat and tried again, this time deepening the tone. "I'm fine." At least she hoped she was fine. "I know what I'm doing." If she could wrap her legs around the thickest part of the branch, she just might be able to shimmy to safety.

"Not trying to argue," the stranger called back, "but from my vantage point you look in dire straits."

Really? His powers of observation astounded Etta. "I can. . .manage," she responded, stretching her left foot.

"Hang on, I'm coming."

What? "No. . .I'll be fine." While she appreciated the gesture, the bobbing branch wouldn't sustain her weight long enough for him to render assistance.

Her pulse hammered in her ears. With a quick *please, God*, she squeezed the offshoot between her thighs, loosened her viselike hold, and wriggled toward the trunk.

Crack!

The limb snapped from the tree. Arms flailing, Etta grunted as her body ricocheted from one branch to the next, her nails tearing at the bark. She slammed into the stranger, jarring her spectacles loose. The pair hurled into the azalea hedge before landing in a bed of daffodils. A freshly manured bed of daffodils, if the odiferous scent assaulting her nostrils was any indication.

"If you don't mind," the stranger groaned beneath her, "you can get off me now."

Etta blinked rapidly as umber eyes, wide as you please, stared back at her. Umber eyes she recognized as belonging to the most heroic member of the town's esteemed fire department.

"Oh. . .um. . .certainly." She scrambled to her feet.

"Leo Eriksson." He stood and swiped dirt and manure from his uniform. "I'm a fireman here at Company No. 1."

"Henry Mason." Etta stepped forward, and a crunch sounded beneath her heel. *Not her spectacles.* She lifted her polished Emerson shoe and squinted at the mangled wireframes and broken glass. With eyesight so poor a bat took pity on her, she'd now have to amble about town trying to find her way home.

"You're Henry Mason? The reporter for the *Brockton Enterprise*?"

Proud her reputation preceded her, Etta stood a little straighter—until it became evident she had more than an inch on the handsome fireman. *Handsome? Keep your wits about you. You're Henry Mason, investigating possible corruption in the fire department and city hall. Not to mention, you happen to be dressed like a man.*

Leo leaned closer, and Etta's heart pounded in her chest.

"I may not be the smartest man in town, but there's one thing I know for certain," he said, yanking the false eyebrow from her face. "You're *not* Henry Mason."

Etta shrieked and rubbed the smarting flesh above her eye.

His brows tented in question. "Henrietta Maxwell?"

"Hello, Mr. Eriksson." Stinging tears dampened her lashes.

"I'm so sorry. The uh. . .uh. . ." He held out the bushy swath of faux hair. "Your eyebrow was askew, so I reasoned something was awry. Please accept my apologies. If I'd known you were behind the disguise, Miss Maxwell, I'd never have ripped it off."

She lifted her palm. "It's not your fault."

Leo guided her farther down the alley. "Wait here."

He returned a few moments later with a wet rag. A large black and white dog trailed behind him.

"You brought a friend with you."

Leo glanced at the canine. "That's Wilson. He's trained to position the horses when we have a rollout."

"May I?" he asked, holding up the cloth. "It will ease the stinging sensation and reduce the swelling."

She nodded, and Leo stepped closer. He cradled her neck in the palm of one hand while gently pressing the cloth against her brow with the other, which triggered an uptick in her pulse.

"Mind if I ask why the heiress of the Maxwell fortune is impersonating an award-winning journalist for the *Brockton Enterprise*?"

Inches away from her now, his warm breath tickled her cheek and she'd nearly forgotten the pain pulsating above her eye. She should distance herself—to concentrate, but her treasonous feet wouldn't budge.

Disclosing the truth meant risking everything she'd worked so hard to achieve the last five years. Although he appeared intelligent and kind, admirable traits in a man, what did she really know of Leo Eriksson? Was he loyal? If she confided in him, would he keep her secret?

"Miss Maxwell?" His brown eyes questioned her. "Why is a Boston socialite concealed in men's clothing climbing a tree behind the Bonner Insurance Company?"

"I'm. . ." Her thick tongue struggled to form the words. She swallowed and tried again. "I'm Henry Mason."

"But Henry Mason is a—" His gaze traveled the length of her slim frame, taking in her tweed cap, argyle sweater, and gaberdine knickerbockers. Then, mouth agape, he stepped away.

She fought the urge to close his unhinged jaw. "It's true, Mr. Eriksson. I'm Henry Mason."

"But how? Why?"

"I'll answer your questions if you promise to keep my true identity secret. No one can know Etta Maxwell is Henry Mason."

"I'm not sure I'm comfortable with participating in your ruse. People count on Henry to get the facts right and hold our government officials accountable."

"That's why I need your help. My editor doesn't believe readers will have faith in my reporting if I write as a female. A condition of my employment is that Henry's identity cannot be compromised. If the city desk manager finds out you know the truth, he'll fire me quicker than you can say 'yesterday's news.'"

Leo glanced toward her prior roost beneath the upstairs window of Bonner Insurance. "Tell me what you were doing in that tree that was worth risking your neck over."

"Working on a story."

His flat expression informed Etta he'd already guessed as much. She eyed the attractive fireman. Should she risk confiding that she was investigating the string of downtown fires as possible arsons for hire? Then again, he already knew her most precious secret.

She forced a heavy breath from her lungs. "An informant gave me a tip that the Bonners are running an insurance scheme related to the fires in the Campello District and that some pretty big fish from city hall might have their hands dirty as well."

"That sounds dangerous."

"Not if you keep my identity and my investigation to yourself. You can't say a word, not even to your family."

She extended her hand. "What do you say, Mr. Eriksson? Can I count on you?"

He scraped his palm over his face. "How about we work together? Swap information and find out who's behind these fires before someone gets killed?"

"If we're going to partner in this investigation, let's do away with the formalities. When I'm not dressed as Henry Mason, I'd appreciate you calling me Etta. May I call you Leo?"

He hesitated. Heat flushed her cheeks. She'd probably way overstepped the bounds of polite society—again.

"My apologies for putting you on the spot, Mr. Eriksson. As Henry Mason, I work in a male-dominated profession and feel more comfortable addressing men less formally than most women."

"No, no. Please, call me Leo."

"Wonderful. And you'll tell no one that I'm Henry Mason?"

"Your secret is safe with me." He offered his hand, and they shook on the deal.

Once again, her pulse took notice of his touch. She was no longer sure if she'd agreed to the bargain with Leo to keep Henry Mason's identity concealed and further her investigation or simply to spend more time with the brave fireman who'd risked his life trying to rescue her grandfather from the icy water three winters ago. But of one thing Etta was certain: Leo Eriksson stirred a deep longing inside her, a longing that went against her independent nature.

And she intended to use every investigative skill in her repertoire to discover why.

CHAPTER 2

Although Etta was wearing men's clothing, there was no mistaking the jolt that shot through Leo, recalling similar sensations when he'd danced with her at the Fireman's Ball last spring.

"Mr. Eriksson?"

Despite the fact she stood more than an inch taller than he did, there was something about the eccentric heiress that drew him to her. *The Brockton Times* reported that she'd left the luxury of her Boston home to strike out independently, something completely unheard of by a woman, no matter what social background she came from. Now it made sense to Leo why little was known of Miss Maxwell unless she popped up in the society column for donating to her favorite charity, the Brockton Fire Department.

"Mr. Eriksson, you can let go of my hand now."

For the love of Pete, had he lost all scruples? He wiped his moist palms against his dark blue shirt. "Sorry."

"May I have my false eyebrow, please? I may be able to reuse that."

"Oh, um, sure. Here you go," he said, offering it to her. "That's a mighty impressive outfit. If your eyebrow hadn't slipped out of place, I wouldn't have recognized you."

"That's good to know." She licked her thumb, rubbed the back side of the postiche, and reattached it above her eye. "How does that look?"

He squinted and shook his head. "May I?"

"Yes, please."

Leo moved closer and, once again, gently placed his hand at the back of her neck and realigned the bushy strip of hair. His pulse quickened. What was it about *this* woman? Cognizant of their proximity, and unsure if his breakfast made his breath reek, he reluctantly stepped away and examined his work. "Much better."

"Thank you." Their gazes locked, and Leo sensed his attraction might not be one-sided. However, the image in his mind didn't match the knickerbocker-clad woman standing in front of him.

"Have you seen my notebook?" Etta held up her fingers and demonstrated the length and width of the tablet. "I dropped it when I fell from the tree." She stepped to the flower bed and dug through the azaleas. "It must be here somewhere."

Before he could assist her in the search, she stooped behind the bush. "Found it." She held up the small tablet, and some dirt fell from within its pages, decorating her nose.

She was the most peculiar woman he'd ever met. Not that Leo could attest to knowing many women, let alone what made them tick—especially after Annika broke his heart. He'd given up on the idea of a family to call his own. But something about Miss Maxwell made his pulse skitter.

Ah, you're a fool, Eriksson. She may be independent-minded, but she comes from a very different world. There's no way Clyde Maxwell would ever let a Brockton firefighter pursue his daughter's hand.

Etta cleared her throat. "I'm glad to hear you think the fires are arson as well. That piece in the *Times* today doesn't square with what I'm learning."

"Nor with what my father has discovered. Someone must have leaked a falsified report."

"When and where can we meet to compare notes on the investigation?"

"Wanna go inside the firehouse now, Miss Maxwell?" *Firehouse*. Leo thunked his palm against his forehead.

"Is something wrong, Mr. Eriksson?"

"I'm late. Roll call was five minutes ago." If he hurried, he could still beat Gunnar, and his younger brother would never be the wiser. "Oh, and you should probably call me Leo when you're Henry Mason."

"Right. Thanks for the reminder. How about the park off Denton Street after your meeting?"

"Fine. Give me an hour."

Gunnar turned the corner. Leo shook his head.

"Is something wrong Mr. Er—uh, Leo?"

"Just my brother headed this way. I'll get some good-natured ribbing for being late."

"Sorry about that. I should go. Remember, mum's the word about who I am."

"Your secret is safe with me."

She hurried past Gunnar and crossed Calmar Street. His brother draped his arm around Leo's shoulders and chuckled. "Looks like I won't be the only one receiving Pops' ire for being late this morning."

"Yeah, but you'll be blamed for dragging me down. He'll think you're a bad influence on me."

Gunnar punched his arm. "Who's that?" he asked, nodding toward Etta.

"Henry Mason."

"The reporter for the *Enterprise*?"

"The same. He fell outta that tree. I made sure he was all right."

"What was he doing up there?"

"I really can't say."

Leo opened the door to the station and whistled for Wilson to follow him inside. "C'mon. We can't put it off any longer."

Etta found a bench in the park facing the duck pond and lowered herself onto the seat. Her bum ached a bit. No doubt she'd have more than a few bruises and stiff muscles from her mishap today. She flipped open her notebook and sniffed the pages then her vest. Manure. The foul smell lingered. Oh well, nothing could be done about that now. Leo should be arriving any minute.

A light breeze blew a piece of hair across her cheek. She'd given no thought to whether her hair remained tucked in her cap. Etta glanced over her shoulder. No children played nearby, and no nannies pushed prams with their charges nestled inside. With the coast presumably clear, she removed her cap and repinned her hair.

She reclined against the back of the bench and stretched her long legs in front of her, crossing her light brown Emersons at the ankle. Despite her costume malfunction earlier, her disguise, coupled with tips from Milton on how to act like a man, had grown Etta's confidence and allowed her to pursue her dream of being a front-page reporter with her own byline. All she needed was to break the perfect story—a story like corruption in city hall—to make that dream a reality.

Masquerading as a male journalist gave her a new appreciation for the opposite sex. They certainly required fewer words and emotions to form meaningful relationships. They also appeared to understand the concept of spending time together without expectations. Some kerfuffle always seemed to rear its ugly head when her fellow society ladies were together.

Her editor at *The Gilded Gown*, a lady's social magazine for Boston's elite, wanted her to write fluff pieces about garden clubs, society marriages, and any scandal she could unearth about the Boston set. She had little interest in her *Gilded Gown* column, but it served its purpose by allowing her to get the job with the *Enterprise*. It also paid for her room at the boardinghouse, ensuring her independence. When the press learned of her unusual living arrangement, she made another appearance in the society columns, and the label "eccentric" became attached to every future mention of her name.

Leo slid onto the opposite end of the bench.

Remembering the tips Milton shared with her about male idiosyncrasies compared to those of females, she lifted her chin in acknowledgment.

He stretched his arm along the back of the bench.

Etta tapped the copy of *The Brockton Times* sandwiched between them. She hated supporting that rag, but the newsboy for the *Enterprise* was nowhere to be seen, and the prop was necessary for the illusion she wanted to create for any passersby: just two fellas sharing opposite ends of a park bench.

"Act like you're reading it," she said.

Leo picked up the paper. "No one's around."

"Not now, but since we'll be meeting regularly to share information, let's establish good habits."

"Sure." He opened the newspaper to one of the inside columns and crossed his ankle over his knee. "Who was in the meeting that would make you climb a tree to get a good look?"

He cut right to the chase. She appreciated that about male communication. Women tended to talk around the subject, often weaving subtle syntax and subtext into their conversation that even an accomplished knitter couldn't unravel.

"If you don't mind, I'd like to ask the first question and weigh your answer. No offense. I just want to make sure you're being on the up-and-up with me."

"Fair enough. What's your question?"

"What makes you certain the fire at Brockton Hardware was an arson? Do you have any thoughts on who would've leaked false information to the *Times*?"

Leo shook his head. "That's two questions, Miss Maxwell."

"Henry," she corrected. Besides the misstep with her name, he'd shown himself to be a clever man. She'd hoped to pepper *him* with questions and learn more information than she relayed.

"My brothers, father, and I were on the scene at the hardware store, and Pops did the investigation report for all three fires." He turned the page of the broadsheet. "There was a match in one of the trash cans, and the soot marks on the wall indicate that was the fire's origin."

Etta made a mental note of the information to jot down in her tablet later. Even though Leo knew of her disguise, keeping her hands hidden (her biggest point of vulnerability) was a rule not worth breaking. She opened her mouth to ask another question, but Leo managed to speak his first.

"Tell me why climbing that tree was so important. Whom did you observe, and how did you know there was a meeting?"

"That's two questions, *Mr. Eriksson*."

He grinned. "So, it was."

His eyes sparkled. *Stay focused, Etta. You're Henry Mason, ace reporter for the* Brockton Enterprise, *not a smitten young lass.*

"I have an anonymous source who tipped me off to a meeting between the Bonner brothers and some city officials."

Leo turned to a new page. "And?"

Etta leaned forward and rested her elbows on her knees. "My source was correct. There were some important suits in the meeting."

"Suits who might have a vested interest in ruining my father's reputation and that of Engine Company No. 1?"

"Possibly, yes." She glanced at Leo. "Any way you can get me a copy of those arson reports?"

"I can do that—"

"Wonderful. How soon—"

"Can you tell me if the commissioner was in the meeting?" he interjected.

"I'm not comfortable naming names at this point, Leo. Just tell your father to watch his back. Please send the reports to the attention of Henry Mason at the *Brockton Enterprise*."

"I can bring them by this evening. My shift is over at nine."

"No. Mail them. It will take a few more days, but we don't want anyone at the *Enterprise* knowing you're my source. And don't forget to seal the envelope. That way I'll know that no one has seen them but me."

She rubbed the fine hair of the false mustache above her lip. "What if I need to get in touch with you with additional questions? Can I send mail to the firehouse?"

"Yes. I also eat three squares at the Drake Tavern."

"Excellent. I'll be in touch." She groaned as she stood.

"Are you all right?"

"Yeah, just muscle aches from the fall." She grinned. "Can't imagine how much worse it would be if I hadn't landed on you."

Leo chuckled. "Don't remind me."

Their laughter turned to uncomfortable silence. Uncertain where to cast her gaze, she settled on her feet. "I. . .uh. . .should probably go write my article."

"Oh. . .I. . .should probably return to the firehouse before I need to account for my whereabouts."

"See ya around, Leo."

"Yeah, see ya around, Henry."

Her steps were light and airy as she began the route to the boardinghouse. She liked Leo Eriksson—probably more than she should. However, she would keep him at arm's length. If the arson investigation uncovered evidence that any of the Erikssons were involved, she'd break the story—attraction or not.

CHAPTER 3

Etta skirted into the alley behind Mrs. Hemingway's boardinghouse. Sneaking through the backstreets allowed her to dodge the neighborhood Nosy Nellies, who at midday were most likely busy with tasks around the house. Since she never knew who might be watching from their window while washing dishes, she always took extra precautions. She knew from experience that by evening, the same sweet, gray-haired ladies would procure seats on their porch rockers with glasses of lemonade, ready to watch the comings and goings of acquaintances. How else would they have anything to talk about at the beauty parlor tomorrow?

You're so hypocritical, she chided herself. After all, she wouldn't think twice about plying information from them if necessary for one of her articles.

She nearly tripped over Midnight, the black alley cat Mrs. Hemingway fed hoping to keep the mice population from exploding. The feline was always underfoot, but without her spectacles, she hadn't properly anticipated the cat's movements.

Etta climbed the stairs to the back porch, pushed open the door, and stepped inside, the squeaky hinge announcing her arrival. The clack of Mrs. Hemingway's shoes brought a sigh of relief. She'd left in a hurry without breakfast, so not only would she have a warm meal waiting, but her landlady would insist on heating water for Etta's bath as soon as she got a whiff of her putrid stench. There was no way she'd let Etta anywhere near her clean linens, and Etta couldn't blame her one bit.

"There you are, Henry. I've kept a plate warm on the back of. . ." She stopped and sniffed the air before leaning closer. "I'm not sure why you smell like a cow patch, but I'll heat some water immediately. You are to scrub from head to toe, young man."

Etta appreciated how Mrs. Hemingway referred to her as Henry even when no one was around. She took her promise to guard Etta's alternate identity seriously, but she wasn't the only one who knew her secret. So did her editor, William Littleton, who approved the entire ruse. Add Leo Eriksson to the mix, and the list of people who knew that Henry Mason was, in truth, Henrietta Maxwell had grown to three. She could only pray each would keep their word and not reveal her true identity. Fortunately, she'd never revealed to Milton why she sought his assistance, and the large sum of money she'd paid him seemed to squelch his curiosity.

She crossed her fingers over her heart. "I promise."

Mrs. Hemingway waggled a crooked finger, a playful grin brightening her face. "You'd better. Now have a seat." She placed a warm dish in front of Etta—roast beef and gravy, mashed potatoes, and green beans. "I'll get the water heating."

Etta blessed her meal and thanked God for the umpteenth time that week for Mrs. Hemingway. Although Etta wanted to be a modern, independent woman, she'd starve to death if she tried to prepare her own meals—something she had in common with Leo.

Famished, she grabbed her fork and knife and cut into the tender meat. After devouring most of her meal, she tugged her notepad from the pocket inside her vest and flipped the small cover open. She could barely decipher her own scribbling. Without her glasses, she'd been lucky to connect pencil and paper. Writing on the lines was clearly beyond her blurry-eyed capabilities. Fortunately, her second pair of glasses were tucked away in her desk drawer upstairs.

"If you're finished there, you could carry one of the buckets of water upstairs, and I'll bring the other."

"Certainly." Although it was customary for a boardinghouse matron to carry the water, Mrs. Hemingway was getting on in years and Etta always did what she could to lighten her landlady's burden.

Etta took the large bucket and led the way through the hall and up the stairs so Mrs. Hemingway wouldn't feel rushed. When she finally reached the hall bath shared by all the boarders, she slowly poured the hot water into the large porcelain tub.

Mrs. Hemingway grabbed the empty buckets. "Thank you," she said, straining to give breath to her words. "I'll be back in ten minutes with a kettle to warm the water a bit."

Etta nodded her thanks and ventured to her room to retrieve a clean blouse, skirt, and underthings before returning to the bathroom and locking the door. Mrs. Hemingway would use her key when she brought the kettle to warm her bath. She unpinned her hair and slipped out of her clothes before stepping into the tub. The hot water tingled against her bare toes. She wiggled them in the water then eased herself to a sitting position.

She untucked her long hair from behind her shoulders, allowing it to hang over the back of the tub. The hot water soothed her aching muscles. Etta relaxed, and her mind revisited all she'd learned this morning. A string of questions flooded her thoughts. What was the Campello District ward boss doing in a meeting with the Bonner brothers? Her informant indicated some kind of insurance kickback scheme. Anders Bergstrom did own two jewelry stores. But even though one was downtown, it lay outside a reasonable proximity to the current arsons. Were they considering expanding their territory, or was Bergstrom just looking to purchase insurance? It had to be more than that, didn't it?

Something didn't make sense to Etta. Why would Nilsson, who was running for fire commissioner in the November election, be involved in a string of suspicious fires? Wouldn't that hurt his chances? Would he risk setting the fires himself? Or had he been advising the Bonners on how to cover their tracks and then falsify reports? She still possessed many more questions than answers, which always led her to believe a story was worth pursuing.

Etta groaned. She had two articles dueling for her attention—the piece for the *Enterprise* countering the *Times'* assertion the fire wasn't arson, and the article for *The Gilded Gown* about the Worthingtons' spring ball. Needless to say, the latter held little interest for her.

She gulped a breath of air and slid beneath the water. When her lungs burned, she resurfaced, soaped the wash rag, and scrubbed her arms and legs while mulling over the arson investigation. The report she needed to prove the fires had been intentionally set was written by Leo's father, Petter Eriksson.

Leo had at least one brother who was also a firefighter with Engine Company No. 1. With at least three family members stationed in one firehouse, they could cover for each other much too easily.

Just because Leo rescued her grandfather, she shouldn't assume he was a straight shooter. She hated to think he could be involved in any of this, but she would make sure of his character—and that of his entire family—before sharing any more information with him.

Although her instincts told her the family was on the up-and-up, she'd stop by the firehouse in the morning and see what she could learn about the Erikssons. Sloppy investigating would not result in a coveted byline, and she didn't intend to derail this opportunity with a rookie mistake.

Leo slid into his usual booth at the Drake. His stomach grumbled to life at the smell of eggs and bacon.

"Your usual?" Eva asked as she poured a cup of steaming coffee into his white porcelain cup.

"You know me well."

"For a firefighter, you sure don't take many risks, do you?"

"Nah. There's enough on the job."

"Your dad or Jens joining you this morning?"

He checked the time. "They should be here already."

"Okay, I'll tell Cook to scramble some eggs for them too." She smiled a little too brightly at him. "I'll be right back with *your* order."

Leo sipped the steaming brew. Eva was a sweet gal, and he hoped she found a nice fella to settle down with, but it wasn't him. There was no spark, no electricity, when she came near. Unlike his interactions with Brockton's unconventional heiress. A little less than twenty-four hours had passed since she'd fallen out of that tree and into his life—again.

They'd only shared a dance or two at the Fireman's Ball, but he'd never forgotten her. She was attractive, but not in the flamboyant way of most wealthy women. No, she was an independent, modern woman: intelligent, hardworking, and ambitious. And that was exactly what he liked about her. The fact she masqueraded as one of the top reporters in the greater Boston area only added to her list of charming eccentricities.

Leo took another swig of coffee and glanced around the diner. He nearly spit the coffee from his mouth when he spied Etta, er, Henry, sitting with Leif Hansen, one of his fellow firefighters from Engine Company No. 1. If he didn't know that was Henrietta Maxwell, heiress to the Maxwell Foundation, he'd never suspect. Her disguise was excellent.

Their eyes met, and she gave him a curt nod in acknowledgment.

Why was she meeting with Leif? Was she looking for additional information, or did she doubt the facts Leo provided?

The bell on the diner's door gave a tinny greeting. He looked up and waved as his father and Jens entered the tavern.

"Good morning," he said, greeting his family. Jens looked as though Pops had dragged him from the bed moments earlier. Although they lived together, Leo preferred to rise early, while carefree Jens was the night owl of the family.

"You're awfully chipper this morning. How much coffee have you consumed?" Jens lifted his cup, signaling Eva to bring the pot to their table.

"First one, brother. I've already run two miles, showered, and spent some time in the Word."

"You're a blight on the Eriksson name."

Leo reached across the table and tousled his youngest brother's hair. "Someone's got to set an example around here." He glanced at his dad. "I didn't mean that as a slight."

Pops held up his palm. "None taken. You boys have always teased one another."

Now that he knew her whereabouts, Leo couldn't help but seek Etta out again. He was surprised to find her staring at him while interviewing Leif. Leif left the table, and Etta jotted something in a tablet she'd taken from her pocket. Notes of their conversation, perhaps?

Eva placed a delicious-smelling plate of eggs and bacon in front of Leo. Her hand barely let go before Jens snagged a long strip.

"Thanks, brother."

Leo gave Jens a stern look he hoped conveyed his annoyance. Out of the corner of his eye, he saw Etta approach their table.

"Good morning, Chief Eriksson," she said, addressing his father. "I'm Henry Mason, a reporter for the *Brockton Enterprise*. I'm doing a story on the string of suspicious fires here in the Campello District. Could I ask you a few questions?"

Without waiting for an invitation, she slipped into the booth beside Leo. "First, could I get your name and rank?"

Pops eyed her. "Is this on or off the record?"

"You tell me. But if it helps, I'll buy breakfast for the table."

"Works for—"

Pops held up his hand again, and Jens stopped talking.

"I'm Petter Eriksson, battalion chief of Engine Company No. 1." He nodded toward Jens. "The young man with the bottomless pit for a stomach is my youngest son, Jens. I think you're already acquainted with Leo. He told me he met a reporter from the *Enterprise* yesterday who wanted to write a rebuttal piece to the *Times'* article about the arson investigation."

"That would be me."

Eva brought two plates of fried eggs, bacon, and toast. "Leo said to order you the same as him." She looked at Etta. "Do you want anything else?"

"No thanks, but add the Erikssons' bill to my tab."

Eva raised her eyebrows but didn't comment on Henry's big expense.

Etta waited for the waitress to return to the counter. "I spoke with Leo yesterday about indications the fire may be arson. Battalion Chief Eriksson—"

"Chief Eriksson will be fine."

"*Chief* Eriksson, would you mind reviewing the clues you found? In your own words?"

Pops returned his cup to the saucer and recounted all the evidence they'd discovered at Brockton Hardware pointing to arson.

Why was she asking Pops to chronicle the same information? Didn't she trust him? And if she wanted to hear those facts again, why wasn't she taking notes? Come to think of it, she hadn't written anything down while talking to Leif either. She'd waited until he left, then jotted something in her notepad. Perhaps she concentrated more on the conversation if she didn't take notes. Still, she was at greater risk of getting the facts wrong, wasn't she?

When Pops finished, Etta peppered him with more questions about his tenure as a firefighter, if he'd been in charge of other arson investigations, and what kind of training the city provided to determine fire causation. Pops handled it all with straightforward dignity and grace, as he responded to any problem he encountered in his personal or professional life.

Leo's posture stiffened. Was Etta implying that perhaps the men of Engine Company No. 1 weren't qualified to determine arson?

"Do you have time for one more question?"

Pops had barely eaten a bite. Nor had Leo for that matter, but Jens had managed to clean his plate and currently eyed Leo's bacon. He gave a curt shake of his head, daring Jens to take a slice.

"One more, then I need to eat and get to the station."

"Wonderful, thanks. I'm curious about the number of Erikssons serving in Engine Company No. 1. Are there any regulations governing leadership supervising family members? Do you think this strengthens or weakens your company and its determinations in cases such as the Brockton Hardware fire?"

Leo lowered his chin. "What are you implying, Henry?"

"I'm not implying anything. I'm just curious as to whether you or Jens would feel free to disagree with any findings your father makes in his role as battalion chief of Engine Company No. 1."

"My father is the most honest—"

Pops raised his palm again, and Leo held his tongue. "It's a fair question, Leo."

His father's gaze locked on Etta's. "We're not the only firehouse in the city where family members serve together. Firefighting tends to run in the blood. Same with policing, Mr. Mason. So, the answer to your question is no, there are no regulations prohibiting family members from working together in the same station. As to your second question, hopefully my experience and integrity will never make it necessary for Leo, Gunnar, or Jens to ever doubt my judgment."

Etta didn't look Leo's way. Probably for the best. He was furious. How could she insinuate Pops could be bought?

"Any other questions, Mr. Mason?"

"Just one. If you believe the fire at Brockton Hardware was indeed arson, and are prepared to turn in such a report today, who do you suspect gave false information to the *Times* reporter?"

"No comment."

Pops stood and placed some coins on the table to cover his meal and a tip for Eva.

"I offered to cover the bill as a thank-you for your time this morning, Chief Eriksson."

"Thank you, Mr. Mason. But to avoid any appearance of favoritism, I'll pay for my own breakfast and so will my sons." He grabbed his plate and shifted his attention to Leo. "Tell Eva I'll return the plate. See you at the station."

He glanced at Etta. "Feel free to stop by the firehouse if you have more questions, Mr. Mason."

Etta stood and shook Pops' hand. "Thank you, sir."

Leo marveled at his father. How could he allow a reporter to ask questions that suggested he might not be on the up-and-up and not only be polite but invite additional questions? He sure could take a few lessons from his father about grace under fire.

Jens shimmied to the edge of the booth and snagged the last piece of Leo's bacon. He hopped to his feet before Leo could grab his wrist and retrieve the coveted slice. "See you at the station, big brother. Feel free to finish my toast."

Honestly. Leo couldn't really complain. He had no one to blame but himself. When their mother had died fifteen years ago, Jens was only seven and Leo stepped in to fill the void left by her passing. No one could replace her, but Leo did the best he could to keep his brothers in school and out of trouble while Pops worked at the firehouse.

Besides, he didn't have time to fuss over the bacon when another breakfast companion was in his crosshairs.

He turned his ire on Etta, who hastily scribbled notes in her tablet. "What was that all about?"

Using her index finger, she pushed her glasses higher on her nose. "What was what all about?"

"Interrogating my dad like that?"

She ceased her recollecting and turned her attention to him. "I'm a reporter, Leo. That's what I do. I ask hard-hitting questions and write what I hope are pithy stories."

"It was insulting."

"I didn't mean to affront anyone. But the public has the right to know if you, Jens, and Gunnar—I assume that's another brother—can challenge your father's findings if you would ever disagree."

"See, that's what I mean. That's insulting to my dad's reputation. Do you have any idea the hero my father is? He's practically a legend in the Campello District. Not only for his bravery but for his love of this neighborhood and the people who live here. There's nothing he wouldn't do for any one of them if he could."

"Actually, I do know. I spoke with Leif Hansen before interviewing your father. I asked him how he felt about the chief supervising his family and if he believed opportunities for his advancement were hindered by your presence."

"*My* presence?"

"Not yours in particular, but by the chief's sons. And you'll be happy to know he practically glowed like a streetlight when speaking of your father. He recounted several episodes of bravery and courage, but what struck me most was what he said about your dad's leadership."

She flipped back a few pages in her tablet. "Here it is. 'Chief Eriksson demands excellence from his crew, but that's okay with me. Not only because I want to be the best firefighter I can be, but because I know he won't ask anything of me he won't ask of himself. He'll be the first man inside a burning building and the last one out. I never worry he'll leave any one of us behind—blood relation or not.'"

Etta's words smacked Leo in the gut like a sucker punch. Why had he assumed the worst about her? "I think I owe you an apology."

"It's not necessary."

"I jumped to the wrong conclusion about your line of questioning."

"I report the truth to the best of my ability. I'm happy to have such a positive profile of your dad to include in my article and also to guide my investigation. I now know with certainty whom I can trust."

"Thanks, Henry."

She closed her notepad. "But, Leo, if I'd learned the opposite, I would have included that as well—friendship or not."

Leo wasn't sure what to make of that comment. He supposed it was a good thing. It showed Etta to be a person of integrity, like his father, as well as a good journalist who would follow the story wherever it took her—unlike those yellow journalists over at the *Times*.

She peered at him over her glasses. "It's *never* personal."

He nodded. His head knew it wasn't personal, but his heart was a bit shakier on the subject. Where would his loyalties lie if her investigation led her to unfavorable conclusions about the Brockton Fire Department? And worse, what would that do to their budding partnership?

CHAPTER 4

Etta sat in the rear of the Boston Horticultural Society's social hall, the weather too chilly and dreary to allow the group to meet outside. Besides, the gardens still lay dormant from winter's frigidness. Only the bravest of flowers poked their heads above ground this time of year—daffodils, crocuses, and a few hyacinths all teased of the beautiful splendor spring would display before long.

She hunched over her tablet, jotting impressions from the mayor's press meeting earlier that morning regarding the Campello arsons on one side and notes about the garden party on the other. She didn't doubt her excellent memory would fail her on either topic so much as finding the exercise a superb way to endure the mind-numbingly dull lecture on "English Ivy: Friend or Foe?"

Her mother placed a hand on Etta's arm. "Not now, Etta." Her pleading tone snagged Etta's attention. "Please draft your article later. And sit up straight, for heaven's sake, before people begin staring."

Compelled by her deep affection for her mother, Etta straightened her shoulders, pushed her glasses higher on her nose, and feigned attention to the horticulturist's presentation on combatting ivy. If her mother possessed one fault, it was that the opinion of Boston's *beau monde* carried far too much weight for her.

Mother smiled and patted her hand, showing her appreciation. If sitting taller in her chair and counterfeiting interest at tiresome social gatherings was all it took to please her, Etta would happily oblige. After all, her mother must survive in the cutthroat world of Boston high society, where people commented relentlessly on her eccentric daughter.

Mother was the one who convinced Father to permit Etta to move into the boardinghouse in Brockton. The one caveat: She would accompany her mother to the Boston Garden Club meetings and other prominent social events. A well-played hand by her mother.

Not all events were as tedious to Etta as the garden club assemblies. She especially enjoyed gatherings that served a higher purpose than hob-nobbing with Boston's elite, such as those that raised funds for orphanages or the abused women's shelter. That was, after all, how she'd first made Leo's acquaintance.

To tell the truth, she enjoyed the opportunity to wear more feminine attire on occasion. While she didn't splurge on as much frippery as most of her peers, she would purchase a stylish gown at the beginning of each new season. Of course, wearing the same gown to multiple events evoked disapproving smirks from her contemporaries, but Etta shrugged it off. She didn't need or want their approval. She wore their disdain as another fine jewel in her unconventional crown.

Marriage had never been Etta's highest priority. While she did long for a loving marriage and brood of children, Beacon Street ballrooms were not the place to find the kind of man Etta desired. One who loved God, sacrificed himself for the good of others, and who would adore her and their children. Not someone looking for societal connections or money to prop up his failing fortunes. Thankfully, her parents never threatened to take Etta overseas and exchange her inheritance for an aristocratic title like many of the *nouveau riche* were doing to earn their place in Boston society.

Applause jarred Etta from her ponderings. As the speaker stepped from the podium, conversations budded throughout the large room. This was the time she usually found information to sprinkle into her column for *The Gilded Gown*.

Penelope Worthington and her daughter Elizabeth glanced her way. Although their smiles refused to reach their eyes, it was invitation enough for Etta to approach their table.

"Good afternoon, Mrs. Worthington. Liza."

"How are you?" Liza asked, rising. She kissed Etta's right cheek then her left. She regained her seat then patted the chair beside her. "How are you managing in that dreadful boardinghouse?"

"In Campello of all places," Mrs. Worthington added with a flutter of her fan.

Etta squared her shoulders and sat beside her childhood friend.

"Quite well. I'm enjoying my independence."

Mrs. Worthington scoffed but didn't interrupt.

"You don't find the society rather. . .limited?" Liza asked.

Etta laughed. "Well, there isn't a garden club to attend, but I don't mind. Living closer to those we are trying to assist through the Maxwell Foundation has shed great light on where the most significant needs are."

"Pishposh," Mrs. Worthington interjected, waving her hand in the air. "Couldn't you ride out in your father's motorcar each day?"

"Certainly, but living in the community helps me build trust and establish partnerships with local businesses. When I build relationships with Brockton residents, I can better ascertain which individuals or families most need our assistance. Speaking of assistance, I hope I can count on both of you to attend our Fireman's Ball this spring to help raise—"

Mrs. Worthington scanned the room. "Yes, yes, we'll be there. We always support your family's foundation." She reached for Liza's hand. "Come, dear, there's Loretta Harrison. Let's see how her daughter, the duchess, is faring."

Someone touched Etta's elbow, and she turned to see the smiling face of Maeve Fitzgerald, one of her closest childhood friends.

"Maeve." She leaned down and kissed her petite friend's cheek.

"I thought that was you, Etta. It's been much too long."

They sat together, and Maeve eagerly spoke of her children and her summer home on the Cape. Despite her friend's smiles, Etta thought she detected a hint of sadness in Maeve's voice when she shared about her husband Martin's business success, his long hours away from home, and his frequent trips to New York City.

"Enough about me," she said. "Are you enjoying writing for *The Gilded Gown*? I always look forward to your column." Her gaze darted to the side of the room, and her joyful expression became circumspect.

Etta glanced in the same direction in time to witness the scowl on Maeve's mother's face, accompanied by a tight shake of her head.

Maeve squeezed her hand. "I'm so glad we could visit today. I promised my mother I'd invite Mrs. Harrison and her daughter for a game of bridge when the duchess visits from England next month. I should do that before I forget." She pursed her lips. "I'd invite you, Etta, but you're a modern working woman with no time for such frivolities."

Her friend stood, and Etta followed suit. "Hopefully, I'll see you at next month's garden club meeting," Maeve said.

Etta nodded and watched as Maeve made her way to her mother, who was engaged in conversation with Mrs. Harrison. She had no ill will toward Maeve, nor did she feel any in return. They'd just grown apart when Maeve married and Etta chose a different path.

Now her friend engaged herself in the activities that all ladies of the Boston gentry did: garden club meetings, card games, dinner parties, and society balls.

Etta glanced around the lecture hall. Every woman in attendance clustered together in groups of three or more.

Every woman except Etta.

That was the flip side of having a strong, independent nature. She longed for a friend she could confide in and share all her exploits as Henry Mason. One who wouldn't judge her. One who would not only celebrate her accomplishments but cheer her on.

"Just one, Lord," she whispered. "That's all. Just one."

Gaslights illuminated the porch stairs of the small white bungalow where Leo's parents raised him and his brothers. He'd worked straight through his supper break, taking inventory at the firehouse. Unfortunately, the Drake was closed when he'd left. He doubted the icebox at home would hold much promise. Perhaps he could scrounge some eggs to silence his stomach's clamoring protest.

Leo shoved the door open. His father sat at the kitchen table, paperwork strewn over the makeshift desk. "Hey, Son," he greeted, without breaking his focus on the station's budget.

"Hey, Pops." His father's familiar greeting warmed his heart as much as the smell of his mother's Swedish stew simmering on the stove. He licked his lips. "Do I smell *kalops*?"

"Yeah," Pops answered in a barely audible tone. "Trude made a double batch, seeing as how we've got inventory and budget due by Friday."

Leo removed the lid and inhaled the savory scent of bay leaf and allspice. "God bless Trude." Gunnar's wife had a soft spot for her father-in-law and her husband's bachelor brothers. "What Trude sees in Gunnar, I'll never know."

Pops chuckled under his breath. "She's a godsend."

Leo scooped a ladle of stew into a bowl and joined his father at the table. He bowed his head and thanked God for His constant provision, the delicious meal, and Trude's kindness.

The first bite settled on his tongue, reminding him of chilly autumn days, snowball fights in winter, and his mother reading to him and his brothers beside the fireplace. Each spoonful tasted like his childhood.

"This is every bit as good as Ma's."

"Yeah, Trude's a good cook. She has a generous heart like your mother too." Pops removed his glasses. "So, when are you gonna settle down with a fine woman like Trude?"

"When do I have time to pay calls on a woman? Besides, I'm married to the job. No woman wants to play second fiddle to the station." A lesson Annika taught him, and one he'd most likely never forget.

"You tell yourself that, but you know it's not true. Gunnar has Trude, and for twenty wonderful years, I had your mother."

"I know, Pops, but both you and Gunnar met your gals before you graduated high school." He gulped another mouthful of kalops and smacked his lips as the tender meat fell apart on his tongue.

"You know, Son, not every woman will feel the same as Annika."

"It's not about Annika."

"I don't believe that. And deep down, you don't believe it either."

His father possessed the ability to look deep into the hearts of his children with an innate understanding of what made each of them tick. There was no point in continuing to deny what his father so astutely sensed. His best tactic was to dodge and evade. "Did Trude bring us any rolls to go along with the kalops?"

"In the bread box."

A feast fit for a king. He cut two rolls and slathered them with butter then returned to the table.

Jens hurried into the kitchen and checked his appearance in the mirror. He faced Leo and their father. "How do I look?"

Leo grinned. "As homely as that alley cat you rescued a few years ago."

"Never mind him," Pops said. "You look handsome."

"Thanks, Pops." Jens grabbed a roll from Leo's plate.

"Don't—" Too late. He'd already ripped off a huge chunk with his teeth.

"Want it back?" he asked, opening his mouth for Leo to see the soggy lump of bread.

Leo wrinkled his nose. "No thanks. What does Genevieve see in you anyway?"

Jens made a play for Leo's other roll, but Leo grabbed his wrist. "Don't even think about it."

"I didn't think you still had reflexes like that, old man. There's hope for you yet. Maybe Genevieve can scrounge up a date for you for Saturday night."

"Thanks, but no thanks, Jens. I'll find my own gal."

His brother rolled his eyes. "You'll actually have to go somewhere besides home, the Drake, and the station to find that gal."

"Very funny. As it happens, I have my eye on a lovely young woman."

"Good for you, Brother." Jens patted Leo's back, grabbed the other roll, and bolted toward the door.

"Jens!"

His brother grabbed his slouch hat and turned the doorknob. "Don't wait up!"

Pops shook his head. "How many times is that boy gonna steal your food before you learn to keep a better eye on it when he's around?"

"It's a game we play— sorta how we say we love each other."

"You mean you let him steal from your plate?"

"Sure, there's a couple more. If it was the last one, I would've tackled him before he got out the door."

Pops grinned. "You mother him."

Leo buttered two more rolls. "Eh, I just try to look out for him. Jens isn't really cut out to be a firefighter like Gunnar and me. He's too sensitive, too artistic. The problem is, he thinks he's letting us down if he doesn't do the job."

"Yeah. I see that too. I've told him that's not the case, but he insists."

"We all have." Leo rejoined his father at the table. "He loves that secondhand camera equipment he bought from the photographic studio. Wonder how he could make a living with that?" He pondered the question while he ate a few more bites of his supper.

"I think you should take Jens up on his offer."

"What offer?"

"To introduce you to some of Genevieve's friends."

Leo rested his spoon against his bowl. *This again?* "Pops, Genevieve's friends are gonna be too young for me."

Pops looked at him over the rims of his glasses. "You make it sound like you're my age. You're only thirty, Leo. You're not ready to be put out to pasture yet."

"Feels like it, Pops. My body may be young, but my spirit feels old."

"That's because you're lacking female companionship. What about that young woman you danced with at the Fireman's Ball last year?"

"Hen-ri—" He choked on his food and thunked his fist against his chest. What would make his father remember that? "Henrietta Maxwell?" he asked, still struggling to find his voice.

Pops slid his glass of water toward Leo. "If I recall, there seemed to be a spark of attraction between you."

Leo scoffed. "She's the daughter of Clyde Maxwell, one of the wealthiest men in Boston. I doubt a fireman from Brockton would be the sort to catch her attention or win her father's approval."

"Why not?" Pops locked eyes with him. "You're a good-looking, kind-hearted young man who is morally focused. The woman fortunate enough to capture your heart will be blessed indeed."

"Thanks, but I'm not so sure my father's glowing endorsement would hold sway with the Maxwells."

Pops shrugged and returned his attention to the budget paperwork. "Besides, Mr. Maxwell started in a shoe factory, just like many men here in Brockton. He doesn't strike me as the type to forget where he came from."

Leo shoveled another heaping spoonful of kalops into his mouth. He had no idea his father was so discerning in the art of romance or that he'd perceived his attraction to Etta. He bit back a chuckle. What would Pops say if he knew his favorite reporter, Henry Mason, was, in fact, Henrietta Maxwell? Her masculine attire had gone unnoticed by Pops and Jens at breakfast earlier that day. Her height aided in her ruse, and Leo suspected if her eyebrow hadn't malfunctioned, he wouldn't have recognized her either.

Etta certainly looked different than she had the night of the Fireman's Ball. She'd been radiant in her lavender gown. Although her dress wasn't as fancy as the gowns of many of the other ladies in attendance, she stood out, since most of the others wore white. Her chestnut hair had been piled on her head in the popular style most young ladies wore, but the loose strands that twisted along her neck had just about done him in. He'd been thankful she couldn't hear his heart pounding when he'd taken her hand and led her to the dance floor, opening the evening's activities.

Miss Maxwell was brave, daring, and foolish all at the same time. She was determined and independent. He liked that about her. Any woman married to a firefighter would need those characteristics when the job required him to be on call for long shifts or when the alarm bell sounded, interrupting family life at any moment.

He tore off a piece of roll and popped it in his mouth. Who was he kidding? Henrietta Maxwell would never consider a firefighter from Brockton.

The lady was way out of his league.

CHAPTER 5

Etta stood on the corner of Calmar and Main, weighing whether or not she should stop by the Drake where Leo most likely dined with his family. What reason did she have to drop in? Other than her desire to spend time with him, of course. In the five days since they'd been reintroduced, she'd had difficulty sleeping. Her wayward thoughts tended to drift to the handsome firefighter.

If she'd disguised herself as Henry Mason, she could've shared a copy of the *Enterprise*'s morning edition bearing her article unequivocally stating the fires in the business district were indeed arson. However, she couldn't think of one plausible reason why Etta Maxwell would dine alone at the Drake, not to mention seek a visit with Leo Eriksson. At least not one she'd admit to.

Resolved to relegate her interest in the firefighter to a passing fancy, she strode toward the Brockton National Bank. The morning sun reflected off the windows of the Grover Shoe Factory, nearly blinding her. She bumped into a stocky man removing a large glass water bottle from the side of a delivery truck.

"Hey, watch where you're going, buster. You nearly plowed me over."

"My apologies."

"Oh, sorry, Miss Maxwell," he said, tugging at the brim of his cap before hoisting the bottle onto his shoulder. "I didn't realize it was you."

"That's all right, Mr.—"

"James Cole, ma'am. Always appreciate what your family does for Brockton."

"You're welcome, Mr. Cole. We're honored to be of service to the community." She apologized again for interrupting his work, skirted around the dolly where he strapped his load, then crossed over Main Street.

Etta slipped inside the bank to make a withdrawal. Unable to arrange for her father's chauffeur to pick her up, she'd need to hire a cab to take her into Boston that afternoon for the engagement announcement she needed to cover for *The Gilded Gown*. She dreaded the thought of spending the day with the likes of the Cabots and Lowells, but Isadora Bassinger's engagement to the Earl of Greystone had all of Beacon Hill atwitter. While she had little interest in another heiress being married off to a poor Englishman in exchange for his title, her readers certainly did.

The short line moved quickly. Before long she was back on the street, hailing a cab. As the driver steered the horses toward the curb, a thunderous boom rang out and the ground trembled beneath her boots. A huge whistling projectile resembling a rocket tore through the roof of the Grover Shoe Factory. Its path intersected with the water tower. The large structure wobbled then toppled onto the building.

She sucked in a breath as the rear of the five-story plant shuddered then folded in on itself like a stack of Mrs. Hemingway's hot cakes. Debris littered the air. Something sharp nicked her face. Her fingers dabbed her cheek, and crimson droplets stained her gloves.

Etta ducked behind the cab while the driver fought to keep his startled rig under control. She peered around the carriage. Pedestrians sought cover wherever they could, while others gaped at the billowing plumes of smoke filling the sky.

A second blast launched flaming debris through the air, alighting the factory as well as shops and businesses on the opposite side of Calmar Street. Hungry flames appeared eager to feed on the wood frames of any building unfortunate enough to cross their greedy path.

The mighty timbers that supported the massive factory buckled. She gasped but couldn't force herself to look away as the building partially collapsed into a monstrous pile of burning rubble, trapping countless workers in a fiery grave.

Leo bolted to his feet "What was that?"

"Sounds like an explosion," Pops answered.

Leo burst through the front doors of the firehouse onto Main Street, Gunnar fast on his heels. His heart sank at the sight of the Grover factory. "The rear quarter is missing," he said, disbelief ringing in his ears.

Gunnar clasped his hands on his head. "Ho-ly smoke."

Flaming projectiles soared through the air, igniting everything they landed on. Passersby ducked for cover. Horses bucked and whinnied, and motorcars came to a halt. Drivers gawked as the plant's water tower crumbled into the remains of the burning manufacturing plant.

Leo pushed past his brother and yanked the firehouse door open. "The Grover plant imploded!"

Leif looked at his watch. "This time of day there must be hundreds of people inside."

Leo's heart hammered in his chest. "Sparks from the blast set fire to businesses across Calmar Street. Some may have landed on the roof of the Churchill & Alden Factory too."

Without a moment's hesitation, Pops shifted from firehouse chief to emergency roll-out commander. He ran to the office then returned to the garage floor, a voice trumpet held to his mouth.

"All men on deck. This is not a drill. We pull out in three minutes. Leif, sound the alarm to notify neighboring fire departments. Jens, open the bay doors, then help Leif and me ready the water trucks."

Wilson sprang into action, herding the horses from their stalls and positioning them in front of the steamer truck while several crew members worked the pulley lowering the harnesses onto the backs of the steeds. The dalmatian then sprinted through the opened garage doors, barking at pedestrians and street traffic to clear the apron for the steam engine to dash into the city street as soon as the crew was ready to depart.

Leo rushed toward the rear of the station. "Gunnar and I are headed to the scene now." He grabbed two axes from the wall.

"But you don't have your protective equipment," Pops said.

"Make sure to throw it on the truck."

Leo sprinted outside the station, but Gunnar was gone. Thick, black smoke poured from the neighboring factory.

Where was his brother?

Etta rose from her shelter and stared at the disaster unfolding before her eyes. She stumbled backward. In a matter of minutes, an entire city block of her beloved Brockton resembled Atlanta following Sherman's March to the Sea. Shrieks of the injured rose with the smoke permeating the scene, raising the fine hair on her arms.

She glanced at the Drake. So far, the diner was safe, but only a few doors down, two businesses were ablaze.

The bell atop the Porter Congregational Church rang, summoning police and firefighters to the scene. A priest burst through the doors of St. Margaret's, about fifty feet from Etta. He paused and took in the scene. His expression blanched. Then the priest ran toward the disaster, seemingly unconcerned for his own safety.

Etta followed suit, glad she'd dressed in her more practical split skirt, and rushed across the thoroughfare as fast as her feet allowed.

A soft whimper drew Etta's attention. Where in the utter destruction before her had the sound come from? Ears attuned, she listened. When she heard the mewling again, she hurried to her left.

Heart pounding, she knelt and rummaged through a mound of debris. "I'm here." She shoved a small chunk of ceiling plaster to the side, revealing the face of a girl. *Good heavens.* She couldn't be more than twelve years old.

Etta stroked the girl's cheek, and her dark lashes fluttered. "I'm going to help you."

She clawed at the rubble, feverishly tossing remnants of the once productive factory to the side. A tangle of wood and twisted iron pinned the girl's legs. Etta strained to move the obstacle, but it wouldn't budge. No use. She'd need to find someone to help, or the child might perish in the fire. "I'll be right back. I need to get help."

"Don't leave me," the girl cried.

She squeezed the child's limp hand. Tears pooled in the girl's eyes, mirroring the ones in her own. "I'll be right back. I promise."

Etta scrambled over the heap of debris until she found solid footing. She stood and took in the scene around her. Flames licked at the wood frame in the portion of the plant still standing. Injured workers crawled from the rubble while others fled down a shaky fire escape. Several employees jumped from windows onto the street below. To her right, men carried an injured woman to safety. Who could help rescue this child?

"Father, I can't do this on my own. Please bring someone to help us," she whispered.

Her gaze darted about. She spied a man working to remove a timber from the wreckage. "Help me," she called, waving her arms to attract his attention.

When he glanced her way, she cupped her hands around her mouth. "Hurry! A child is trapped." She motioned for him to follow her.

Thank you, Father.

Etta led him to where the child lay. Using a nearby timber, he leveraged the rubble off the girl. His face reddened as he strained. "Okay, lady," he said. "Grab her, quick."

Etta reached out, but the girl's apron snagged on a jagged piece of metal.

"Hurry," the man shouted.

With frantic hands, she yanked the fabric, freeing the child whose arms now clung to Etta's neck. "It's all right, my darling. You're fine," she cooed, rubbing the girl's back.

"I'll take her," the man said. "Those flames are moving fast."

Etta relinquished the child to her rescuer. The trio clambered over the debris and finally made it to safety in front of St. Margaret's church.

"Thank you," she said as the man returned the girl to her care.

"Glad I could help."

She sat on the church steps, cradling the girl in her lap. "Are you hurt? Let me look at you."

The child shook her head and nuzzled against Etta's neck. "Is my mama dead?"

"Was she in the factory?"

"Uh-huh."

Etta pulled the girl close. "I don't know, sweetheart, but we'll pray she's fine. Can you tell me your name?"

"Nellie Hurd. My mama's name is Lilian, but my papa calls her Lily."

"Father God, keep Lilian safe. Help the rescuers to find her quickly. Amen."

As Etta comforted the girl, she surveyed the scene, engraving the images in her mind so she could recall them later. Scores of men rushed from the Churchill & Alden Shoe Factory to Grover's Shoes and aided in the effort to locate those sandwiched between the building's collapsed stories. Several men had procured a ladder, from where she couldn't imagine, and propped it against the eastern side of the burning factory to reach the second floor.

Helplessness plagued Etta as she soothed the crying child. How many would be as fortunate as Nellie? How many would perish?

She glanced toward the Drake. Flames now licked the roof of the Erikssons' favorite diner. Since the explosion occurred before eight o'clock, the family might have been in the restaurant enjoying their morning meal.

A barking dog drew her attention to the firehouse. Was Wilson warning people and motorcars to clear the front of the station? She pinched her eyes shut. Leo and his family would battle the inferno engulfing the shoe factory.

A shiver snaked down her spine. *Wherever he is, Lord, keep him safe. Keep them all safe.*

When he arrived on the scene, Leo organized some of the male passersby into teams, directing them to specific sections of the collapsed portion of the factory. He charged a woman who'd escaped the disaster unscathed to send other victims to St. Margaret's, where they could begin a list of survivors.

An older man, probably close to his father's age, approached him. "I'm Thomas Lindgren. What can I do?"

"We need to establish a morgue. It's a grim task, but we need a place to lay out the dead."

"I can do that. Where?"

"Across the street, in front of the Churchill & Alden factory."

"Direct the bodies there. I'll find more volunteers to round up blankets from neighboring houses."

Leo clasped the man's arm. "Thank you, Thomas."

Horns blared on the fire truck and tanker as the men of Engine Company No. 1 rolled out of the station on the other side of the Grover factory. The stiffness in Leo's shoulders lessened. He could now concentrate on locating survivors and relinquish the task of establishing a command center to his father's capable hands.

He briefed his father with what little he knew. "We need to find a volunteer to begin prioritizing the injured so when medical arrives, they know who to take to the hospital and who can be treated on-scene."

"Excellent job, son. I'll put Jens on that right away." He handed a set of protective gear to Leo. "Have you seen Gunnar?"

Leo tugged on his rubber jacket and boots. "The worst damage is in the rear." He pointed to the portion of the factory bordering Denton Street. "I'm guessing that's where he'll be."

"Go find him."

He grabbed Gunnar's gear and the two axes then hustled toward the corner of Calmar and Denton Streets in search of his brother.

"Leo," Pops called.

He turned around.

"Be careful, Son."

"You too, Pops."

As Leo neared the collapsed section of the factory, cries for help halted him. His gaze swept over the area. Where were they coming from?

"Help us! We're trapped in here!"

He darted through what once had been the sturdy outside wall of the plant and climbed over broken pieces of machinery. "Where are you?"

"Over here!"

He followed the sound of their voices. Three Grover employees were trapped behind a thick metal gate, smoke billowing over their heads.

A woman shook the bars. "We can't get out."

Leo lay one of the axes by his feet. He tugged a kerchief from his pocket and covered his mouth. "Stand back!" Although his voice was muffled, all three stepped away from the gate.

He swung the axe at the padlock multiple times. Finally, its sharp blade broke the shank, and one of the men yanked the gate open.

"This way," Leo said. He grabbed the axe he'd brought for Gunnar.

Gunnar. He'd promised Pops he'd find his brother.

Once he'd led the rescued factory workers to safety, he inquired about injuries. Each reported only minor cuts and bruises. The two men offered to help Leo look for survivors.

"Thank you," the woman said, tears pooling in her eyes. "You saved our lives. I thought for sure we were goners."

"I'm glad I heard your cries for help. Will you be okay?"

"Yes. Go now, find other people to save."

Leo and the two men he'd rescued continued to the fully collapsed portion of the plant.

He found his brother straining to lift a thick stanchion.

"Gunnar." His brother turned toward the sound of his name. "I brought some muscle. Put these on."

Leo tossed Gunnar his rubber jacket then handed an axe to one of the volunteers. "Let's chop the beam into smaller segments."

"Good idea," one of the men said.

They swung the hatchets into the thick timber until it broke. Then Leo motioned for the other men to clear the massive chunks of wood and to search for survivors. He and Gunnar took the axes and moved to another support beam and repeated the action.

"Help. . ."

Leo stood upright, his trained ears listening for another plea for assistance. "Did you hear that?"

"Yeah, I think it came from over there," Gunnar said.

The brothers climbed over piles of twisted machinery and office furniture in a desperate attempt to find the wounded person.

"Help. . .me," the faint voice called again.

A brawny arm clad in blue cloth protruded from beneath a mound of roofing tile. Gunnar tossed his axe aside and frantically sifted through the remnants of the once bustling factory.

Leo stooped and rested his fingers on the injured man's wrist. "It's no use, Gunnar. He's gone."

His brother heaved another handful of shingles behind him. "Are you sure?" He gulped a breath. "Maybe we can save him if we get this rubble off his chest."

Leo stood and shook his head. "Not this one. Looks like he was impaled by jagged metal. The patch on his shirt pocket indicates he works for a water delivery company. We'll make a note we found his body. Let's find someone we can rescue before those flames get any closer."

"Over here."

Gunnar grabbed his axe and pointed. "Sounds like she's calling from that direction."

They moved toward the center of the building, where indigo flames feasted on the remnants of the factory's wooden frame. Despite his protective gear, warmth from the blaze heated Leo's skin. "The fire is burning fast and hot. Natural gas from severed pipes must be feeding the flames."

Gunnar nodded. "We don't have much time."

"Don't leave me. I'm here."

"We won't leave you," Leo said, praying the encroaching inferno wouldn't make him a liar. He couldn't imagine anything worse than burning alive, and he had no intention of leaving this woman behind.

"I think the voice came from over here." Gunnar lifted boards and a broken desk. "Found her!"

Leo scrambled over the debris, spying another corpse. This time a woman stared wide-eyed toward heaven. He paused long enough to slide her eyelids shut.

"We're over here," Gunnar said. "Hurry, Leo!"

He hated leaving the young woman who'd met death alone simply for reporting to work on what should've been a normal Monday morning, but there was nothing more he could do for her.

He scrambled toward his brother, toward a victim he could assist—toward life.

Together, Leo and Gunnar heaved a huge bolster, straining against its massive weight.

"My leg," the injured woman cried, moaning as they lifted a chunk of wood from her mangled limb now lying at an unnatural angle. "It hurts."

Leo knelt beside her and examined her injury. Nails and wood shards pierced her thigh. He was no doctor, but it didn't take a physician to recognize her leg was broken, most likely in several places. He locked eyes with Gunnar. "She's not walking out of here."

Leo shifted his attention to the injured woman. "This will be painful. We'll be as gentle as we can, but we need to hurry."

She whimpered her acknowledgment.

"You can do this," Gunnar added. "We're gonna count to three and then tug you free. One. . .two. . .three."

"Ah," the woman groaned, biting her lip against the pain.

"You're doing great," Leo said.

Once they had her liberated, Gunnar scooped her into his arms. "I've got her." He nodded to the fire licking at the broken beams less than ten feet away. "We don't have much longer. See if you can locate anyone else. I'll return as soon as I find a safe place for her to wait for medical help."

"Pull back."

Gunnar froze, his wounded burden cradled in his arms.

Leo turned toward his father, whose voice projected through Engine Company No. 1's red and white megaphone. "I repeat, pull back. Immediately."

What? How could they halt the search for survivors so soon? His suspicions about leaking gas lines must've been spot on.

Firemen throughout the wreckage repeated his father's call to cease the rescue mission. One by one they climbed from the ruins and abandoned the search.

"C'mon, Leo. We gotta go."

Gunnar stared at Leo, waiting for him to move in his direction, but he couldn't do it. How could he?

"Leo." Desperation peppered his brother's voice.

Didn't the Bible say there was no greater love than laying down his life for another? Shouldn't he be willing to lay down his life now to save one more man, woman, or child?

Determination swelled through him. The moans of trapped victims filled his ears, intensifying his pulse. "Go, get her out of here."

"I'll be back for you, big brother." Gunnar turned and navigated his way to safety.

Leo ferreted through papers, ceiling plaster, and broken machinery, through file cabinets, flooring, and twisted metal, all to no avail. He moved to a new spot, staying ten to fifteen feet ahead of the rapidly moving fire hindering his effort to save lives.

Just one more, God. Please, just one more.

CHAPTER 6

After finding a Grover Shoes employee who knew Nellie and her mother, Etta assured the child she'd be all right then made a beeline for the Drake, its roof now ablaze. Her less-than-fashionable boots allowed her to maneuver the streets littered with debris from the explosion while being mindful not to twist her ankle. She'd be of no use to anyone if she was injured, nor did the medical teams need another wounded person to care for.

Etta jostled her way through the throng of onlookers outside the diner. Her unusual height gave her an advantage as she stood on tiptoe looking over and around the heads of those watching in horror as nearly an entire city block burned. Where was Leo? Her pulse resounded in her ears. Had he and his family been inside when the explosion happened? Had they been injured? Could they be trapped inside?

Where were the water trucks? Some of the spectators had formed a bucket brigade.

Without hesitation, she stepped into the line and grabbed a leather handle. Again and again the pails flowed to and from the cistern beside the Drake. Before long, her muscles strained under the weight of the water-laden containers as she passed bucket after bucket to the woman beside her. Their efforts yielded little to slow the pace of the flames gorging on wood, fabric, paper, and anything else consumable inside the homes and businesses on this side of Calmar Street.

A horn blared. A light breath escaped her lips. Fire trucks were rolling toward the scene. Help would soon be here. "Thank you, Lord," she whispered.

"Help!"

Etta jerked her head toward the desperate plea. A woman holding an infant leaned out a second-story window above the dressmaker's shop.

The woman tossed a blanket to the ground. "Catch my baby!"

Bile rose in Etta's throat. Would she really throw her infant from the window? What a horrible choice to have to make.

Two men unfolded the quilt. A woman and a teenage girl joined them and each grasped a corner. The crowd stepped back so the volunteers could spread wide apart until the blanket was almost taut.

Etta's stomach roiled as the despondent mother prepared to toss her baby to strangers below.

A policeman blew a whistle. "Outta the way. Make room for the water truck."

"Wait! The fire truck is comin'," an onlooker yelled.

"There's no time. Catch my Joseph."

"Okay, we're ready," one of the men holding the blanket called.

The woman kissed the infant's forehead and dropped him. Etta clutched her bodice and turned away, bracing for the sound of the baby's head cracking against the pavement.

Cheers erupted from the crowd. Etta's fingers flew to her lips. Barely able to contain her joy, she praised God for sparing the child.

An engine from Company No. 3 eased to the edge of Main Street and came to a stop. Four firemen quickly disembarked from the vehicle. The policeman whistled again for the crowd to move aside.

"Make way!" A fireman carrying a ladder rushed to the dressmaker's shop and leaned it against the brick exterior. The woman screamed, and Etta saw flames eating at her clothing. The fireman tossed the blanket over his shoulder and climbed to her aid while another held fast to the ladder.

The woman disappeared from the window, and a collective gasp rose from the crowd. Etta clamped her eyes closed and covered her ears to block out the woman's agonizing cries. If only she could pinch her nose against the scent of burning hair at the same time.

"Get down the ladder so we can use the hose."

Etta opened her eyes as the fireman jumped from the third rung and his crew members sprayed water on the fire. She nudged her way through the crowd and onto Main Street. Uncertain of Leo's whereabouts, her gaze drifted to the blazing shoe factory.

Protect him, Lord.

Leo lifted the heavy chunk of ceiling plaster from the wounded man's chest. Dried blood streaked his face. Leo lowered his ear to the victim's mouth and was rewarded with the faint sensation of warm breath against his cheek as flames devoured the debris only a few feet away.

"We need to go," Gunnar said, his voice breathy from exertion. He squatted beside the injured man and slid his fingers over the major artery in his neck. "He's got no pulse."

Leo snapped his head in Gunnar's direction. "I felt his breath."

His brother shrugged. "Not any longer."

Screams of anguish lifted on the air. Leo grabbed his axe and sprang in the direction of the cry.

"Leo!"

"Go back before you get hurt, Gunnar. I couldn't take it if you didn't make it out. Not after Patrick."

Leo frantically chopped at an upside-down worktable laden with a metal contraption that trapped a pair of women beneath it. Smoke burned his eyes and lungs, but the horrid smell of burning hair and flesh fueled his determination.

Gunnar joined him, chucking pieces loosed by Leo's axe over his shoulder.

"I thought I told you to leave," Leo said.

"Not without you."

After hacking the obstacle into three sections, they leveraged one of the table legs to lift the machinery, freeing one of the women. Fire ate at her garment, and she screamed as Leo splayed himself over her legs, smothering them with his rubber coat. They propped the rescued woman against the remainder of a stairwell and returned to help her coworker.

A steel pin pierced the second woman's arm, pinning her to the ground. Gunnar kicked burning debris away from them. "We can't save this one," he whispered. "The fire is spreading too quickly. But we can save the other one."

Leo looked at the woman he'd dragged free. Loose hair from her bun fell over her unconscious face.

"You take her. I'll see what I can do for—"

"No. I promised Pops I wouldn't return without you. It's both of us or neither of us, Leo. Your call."

"My daughter—" The trapped woman winced. "Nellie. Have you. . .found her?"

Leo's gaze darted to Gunnar.

His brother shook his head. "We gotta go, Leo. Pops' orders."

Leo squeezed her hand. "Not yet, but a lot of folks made it out. We'll look for her, ma'am."

She whispered a thank-you and closed her eyes.

Gunnar hoisted the first woman over Leo's shoulder then grabbed his axe. "Follow me. And don't stop."

"Got it," Leo said.

An agonizing scream rent the air. Leo turned back to see the second woman's clothing alight. "Father, take her into Your arms quickly."

As they navigated through the unsteady maze of rubble, Leo's spirit stilled. The faint whisper of prayers and voices reciting Psalm 23 rose above the cries of human misery. The sound of the condemned making their peace with God.

Hopefully, he'd make his own peace with leaving them behind.

"You should've left straightaway, Son. You and Gunnar could've been killed."

"But we weren't, and we saved another person."

Pops scraped a hand along his jaw. "Your desire to save lives is admirable, but not at the risk of your life or another member of our crew."

"But—"

"No protests. You do that again, and I'll put you on report for dereliction of duty, Lieutenant Eriksson. Understood?"

When Pops mentioned anyone's rank in affiliation with his stern, take-no-prisoners tone, there was no use disputing the matter. "Understood."

"Good."

Leo's attention shifted to the fires on the opposite side of Calmar Street. He motioned to the diner that had become a second home and the people who worked there like a second family. "Looks like the Drake's on fire."

Pops grabbed his arm. "Not now, Son. The largest number of wounded and dead will be right here at Grover's plant. *This* is our priority. I've tasked Engine Company No. 3 with the Drake and other businesses on the Dahlborg Block."

Leo's gut twisted. Pops was right, but still it seemed like he was abandoning his own flesh and blood.

His gaze narrowed to a young woman pushing her way out of the crowd onto Main Street. Even at this distance, she resembled Etta. Had she been at the diner when it caught on fire? Was she hurt? Perhaps she was covering the story for the *Enterprise*. If she was, why wasn't she in her disguise? Either way, she had put herself at risk, and for some unexplainable reason, that was unacceptable to him.

"Pops, I'll be right back. I want to see how the rescue crews at the Drake are coming along."

"I need you here assisting with situation control and managing the shift from a rescue mission to search and recovery."

"I won't be long. Ten minutes, I promise."

"Five minutes, or I'll be adding abandoning your duty station to that report."

"Yes, sir."

Leo took off at a sprint. His lungs protested from the morning's exertion, but he didn't let that deter him from reaching Etta.

Five minutes wasn't long, but it was long enough to determine if she had any injuries and get her to safety.

Snap out of it, Etta.

She had to trust God to protect Leo. That wasn't her job and she, like many others, would live with the consequences of today's events, with the horrid sound of those trapped in the burning wreckage.

She needed to wrap her head around the fact the Grover plant had exploded. The time had come for her to switch from bystander to reporter. First, she would swing by the boardinghouse and change into her Henry Mason garb so she could begin investigating what kind of projectile burst through the factory's roof. Her hunch was the boiler. She didn't know much about mechanical devices, but she had read about boiler explosions, including the infamous tragedy aboard the *Sultana* when over one thousand souls lost their lives.

This incident had many of the same earmarks. How many had been working in the plant this fateful morning? How many perished?

"Etta! Etta!"

Leo? She spun to face him, her heart thundering in her ears.

He lowered the kerchief from his mouth and nose. "You're safe," he said, tugging her against him.

Could he feel the pounding in her chest?

"I was worried about you as well."

He stepped back but held her forearms. "What are you doing here?"

"I was looking for you."

"Me?"

"Yes. I was worried you and your family might have been at the diner when it caught on fire."

His gaze softened. "We're fine. We were at the station." He swiped her cheek with his thumb. "Are you hurt?"

"I was across the street from the factory when it exploded and something nicked my cheek. I'll be fine."

He took her hand and led her to the opposite side of the street in front of St. Margaret's, nearly the exact spot where she'd witnessed the horrific explosion. "You need to be out of harm's way."

"But—"

"No buts, Etta. I need to concentrate on setting up a command center for the search-and-recovery operations. I can't do that if I'm worried about your safety."

"Search and recovery? But people are"—she shuddered—"still alive."

"We can't. . ." His voice caught in his throat. "The fire is too hot and spreading too quickly to continue locating survivors."

A haunting sadness captured his usually brilliant umber eyes—a look she was unaccustomed to seeing. Was he ashamed? Disappointed in himself? Did he disagree with that decision? There was so much she wanted to ask him, but this wasn't the time or place for conversation. "That must've been a very difficult decision."

He gave a tight nod.

"Listen, I have to get back or Pops will put me on report, but I need a favor."

"I—" She'd been planning to start her investigation. Her editor would be expecting a story from his ace reporter. But how could she disappoint Leo? "Sure, what can I do?"

"It won't be long before the families arrive looking for loved ones. We'll direct survivors here to St. Margaret's. Can you stay here and formulate a list of names? Note their injuries and send them inside the church. Medical teams will arrive soon to assess and treat the wounded."

"I can do that."

He squeezed her hand.

She wanted to tell him how thankful she was that he wasn't seriously hurt, but there was no time for that now.

"Anything else you need?"

"Pray."

He jogged toward his fellow firemen waging a futile war against the burning factory, and Etta lifted a silent petition. *God protect him. Protect them all.*

CHAPTER 7

Etta scribbled the names of survivors on paper attached to a hinged clipboard she'd found in the church office. In a separate column, she included a brief description of each victim's injuries. She possessed little to no medical knowledge but hoped notations such as damaged ribs, broken bones, twisted ankles, cuts, or contusions would be helpful to the medical staff.

Some of the survivors had such severe burns, she feared they'd die of infection. Remarkably, many people had crawled out of the wreckage with nothing more than cuts and bruises. They were the lucky ones. She glanced at the burning factory, nothing remaining except its smokestack. No, luck had nothing to do with it. Only a miracle had allowed anyone to escape with minor injuries, let alone their life.

A man shuffled toward her, a blood-soaked rag held to his face. He pulled the cloth away, revealing a nasty gash at his temple that ran to the corner of his left eye. "Name," she said.

"Henry Nash."

She jotted his name on her paper along with the notation, 'cut on forehead,' and directed him to the front of the church.

Several men hurried toward the door of St. Margaret's, carrying an unconscious man on a makeshift stretcher.

"I need his name before you take him inside."

"Don't know his name, miss. A fireman pulled him from the rubble earlier and asked us to bring him here so the docs can treat him."

The man moaned and turned his head toward Etta. She winced. Charred skin on his face, neck, and arm greeted her. Her stomach revolted, and she forced herself to keep her breakfast in place.

She hastily wrote, *Male, approximately 30 years, severe burns.* "Find a place for him near the right-side door. That's where the most severely injured are located."

The ambulance from City Hospital drove past her. She waved her arms, trying to flag them down, to no avail. On their next pass, she put her fingers in her mouth and whistled. Every head on the block turned in her direction. She shrugged. One more eccentricity to add to the list. If it wasn't for the disaster unfolding in the Campello District, tomorrow's headline would dub her the Whistling Heiress.

She'd learned what Mother called an unladylike habit from her father when she traipsed along on his hunting and fishing expeditions. The trick had proven handy when calling the family's ornery dog, but Mother made Etta promise not to whistle in public. She'd kept that promise—until today.

The ambulance pulled to a stop at the corner. Three men and two women disembarked.

"I'm Etta Maxwell. A fireman from Engine Company No. 1 tasked me with making a list of the injured."

"I'm Dr. Reid," one of the men said.

After he introduced his colleagues, she handed him the clipboard. "Follow me." She opened the side door of St. Margaret's. "I wrote a description of each person's injuries, which I noted to the right of their name and physical description. What I deemed minor wounds are located near the altar while those with severe or possibly life-threatening injuries are located near this side entrance for easy transport to the hospital."

"Thank you," Dr. Reid said. "Excellent work." He began barking orders to his coworkers.

"If you like," she said, interrupting him, "I can recruit a few of the onlookers out front to help you unload your supplies so you can begin examining the wounded."

"Thank you, Miss Maxwell. I'll have one of my orderlies unload the items we brought, but if you could find us additional blankets, material for bandages, and volunteers with scissors to cut the fabric, that would be beneficial to our effectiveness."

Dr. Reid removed her list and handed the clipboard back to her. "You'll be needing this."

He hurried off to tend to his patients, leaving Etta with a challenging set of requests, especially considering that she needed to record more survivors before they took it upon themselves to enter the church for medical treatment without registering with her.

She closed her eyes and massaged her temple. How was she to find the supplies and the volunteers to satisfy the doctor's petition? She didn't want to disappoint either Leo or the medical team, both of whom were counting on her.

C'mon, Etta. Where is your faith? Your fortitude? She wasn't in this battle alone.

She hurried to the front of the church, whispering a prayer as she walked. "Lord, please help me find dependable volunteers and the materials the doctor requested to treat the wounded. I can't do this without You."

She stepped into the late morning sunshine. The line of people either self-reporting or searching for family members now stretched around the block.

Three women had arrived, two pulling a child's wagon and the third, a wheelbarrow, each piled high with blankets. The oldest of the three women approached Etta, her smile warm and genuine.

"I'm Peggy Hartzell. We heard the survivors are reporting to St. Margaret's. We were told to find you, Miss Maxwell, to see how we can help."

Warmth spread through Etta's chest. God knew what was needed and had made provisions even before Dr. Reid made his request. Why had she worried?

She tucked the clipboard under her arm and shook the woman's hand. "You're a godsend, Peggy. I need someone to assist me with registering survivors. Perhaps start by dividing them into two groups: those who need medical assistance and those simply notifying us they are fine and survived the disaster. I'll take the wounded."

Peggy nodded and immediately began separating the survivors as requested.

Etta tasked the other women with visiting nearby homes to gather blankets, scissors, and material for bandages. She also asked them to recruit anyone they could find to bring water to the church for cleaning wounds. Dr. Reid hadn't mentioned that, but Etta thought it might've been an oversight.

She surveyed the scene. Things seemed to be running much more smoothly. Peggy had even taken it upon herself to find another clipboard and pencil from the church office.

Some might look at the morning's tragic events and question God. Etta saw His love and mercy in the volunteers and the provisions that had miraculously arrived. Even in the midst of calamity, God worked behind the scenes for the good of His flock.

She'd never doubt that again.

Leo and Gunnar accompanied their father to the fire truck. Since the Grover plant was located on the same block as Engine Company No. 1, they'd been first on the scene, making Pops the incident commander.

Their father climbed on board and stood on the bench, where he could address the men from the various fire departments across the city who had responded to the alarm. Jens held the reins, guaranteeing the rig would be steady. Wilson sat proudly at his side.

"Excellent work, men. I couldn't be more proud of the bravery and professionalism I've seen today," Pops said through the large megaphone. "After more than two hours of grueling work, the fire has been extinguished. I'm happy to report that we didn't lose a single firefighter, with only one report of injury from smoke inhalation."

Normally the men would cheer following such a report, but no one who worked the scene could find solace in that statistic when they'd heard the horrifying screams of those trapped in the burning debris.

"Robbins Grover estimates 360 employees were in the building at the time of the explosion. As of now, we have only accounted for 231. It will be our job, and the job of the volunteers who will be assisting us, to locate the remains of those who perished."

Could they really have lost nearly 130 members of their community? Leo inhaled deeply, until his lungs ached from holding his breath, and slowly allowed the air to seep between his parted lips. The thought still unsettled him, even though he'd been the one to gather the current count from Etta.

"Our search-and-recovery efforts will begin immediately. We've divided you into two teams that will work in twelve-hour shifts. Each company should send a representative to report to Gunnar Eriksson."

Gunnar stepped forward and raised his hand. "Your representative will relay your assigned shift and quadrant for the search-and-recovery mission."

He paused then said, "I'll be meeting with the mayor shortly to let him know what we need from the city. Are there any questions?"

"Yeah." A fellow in a tweed cap raised his hand. "What was the cause of the explosion?"

Another man yelled, "Any guess on the number of injured? Are all 129 unaccounted for presumed dead?"

Reporters. Leo shook his head. *Just what they needed.*

"I have nothing to say to the press at this time," Gunnar said. "Any response would be pure speculation."

Leo glanced toward St. Margaret's and saw Etta assisting a limping man entering the church. He had to hand it to her for stepping up and pitching in. She hadn't hesitated when he'd asked her to help track the names of survivors and their injuries.

He had no doubt she'd rather be shouting questions at Pops or interviewing witnesses, but she'd put that aside for the good of the wounded and the families of those missing. He could only pray her sacrifice wouldn't jeopardize Henry Mason's position at the *Enterprise.*

Etta's feet hurt, and her back ached. She hadn't sat down for hours. As soon as the complaint entered her thoughts, she chastised herself. Compared to what the injured were experiencing, her aches were trivial.

As the morning wore on, more and more injured had made their way to St. Margaret's. She'd not only seen a lifetime's worth of pain and suffering, but she'd learned more details about the explosion.

Across the street, the factory fire had been extinguished and a crowd of fireman gathered around Chief Eriksson. From the size of the group, Etta estimated every firefighter in Brockton had responded to the disaster.

While honored to be of assistance at St. Margaret's, curiosity was beginning to get the better of Etta. She itched to hear the chief's announcements, toss him a few questions, and begin sorting through the events of the morning. Did he have any information about the origin of the explosion or the number of dead?

Based on her own observations, she believed the factory's boiler was the culprit. Her reporter's brain immediately wondered when the machine had last been inspected. Overworked boilers were a huge cause of property loss, injury, and death.

Could it have been tampered with? Could it possibly be related to the series of arsons in town? Although there were striking differences, Grover's factory was located in the Campello District. She made a mental note to follow up on the age of the boiler and its maintenance schedule. She also needed to identify where Grover had purchased insurance for the factory and if he'd received any pressure to buy it from the Bonner brothers.

"Pardon me, miss."

Lost in thought, she hadn't noticed the woman approach. She held the hand of a young child clutching a doll.

"I'm Olive Smith. A gentleman over there said you was keepin' a list of survivors."

"If the person you are seeking self-reported, I should have them on my registry. Who are you looking for?"

"My husband was working this morning, George Smith." She bit her bottom lip and peered at the papers on Etta's clipboard.

Etta scanned the list, which had grown to nearly five pages. She'd been in such a hurry, she hadn't been able to alphabetize the names. "I'm sorry, ma'am. I don't see him."

The woman slid her free hand over the girl's chest and pulled her close. "Do you mind checking again?" Her voice warbled as she spoke. "I can't lose him. I just can't."

Etta offered a sympathetic smile. "Of course." When her second look didn't yield different results, she wrapped her arm around Olive.

"It's very early, ma'am. Some victims—"

Tears spilled from the young mother's eyes and her shoulders quaked.

"I'm sorry, Olive, I didn't mean to upset you." She searched her mind for something to comfort the young woman. "Let's not give up hope. Some of the injured were brought here by coworkers, firemen, and passersby who may not have known the names of the people they were helping. And if the wounded person wasn't able to tell me their name, all I could do at that point was jot down a brief description. Would you like to look over the descriptions and see if anyone matches your husband?"

Olive nodded and swiped the tears from her cheeks before examining the list.

When she finished, she sniffled. "None of those details match my

George." She handed the clipboard back to Etta.

Etta wanted to take the woman in her arms and tell her everything would be all right. But how could she say that? While some people had escaped the explosion with only minor injuries, others died a harrowing death.

"I'm so sorry. I can't imagine how difficult this must be. Not all survivors knew to register with me. It's possible your husband is on his way home right now."

Olive straightened her shoulders. "I'm sure you're right." She placed her hand on Etta's. "Thank you."

As Olive and her daughter walked away, Etta prayed George Smith had indeed found his way out of the burning factory and would be home waiting for his wife and child to return. And if he hadn't, that God's peace and comfort would surround the young widow—and all those who'd lost loved ones today.

CHAPTER 8

Leo dragged his weary body back to the firehouse for a brief reprieve from the day's daunting tasks. He'd have to return to the disaster scene in a couple of hours to assist city workers stringing electric lights around the burned-out factory. Just enough time for a bite to eat and a short nap. Showering would have to wait until the evening.

He rolled his shoulders. The day had taken a toll on him. His muscles ached from the laborious work of searching for survivors and fighting the massive fire, but the pain was nothing compared to the angst in his spirit. He'd not been emotionally prepared for the horrific recovery work that occupied most of his day. So far, all of the bodies they'd recovered, save one, had been burned beyond recognition.

Jens paced outside the station. If the day's events had been brutal for Leo, he could only imagine how difficult they'd been for his tenderhearted younger brother. "You all right, Jens?" he asked.

His brother combed his quaking hand through his disheveled hair. "I don't know." He paused and cupped his ears. "The heartrending cries of trapped victims, burning alive. The horror of it made me think of Patrick. Is that what he experienced?"

What could Leo say to him? He couldn't lie, yet the truth seemed too much for Jens at this moment. He settled for a brotherly embrace.

Jens swiped a tear from his cheek. "What if they don't stop, Leo? What if they torment me in my sleep?"

Leo placed a hand on Jens' arm. "Take a few deep breaths and let them out slowly."

Jens followed Leo's advice. In a few minutes, his breathing calmed.

"I hear them too, but it's over now. They're at peace. No more pain. No more suffering. That's what we must remember every time those thoughts creep back in."

Jens scrubbed a hand over his face. "I know you're right, but that sounds easier said than done."

"It is, but with discipline of mind and consistency, it becomes easier."

Jens nodded, but his brother's harrowed gaze troubled Leo. He wasn't sure he should leave Jens alone. "I volunteered to assist the municipal workers stringing lights for the night shift. Why don't you help us?"

"I think I'll grab my camera and photograph the scene."

"Are you sure it's a good idea to be by yourself right now?"

Jens shrugged. "I see things differently through the lens of my camera. Besides, doing something like documenting the scene will make me feel like I've done something meaningful."

"Okay. But if the voices haunt you again—"

"I'll come find you."

Leo patted his brother's shoulder. "Good."

He hadn't been able to offer Jens much solace, but hopefully he'd said enough to see the kid through. His brother wasn't cut out for firefighting. After the search-and-recovery mission concluded, he would press his father to speak to Jens again and give him his blessing to find a new occupation.

Something that wouldn't crush his spirit.

They stepped inside the station, and Leo headed straight for the bunkroom. Sleep was calling his name.

"Leo. Jens. Perfect timing."

He and Jens exchanged glances.

"I'm meeting Stanley Wingard over at the house on Denton Street where the boiler landed."

"Sure, Pops," Jens said. "I'm gonna grab my camera equipment and take pictures of the disaster scene first, then I'll head over. You got an address?"

"Yes, 74 Denton Street."

Pops gripped Leo's shoulder. "How about you? I sure could use your eyes on the scene."

"Count me in." He was bone tired, but Pops had always been there for Leo and his brothers, especially after their mother died. If Pops wanted Leo by his side now, that's where he'd be—without a complaint.

Etta stooped beside the remains of the Grover Shoe Factory and jotted notes in her tablet. Charred bits of leather, thread, and foot lasts were littered among the bent and broken machinery, all used to make the Emerson shoes the Grover plant was famous for.

Ropes strung between wooden stakes divided the scene into quadrants. Most of the activity centered in the left rear quarter of the lot, the portion of the factory Etta had seen collapse as the projectile hurtled through the building's roof, toppling the water tower. The smokestack, the only evidence of the mighty factory's storied existence, paid silent homage to those injured or perished.

A policeman approached her. She stood and tucked the notepad into her shirt pocket beneath her vest. After Peggy and the other volunteers relieved her, she'd dashed to the boardinghouse and slipped into her Henry Mason disguise. Hopefully, her hasty efforts would hold up under the officer's scrutiny.

"I'm afraid you'll need to leave the area, sir. We have an active search-and-recovery operation underway."

"I'm a member of the press."

His eyebrows arched. "Do you have credentials?"

"Yes, sir." She reached into the rear pocket of her knickerbockers. Finding nothing, she patted the garment's front pockets. Nothing. She'd left in such a hurry, she must've forgotten to grab her press card from her desk drawer.

"I'm Henry Mason, a columnist for the *Brockton Enterprise.* It appears I'm without my press pass."

"Sorry, Mr. Mason. No exceptions."

"Leo Eriksson, a fireman with Engine Company No. 1, can vouch for me."

"I'm sorry, sir. It's not my job to track down your references. You'll need to stay on the other side of the street." He straightened his shoulders and clasped his hands in front of him, signaling the discussion was finished.

She was about to challenge him when she spied a man with a camera and tripod in front of the Churchill & Alden Shoe Factory taking photographs of the scene. Perhaps she could pry information from him to include in her article.

She glanced each way before crossing Main Street. Curiosity seekers craned their necks to view the happenings at the disaster site while family members hoping for a miracle huddled together outside of St. Margaret's.

Etta waited while the photographer focused the lens and took the image. Leo's brother, Jens, emerged with a glass plate in hand from beneath the black tent he'd constructed over his camera and startled at the sight of her.

"Hello again, Mr. Eriksson. I'm Henry Mason, a reporter for the—"

"I know who you are. We met briefly at the Drake. I'm Jens. Pops is *Mr.* Eriksson."

She nodded.

"I need to develop this image immediately or the sunlight will ruin it. Keep talking." He disappeared under another black cloth, this one draping a portable dark box.

"Do you have any insights on the fire or the search-and-recovery operation I can include in my article? Do you know how many bodies have been recovered? Has the fire department confirmed the cause of the explosion?"

The clink of glass resonated from the confines of his dark box. She assumed it was the bottles housing the chemicals he used to develop his photograph. "Nothing I can share with you at this time. Not until we close our investigation."

She'd expected as much. Those Erikssons were a tight-lipped bunch, but she didn't want to end their conversation having gained nothing useful, so she tried a different tactic.

"So, you're a fireman and a pictorialist."

His muffled chuckle rose from beneath the black hood. "I'm hardly a pictorialist. My photography is more. . .practical." He stepped into the sunlight and attached his image to the curtain with a clothespin. "I thought I'd document the scene. Perhaps it will help with the investigation."

"May I?"

"I'd be honored, Mr. Mason."

"Please, call me Henry." Etta stepped closer and examined the photograph. Clean and crisp, no blurred lines. Jens had talent. "This is an excellent image, Jens. You come from a family of firefighters. How'd you learn to take pictures like this?"

"I once worked at the Enchanted Memories Portrait Studio on Grassley Avenue. Mr. Todd taught me everything. It's just a hobby, but I enjoy it."

"With this gift, Jens, you should be working for a newspaper."

"You really think so?"

"I do."

He shrugged. "Maybe someday. . .but it would be hard to leave the family business, as we Erikssons call it."

He packed his camera equipment in a wooden box and surrounded it with straw. "Hey, why don't you come with me to the house on Denton Street where the boiler landed? It's only a few blocks from here."

So, the fire department thought it was the boiler too, just as she'd suspected. "Was anyone hurt there?"

"I don't have any details." He unpinned his picture and placed it inside a large pocket in the velvet-lined lid of the camera box. "They aren't letting the press beyond the street, but I think we could make an exception for Henry Mason."

"Great." Maybe she could sweeten the pot. "If your dad will promise I get new details first, I'll pitch your photographs to go along with my story."

His eyes beamed. "My images. . .in the *Enterprise*?"

She nodded. "Perhaps if the newspaper uses them, your family will see your true talents lie outside the fire station."

"Don't get me wrong, they're supportive. Pops just doesn't see how taking photographs can put a meal on the table."

"If you were hired by the *Enterprise*, that might change his mind."

Jens secured the wood crate containing his portable dark room and solutions to the bottom of a hand cart and then strapped the camera box on top. "Ready?"

Ready? She'd been eager to investigate the facts surrounding the explosion all day. If Chief Eriksson could get her behind the ropes, where she could gain inside information as to why the boiler overheated, she'd have not only Jens' photographs but exclusive details no other reporter at the *Enterprise* would have—yet. Not even that cub reporter, Declan Gibney.

Leo ducked beneath the rope surrounding the front of Mary Pratt's house. A small crowd had gathered out front. Several police officers stood guard to prevent the press and curiosity seekers from disrupting their investigation.

"When my brother Jens Eriksson arrives," he said to the officer, "please let him through. He'll have a handcart with photography equipment."

"Yes, sir."

"Leo!" Jens called.

"Oh, there he is now."

"C'mon through. Dad and Chief Wingard are already examining the boiler."

Jens thumbed over his shoulder. "Henry Mason came with me. He's going to do some interviews. He says neighbors always seem to know what's happening and usually don't mind seeing their names in the paper."

Leo bit back a smile. That sounded like something Etta would say. "How did you pair up with Henry Mason?"

"He saw me taking pictures of the burned-out factory. He really liked my work. Any chance we can let him behind the ropes and give him an exclusive, up-close peek? He said he'd pitch my photographs to accompany his article."

Leo rubbed his jaw. That could be a real benefit for his brother. Jens had a good eye, and Etta noticed his talent as well. All the kid needed was an opportunity, and this could be it. "Bring him over."

"Take the handcart. I'll be right back."

Jens returned a moment later with Etta dressed in her Henry Mason disguise. Her practiced male mannerisms showed in her long, purposeful gait that varied drastically from the gentle swaying motion of most females. How did she do that?

"Good to see you again, Henry."

"Thank you, Leo. You as well. Jens said you might be able to give me a close-up view of the boiler and the damage it did to the house. Perhaps ask a few questions of Chief Eriksson?"

"I can arrange that, but you should know I already spoke to a reporter from the *Enterprise* before you arrived. So I'm not sure if I'll have information for you that he doesn't already know." He searched his memory. "Dent. . .no, Dexter. . ."

"Declan Gibney."

Leo snapped his fingers. "That's him."

She lowered her chin and frowned.

"He is from the *Enterprise*, right?"

"Yeah. He's got excellent instincts for news, but if I'm not careful, that little scrapper will put me out of a job."

Leo raised the cord partitioning the house from the small crowd gathering in the street. "I may have answered a few questions for Gibney, but he didn't have a private tour of the scene."

Her smile crinkled the tiny lines beside her eyes. "For that, I'm grateful."

"It's the least I can do for Brockton's leading journalist."

Jens walked past them, dragging his equipment.

Now alone, he leaned closer to Etta and lowered his voice. "Since you were assisting at St. Margaret's all morning, the other reporters have several hours lead time on their investigations. This just levels the playing field."

"I appreciate that. I have a six p.m. deadline, and I'd hate to miss out on the biggest story in the city—if not all of Massachusetts."

Jens immediately surveyed the damage to the house, chose the best location to take his photograph, and unpacked his equipment.

"Chief Eriksson, you remember Henry Mason," Leo said, keeping his address professional on the job site.

"I do. Good to see you again, Mr. Mason."

Etta gave a tight nod of her head.

"Mr. Mason, this is Stanley Wingard, the battalion chief from Engine Company No. 2 and a close colleague of my father's. He's assisting with the preliminary investigation."

"Preliminary?" Etta asked as she squatted beside the boiler.

"Inspectors from the American Society of Mechanical Engineers will be on site later this week to begin their assessment of the boiler's malfunction," Chief Wingard said.

She pointed to the twisted and mangled pipes protruding from the end of the boiler. "I've never seen anything like this."

"Sadly, boiler explosions are not uncommon. Oftentimes, manufacturing plants push the machines beyond their limit, too much pressure builds up, and they explode."

Etta stood. "Is that what you think happened, Chief Wingard? You believe the plant engineer overworked the boiler? In that case, the fault would lie with him and Grover, correct?"

The chief lifted his palms. "It's too early to determine the cause of the explosion. *That* is my official statement."

"What do you know about the plant engineer?"

"I just said I don't know the cause, and I won't have my name associated with slandering a man without evidence."

"Yes, sir. Have you interviewed the engineer?" she asked.

Wingard tossed up his hands and walked away.

"David Rockwell, the engineer, hasn't been located," Leo responded, his tone somber. "His wife saw him in his office moments before the explosion. Their home is—*was* located on the property as well. It appears the boiler traveled through Rockwell's house before landing here. His wife is fine but shaken."

If the engineer didn't survive, then Grover might be her only lead. She shoved her hands in her pockets. "Has anyone spoken with Grover?"

"He's been cooperative," Leo said. "He's provided us with the factory floor plan."

"Grover told us Rockwell is a first-class licensed engineer with twelve years' experience," Wingard called from the opposite side of the boiler. "Be sure to print that in your story."

Leo marveled at Etta's ability to rattle off questions and keep the facts straight in her mind to recall later without taking notes. Making a simple grocery list challenged his memory. Her keen intellect served her well. Warmth swelled his chest. He was proud of her.

"Chief Wingard, my objective isn't to paint an unflattering picture of either Rockwell or Grover. I want to provide the victims and survivors, as well as the other citizens of Brockton, with answers."

Chief Wingard jumped to the same false conclusion Leo had when Etta questioned his father. In hindsight, her questions had been as simple and direct as the ones she'd asked Wingard. Even though they'd both felt defensive, Etta didn't take it personally. She seemed to understand that getting to the truth would make people uncomfortable. He hadn't considered how much animosity she must endure during an investigation, yet she pushed through. He admired her resilience.

"Can one of you tell me how far it is from the factory to this lot? And how large would you estimate that boiler to be?"

"The boiler is roughly seventeen feet tall by six feet wide, and we guess it's about two hundred feet from the boiler room to this location," Chief Wingard said. "When it overheated, the pressure sent it flying through the factory, knocking out one of the rear support beams, severing gas lines, and compromising the water tower, which then fell onto the roof. The perfect witch's brew, if you will."

"May I quote you on that?"

"Certainly."

"Chief Eriksson, Chief Wingard mentioned severed gas lines. It's my understanding that a spark of some sort would be necessary to ignite them, such as burning coal from the boiler that would have been flying through the air."

"Yes, that's correct," Pops answered.

"What do you suppose caused the second explosion? The one that sent flaming projectiles throughout the factory, setting alight the portion of the building left standing after the initial blast?"

Pops glanced at Chief Wingard, who gave a slight shake of his head. "We're not prepared to comment on that at this time. We'll need to wait until after the search-and-recovery operation is completed in order to make our determination."

"Any chance someone tampered with the boiler, perhaps linking the explosion and fire at Grover's to the arsons in the area?"

"What?" Pops stared at her.

Leo didn't often see Pops rattled, but he could see his father didn't like the implication of Etta's question, that was for certain. He took his position as battalion chief very seriously, and he understood the weight his words carried. He'd been misquoted in the press before and most likely wanted to avoid that happening again.

"Not at this time. *Again,* this is a preliminary investigation." His voice grew terse. "Inspectors from the Hartford Steam Boiler Inspection and Insurance Company will make the final determination."

"And when will that be?"

"We don't know yet."

Sensing his father's growing irritation, Leo redirected Etta's attention.

"You can see where the boiler knocked the house at least two feet off its cement mooring."

"Incredible. Was anyone hurt?"

"No. The occupant, Mary Pratt, left the house shortly before the boiler struck. If she hadn't, there's a very good chance she wouldn't be alive right now."

"Chief Eriksson," Etta said, "when do you think you'll have information on the number of dead and missing?"

"It could be days, possibly weeks, before we know for sure. Our most recent number is 231 accounted for. Make sure your readers understand this is a fluid situation and the numbers will change daily for the next several days."

"I will, sir."

"Thank you. Also, please include a plea for any survivors who haven't self-reported to do so at the Campello Police Station as soon as possible. That may be the only way we know for certain how many survivors there are."

Etta's face went slack, as if uncertain of his father's meaning.

Pops shoved a heavy breath from his lungs. "The recovery process will be grisly, and we anticipate many of the dead will be difficult to identify."

Her eyes pinched closed briefly.

Sometimes when Etta took on her Henry Mason persona, she seemed uncaring—callous even—in her determination to uncover facts and discover the truth. He supposed, like himself and the firefighters he worked with on a daily basis, she'd developed a tough outer layer to protect herself from the harshness of life she often wrote about.

But in her slackened expression, Leo saw the truth. This story pierced her armor, and he was absolutely certain that the catastrophe they'd witnessed that morning would change all of them forever.

CHAPTER 9

Etta climbed the stairs to her room on the third floor of Mrs. Hemingway's boardinghouse. She needed to write an article and get it to her editor before the six o'clock deadline for tomorrow's edition—no, earlier than that—before Declan Gibney, the cub reporter at the *Brockton Enterprise*, filed his story.

She'd been sidelined for a while tracking the names of survivors and their injuries. Although she hadn't volunteered for the job, she couldn't refuse Leo, and the opportunity to help the injured and assist victims' families locate their loved ones had been rewarding. As it turned out, the position gave her a bird's-eye view of the disaster and knowledge she doubted other reporters would have.

But the details she'd learned about the boiler coursing through the engineer's home and crashing into another house, knocking the latter off its foundation—particulars no other reporter would have, including Declan—is what would set her story apart. Chiefs Wingard and Eriksson had been very forthcoming, and she would repay them with a top-notch piece sans any insinuation about Rockwell's or Grover's potential complacency about the boiler. She'd let the facts play out on that score.

Although she needed a bath, cleanliness would have to wait. She grabbed a sheet of paper from her top drawer, inserted it into the carriage of her Underwood typewriter, and turned the knob until the paper rolled into position. Her fingers barely kept up with the sentences forming in her mind, each filled with details about the explosion, the boiler punching through all four floors of the factory before bursting through the ceiling, toppling the water tower, and then traveling north and knocking the house on Denton Street two feet off its foundation. She recalled the sound of the boiler, the sight of glass raining down over the street, and the stench of burning flesh. Perhaps she should strike that last bit...too gruesome. She devoted a large section to the heroic measures of the Brockton Fire Department and the difficult decision to call off the rescue operation to combat the raging inferno.

Etta made a notation in her tablet to follow up on the cause of the second blast and any possible negligence by Rockwell or Grover. She yanked the sheet from the carriage and quickly inserted a fresh one. Her fingers deftly struck the metal keys as she recounted the types of injuries she'd seen at St. Margaret's and provided an estimate of the missing and unaccounted for. A statistic she had exclusive knowledge of due to her volunteer position.

She flipped to a clean page in her tablet and scribbled a list of questions for follow-up stories:

1. Get updated numbers of survivors, dead, and missing.
2. Cause of the explosion—boiler malfunction, overuse, or tampering? Chief Eriksson seems adamant the boiler hadn't been tampered with but need to talk to Grover about his insurance carrier all the same.
3. If the cause is suspicious, is the explosion related to the string of arsons?
4. How long will search and recovery take?
5. What aid will be available for victims' families?

That last question grieved Etta. Did any of the victims have life insurance? Did the injured have money set aside for medical bills? She sucked in a breath. It hadn't occurred to her until this very minute that hundreds of survivors were now unemployed. How would they feed their families or keep a roof over their heads?

She made a notation in the margin to see how the Maxwell Foundation could help. In the morning, she'd pay a visit to Mayor Keith to offer financial assistance. Perhaps she could organize a collection drive for affected persons and their families.

She glanced at the clock on the wall. Five thirty.

Time to go.

If Littleton accepted her article unedited, the typesetter would know how much space to allow for her copy, and she could make any necessary changes right in the newsroom. To keep Henry's profile low and reduce the risk of discovery, she rarely worked at the office. However, if she didn't arrive at the *Enterprise* by six, someone else would get the front-page headline.

She grabbed her portfolio, placed the article inside, and raced from the boardinghouse. When she arrived at the *Enterprise*, Jens waited outside.

"Where've you been?" he fussed. "It's six o'clock now."

"Never mind that. Those pictures are the key to our success. C'mon."

Jens opened the door. They hurried up two flights of stairs and dashed into the newsroom. Littleton leaned over Declan Gibney's desk, probably reading the kid's copy.

She tugged the story from her portfolio. "I've got an article with exclusive details."

Declan glanced at the clock. "You're too late, Mason. It's 6:03."

"You'll want to see this, boss. I've got details there's no way the kid could have. And at least one photograph, possibly two."

She motioned for Jens to step up beside her and show the images he'd taken. "This is Jens Eriksson, an amateur photographer *and* a fireman in Engine Company No. 1, which gave him access to the other side of the rope."

Littleton's eyes widened. That got his attention. Her boss loved an exclusive.

"Go ahead, Jens. Show him."

Jens slipped the photograph of the burned-out factory to Littleton first, just as they'd discussed. "This is from the southeastern corner of the building. You can see the smokestack here, and that's the search-and-recovery crew."

"Yeah," Littleton said, slumping back in his chair. "Our guy got that."

Jens pointed to a smaller structure, its partially burned frame still standing, a distinct hole in its side. "The boiler tore through the engineer's house before shooting up through all four levels of the factory and arcing over several blocks before landing in the house on Denton Street."

Littleton straightened and examined the image through the spectacles perched on the end of his nose.

Jens pulled the second photograph from his portfolio. "Knocking the house several feet off its foundation."

That did it. Etta could see it in Littleton's eyes. He coveted that picture the way she coveted her own byline.

"And you're the only one who got this?" he asked.

"Definitely. My father is the battalion chief and the lead investigator at the scene. My brother, a fireman in Engine Company No. 1, lifted the rope, granting Mason and me access."

Declan scrubbed his jaw. "He told me no reporters were allowed."

Etta tapped the kid's chest with the back of her hand. "It's all about connections, Declan. You haven't been around long enough to have any—at least not any that matter."

Etta tugged the picture from her editor's hand. "But these are only available if they accompany *my* story, which has a preliminary estimate of the missing, wounded, and deceased."

"How'd you get that information?" the kid asked. "None of my sources would release numbers."

"I'm personally acquainted with Henrietta Maxwell."

"The society dame?" he asked, seemingly impressed.

"Yeah, that's her. Leo Eriksson tasked Miss Maxwell to keep a list of the injured and survivors who reported to St. Margaret's."

Declan crossed his arms. "Doesn't matter. You didn't file on time. Number one rule of the newsroom is you gotta make deadline."

She scooted around the cub reporter and sat on the opposite corner of Declan's desk. "So, what do ya say, boss?"

Declan leaned against the desk. "It's past deadline, sir."

Littleton waved him off. Etta bit back a grin. He wanted the photographs. He was practically salivating. She shouldn't overplay her hand, but this was the time to ask for what *she* really wanted—her own byline.

She waggled the picture in front of Littleton. "Can I speak to you privately, sir?"

"Shouldn't I come too?" Jens asked. "After all, they are my photographs."

She eyed Jens. She didn't want the aspiring photographic journalist getting twitchy and cutting a deal with her boss that excluded her article.

"I won't change the terms of our agreement. He takes my story and your photograph, or there's no deal."

"Then why can't I come?"

Jens posed a fair question, but what was she to say? *I'm really Henrietta Maxwell masquerading as Henry Mason, and I need to talk frankly to my editor, one of only a few people who know about my ruse?*

"It's personal, Jens. . .regarding my contract." That was the truth, if only part of it.

Jens seemed to weigh her words. Did he think she might betray him? "You can trust me," she added.

With that, Jens consented. Declan protested, but Littleton didn't bat an eye. Etta followed her boss into his office and closed the door.

He flopped in his chair and held up his palms. "I know what you're going to ask, Etta, and I can't. Maxwell Business Machines is a major advertiser in our paper. You know this. If your father discovers his daughter has been working as an investigative reporter for our paper, he might pull those dollars and go elsewhere. If that happens, I'll lose my job and so will you."

She planted her fists on his desk and leaned closer. "You owe it to me. You've told me my writing is better than any other reporter at the *Enterprise*. Henry Mason is getting a reputation for solid journalism. I'm bringing in readership and advertising."

He scrubbed his face. "It's not about your work. It's—"

Etta folded her arms over her chest. "It's because I'm a woman. I know. I've heard that excuse before."

She'd been told her entire life what women could and couldn't do in society. She was fortunate to have been born into a family who'd only recently achieved financial success, and her parents were more progressive than most of Boston's well-to-do. But Littleton was correct. Her parents wouldn't be pleased. Especially if they were blindsided. She'd need to reveal herself to them as Henry Mason before they saw her byline or heard it from the Beacon Hill gossip brigade.

"I may not get a better opportunity or a bigger story than this." She held his gaze and bade her tone to remain even. Now was not the moment to let her emotions flow unchecked. Besides, Littleton had hired her. She doubted any other editor in Brockton would have done the same. He deserved her respect—even now, when so much was on the line.

He steepled his fingers and stared at Etta. "I'm sorry, Etta. The story runs credited to Henry Mason, or it doesn't run. Those are the terms you accepted."

Etta fought the urge to lower her chin. She'd hoped her boss wouldn't dig in his heels, but she refused to show how his decision had crushed her dreams yet again. If she hadn't promised Jens, she might renege, if for no other reason than to prove to Littleton how much getting a byline of her own meant to her. But she did promise Jens, and it wasn't right to force him to miss his chance just because society wasn't ready to give Etta hers.

"I need to get something for this, sir. Even if I'm the only one who knows it."

"Like what?"

"Jens has an eye for photography. I want you to hire him as a staff photographic journalist. After all, high-quality front-page images sell papers just as well as a Henry Mason article."

"And this will satisfy you?"

"It will do for now. But don't think I'm giving up."

"Why would anyone who has ever met you think that?"

She offered her hand. "So, we have a deal."

"Deal," he said, accepting her hand.

She'd become quite adept at swallowing her disappointment. At least this time she could rejoice for Jens and what the future held for him while she waited for the byline she craved.

Leo shivered as the sun dipped below the roofline of the homes and businesses lining Main Street. Whether the chill sprang from the crisp temperature or the sight of the burned-out diner that had been his second home since his mother died, he didn't know.

He stooped and dug a singed menu from the rubble. Already he longed for the place where he'd gathered with family and friends, chatted about everyday events over coffee and apple pie, and engaged in evasive maneuvers to protect his breakfast from the bottomless pits better known as his brothers.

It's a diner, Leo. Grieving the loss of a restaurant when so many people had lost their jobs, homes, and businesses—not to mention their lives—was downright ridiculous. Besides, the people who made the Drake special were all safe. For that he would be eternally grateful.

He'd learned from Etta about the young mother who'd perished above the seamstress shop next door after throwing her infant son from the window. His chest tightened. The fireman who'd been unable to save her would carry the weight of her loss forever. It was their worst nightmare scenario.

Well, almost.

The only thing worse was losing a fellow firefighter.

The memory of Patrick's hearty laughter warmed him. He shouldn't have gone back in. But Patrick couldn't withstand the little girl's tears over the cat she believed trapped inside, so he'd made another pass. How foolish. People were the priorities—not property and not pets.

When Patrick chose to disobey Pops' command, Leo should've disobeyed too. Preventing Jens from following after Patrick may have saved his brother's life, but it had tarnished their relationship for several years—a relationship that only recently appeared to be getting back on track.

Leo forced a heavy breath from his lungs. Why hadn't he disobeyed orders and gone after Patrick? If he'd been willing to risk his own life, maybe he could've rescued Patrick, and then Jens would have been spared the prolonged melancholy that his best friend's death had triggered.

Or both Leo and Patrick would be dead.

He shook his head. Had he learned nothing from Patrick's death? Why had he thought he knew better when Pops gave the order to pull back?

Because he'd wanted to be a hero this morning when he saved Teresa, just like Patrick had when he returned to the burning house in search of the little girl's cat.

Risking one's life to save others was part of the job. Wanting to be a hero, and not following protocol, got people killed.

Just. Like. Patrick.

No, Pops made the right call. He was sure of it.

"Leo?"

Etta's voice broke the silence. He stood and faced her.

"I just came from the newspaper office. My editor wanted Jens' photographs. Don't be surprised if they're on the front page tomorrow."

"That's great," he said, his lackluster tone failing to convince even himself of his happiness for Jens.

"Are you all right?"

"Sure. Just thinking over the day's events, what we might've done differently." *What I might've done differently.*

He pinched his lips shut. If he said any more, he risked the tangled mess of thoughts and emotions simmering inside him tumbling out, revealing his doubts despite his resolve moments earlier to accept that nothing more could have been done.

"Perhaps you need to shift your thoughts to those you were able to rescue."

"Yeah, you're right. Pops and Gunnar said the same thing, but it still feels like I failed them."

"*You* failed them?"

Ugh. He hadn't meant to say that out loud.

"The loss of life from any disaster is not borne by one man alone," she said, her voice steady and constant. Something he appreciated in a day filled with so much turmoil. "There was nothing more that could've been done this morning without putting others' lives in danger."

"Do you believe that, Etta?"

"I do." She waved her hand over the rubble from the Drake to the corner of Calmar Street and on to the factory lot. "Honestly, looking at this destruction, it's amazing anyone survived."

She shoved her hands in her pockets and rocked on her heels. "I hope you don't find my optimism trite, but more than two hundred people escaped with their lives today. *Two hundred.* No matter how you look at it, Leo, that is a miracle."

"I know you're right, it's just—"

"It will take some time for your heart to follow your head's lead."

This woman. If he possessed an ounce of brains, he'd cast off his fears and pursue her hand. But no one ever accused him of being overly intelligent. Time to change the subject, or he'd end up in an entirely different quagmire of emotion.

"I got your message that you have some information for me about the fire."

"One of the men who checked in at St. Margaret's was employed as a janitor at Grover's," she said. "I overheard him speaking with a coworker about how the factory floors were treated nightly with linseed oil to keep the dust down in the plant. And linseed oil is—"

"Highly flammable."

"Exactly. Once the sparks caught the floorboards on fire, a raging inferno ensued. I think many factors collided today to make the 'perfect witch's brew' as Chief Wingard said."

She cupped her hands in front of her mouth and blew warm breath on her skin. "It's getting chilly out here. I should head to the boarding-house. Good night, Leo."

"See you tomorrow, Etta."

"You'll definitely be seeing Henry Mason."

She'd only walked a few feet away before he called after her. "How'd you know where to find me?"

She traipsed back to him, a knowing grin on her face. "I stopped by the firehouse to follow up on my message and tell you about the linseed oil. When Gunnar didn't know where you were, I figured you'd be here, saying goodbye to the Drake."

"Why's that?"

"Because it was your spot."

"My spot?"

"Yeah. The place where you and your family met on a daily basis. I know the Drake was important to you. Just because it's a place and not a person doesn't mean you can't mourn its loss."

Lord have mercy, she understood.

Of course she did. What he didn't understand was the strong bond forming between them, and in such a short time. A bond that lured him closer and, at the same time, demanded he keep her at arm's length before she wreaked havoc in his life like Annika.

The latter would be much easier if she donned her Henry Mason disguise twenty-four hours a day. Because the only thing stopping him from taking her in his arms and kissing her soundly was that bushy mustache.

CHAPTER 10

Etta stepped from the cab outside city hall and slipped several coins into the driver's waiting palm. She didn't have an appointment. However, the Maxwell name opened doors other surnames did not. As a general rule, she was morally opposed to using her family's wealth and influence for personal gain. But since her errand today would benefit the survivors and grieving family members, she would demand an audience with the mayor if necessary.

Hopefully, it wouldn't come to that.

Mayor Keith was well respected in town and, based on the city's quick response to the disaster, he may have already given thought to a relief fund—the matter foremost on her mind this morning.

She tugged on the jacket of her smart suit before climbing the stairs to the city offices on the second floor. Several men chatting about the fire damage to the factory whizzed by her on the wide staircase, one an aide to Mayor Keith. When she overheard them discussing the factory's insurance policy, every investigative bone in her body ached to linger and discover what they'd learned.

She sighed. No time for that now. Today she had a different mission.

At the top of the stairway, she followed the sign that pointed to Mayor Keith's office. She turned the knob and stepped into a whirlwind of activity. Typewriters clickety-clacked, a woman filed a stack of papers, and two gentlemen in suits and ties studied some sort of representational drawing they'd tacked to the wall. Was that the Grover Shoe Factory? She inched closer and squinted. Although she confirmed it was the ill-fated manufacturing plant, she couldn't decipher any details.

Three people stood in line at Mrs. Stanhope's desk. Etta liked to think of her as the mayor's gatekeeper. No one saw Mr. Keith without first getting the approval of his personal secretary. This she'd learned from reporting on city policy as Henry Mason.

However, she had one thing going in her favor she doubted the men in line in front of her could claim. Connections. She did hate to jump the line, but she assumed at some point today the mayor would hold a press conference, which meant as soon as she finished her discussion with him about establishing a relief fund, she would need to sprint back to the boardinghouse and don her Henry Mason disguise. She scooted closer to Mrs. Stanhope's desk and cleared her throat.

"No way, lady. We were here first," the man next in line said.

"Yeah, you can wait your turn like we did."

Etta immediately recognized the second voice as Declan Gibney—the cub reporter for the *Enterprise*. She had to admit, the kid had tenacity.

He eyed her as if there was a tad bit of recognition. "Do I know you?"

An empty pit formed in the hollow of her stomach. This would never do. If Declan recognized her, everything she'd worked to achieve would come to a screeching halt.

She sheltered her face beneath the wide brim of her hat, raised her chin, and summoned every bit of haughtiness she'd heard in the tone of Boston's garden club set. "Henrietta Maxwell." She scanned his appearance from head to toe. "And who might you be?"

"Declan Gibney, a reporter for the *Brockton Enterprise*. I heard you volunteered at St. Margaret's—"

Mrs. Stanhope shot to her feet. "Miss Maxwell, the mayor will be delighted you've come."

The muscles in Etta's shoulders eased, and she made a mental note to send flowers to Mrs. Stanhope later that day.

The stout woman rounded the desk and motioned for Etta to follow her. "Right this way."

"Hey, that's not fair," the man at the front of the line responded.

"Oh, shush up," Mrs. Stanhope replied.

Etta followed the secretary to the mayor's door and waited patiently while Mrs. Stanhope knocked then entered his office. She returned before Etta counted to three. "Mayor Keith will see you now."

"Thank you."

"My pleasure, Miss Maxwell."

The mayor stood and offered her a seat opposite his desk. She'd always appreciated this room. While his office afforded an excellent view of Brockton and the town green, her favorite feature was the wall-to-wall cherry bookshelves behind his desk. Someday, when she had a permanent residence, she would hire a carpenter to create such splendid houses for her growing book collection.

"I'm delighted to see you today, Miss Maxwell," he said. "I'm hoping you've come to offer assistance to the survivors and their families."

"You've read my mind, Mayor. I'd like to lend my name and my considerable fundraising talent to any effort to aid the disaster victims."

His eyebrows peaked. "You mean more than a generous contribution?"

"Yes, sir. As you know, as chairwoman of the Maxwell Foundation, I have considerable experience organizing charity events such as the annual Fireman's Ball to benefit the Brockton Fire Department. I have an established network of donors to provide cash assistance as well as plenty of people who will eagerly donate their time to coordinate efforts on the ground."

"That is very generous of you, Miss Maxwell."

"I love the city of Brockton, and it's my deepest joy to assist her and her citizens during this crisis."

"Your offer is accepted. And I'm delighted to say we're already receiving donations."

"Already? Without solicitation?"

He nodded. "The first came in yesterday afternoon, just hours after the explosion. The United Shoe Machinery Company of Boston sent us $1,000. Last evening the Joint Shoe Council of Brockton met, approved a $500 gift, and directed us to apply it toward a General Relief Fund."

A soft gasp escaped her lips. "That is marvelous. It truly warms my heart to see people helping their neighbors."

She removed her gloves and laid them in her lap. "Now, what needs to be done for the firemen and other people aiding in the recovery efforts? Can I arrange for food and drinks to be available nearby?"

The worry lines creasing the mayor's forehead upon her arrival faded from his brow. "Speak with Mrs. Stanhope. A donation of any size will ease our burden and assist the men on the ground."

"I'd like to be more personally involved, sir."

"Well, we certainly can't have a woman of your position digging in the rubble." He chuckled, and his amused smile lighted his eyes. They were indeed blessed to have such a kindhearted man at the helm of the city. "What did you have in mind, Miss Maxwell?"

"What plans have been made for a memorial service?"

Mayor Keith eased back in his chair, fingers steepled. "None so far. It's only been twenty-four hours. I have a city council meeting scheduled for this afternoon. A memorial service and a relief fund are on the agenda."

"The Maxwell Foundation wants to ensure every man, woman, or child lost in the disaster has a proper casket and headstone. I realize many families may wish to provide their own as the last thing they can do for their loved one, but many cannot afford it."

"That's very generous of you, Miss Maxwell. Thank you."

"No thanks are necessary. The Maxwell Foundation exists to improve the lives of those who call Brockton home." She paused and licked her lips. "I hope you do not consider this impertinent, Mayor, but has any consideration been given to the remains of those who are not identifiable?"

He sighed. "I've spoken with Chief Eriksson, and he has indicated that many of the bodies are burned beyond recognition. I plan to propose a memorial to honor them, and perhaps a mass grave at city expense."

"If the town council approves a memorial, the Maxwell Foundation will contribute $1,000. More if needed, but I'm confident that families and friends of the victims will want to donate as well."

"We are grateful that your family hasn't forgotten us, especially in our time of need." He stood. "I have a town council meeting to prepare for later today."

Etta rose. "Of course. Just one more thing before I leave. I have a few contacts at the *Enterprise*. May I ask them to advertise the funds available for burial assistance in their next edition? I would like to relieve the burden of victims' families who may not be able to pay for their loved one's final expenses as soon as possible."

"Another excellent idea." He opened the door. "Please ask Mrs. Stanhope to introduce you to my assistant, Frances Lehr. Let Miss Lehr know that she is to assist you with any of the undertakings we've discussed today."

"Thank you, Mayor."

"Good day, Miss Maxwell."

Five people waited in line to speak with Mrs. Stanhope when Etta returned to the front office, Declan Gibney still among them. The secretary's brows lifted in question at the sight of Etta.

"Miss Lehr's office?" Etta asked.

Mrs. Stanhope pointed to a corridor on the opposite side of the room. "Second door on the left."

Etta thanked her then crossed the large office, dodging a woman with a tall stack of file folders in her hands. She paused. What if she gave Declan the scoop about the funeral fund and aid for the victims' families? It was just the kind of fluff, human-interest piece the kid loved. And it would distract him from the more tantalizing, headline-grabbing stories she wanted to write.

Besides, she owed him one after getting the front-page headline this morning for a story submitted after the deadline—a cardinal sin at the *Enterprise*. Although a conversation with Declan could prove risky, she'd managed to fool him once with her pompous airs. If she kept her face shrouded beneath her wide hat brim, she could do it again, couldn't she?

She backtracked and approached Declan, who still waited for Mrs. Stanhope to finish her conversation.

At the sight of her, he thumbed over his shoulder to the rear of the line. "No way, lady. Maxwell or not, I need something to run in today's paper."

"That's exactly what I want to speak with you about, young man." She kept her voice soft and her tone supercilious. "I have something straight from the mayor, and you'll be the first to know about it."

"What kind of information?" Despite his flat expression, Declan's voice betrayed his curiosity.

"Aid for victims' families."

His eyes sparkled. That enticed him.

He left the line and joined her near a large oak file cabinet.

Declan lifted his tablet, pencil at the ready. "This better be good."

"Not yet. I need to introduce you to someone first. Follow me." Declan stuck close, like a puppy—an image that pleased her more than it ought.

Etta located Miss Lehr's office and poked her head inside. The petite woman sat hunched over her desk, scanning the Brockton Business Directory, a book Etta knew well from her fundraising endeavors.

Miss Lehr glanced toward the door, held up her index finger, and then jotted notes on a legal pad. When she finished, she stood and welcomed them to her very tiny, yet orderly, office.

"Aren't you Henrietta Maxwell?"

Etta dipped her chin.

"I recognize you from the newspapers. I'm Frances Lehr." She tugged her desk chair to a small portion of unoccupied space near the window. "Would you like a seat?"

"No, thank you. We won't be long."

Miss Lehr leaned against the side of her desk and folded her arms. "How may I be of assistance, Miss Maxwell?"

"I just finished an impromptu meeting with Mayor Keith. The Maxwell Foundation has offered to cover the funeral costs for any of the victims whose families would like assistance. He suggested I speak with you about spreading the word. The sooner these grieving families learn assistance is available, the sooner we may lighten their burden."

"All of them?" Her mouth fell agape, but she quickly regained her composure. "That's very generous."

"It's the least we can do. We are looking for other ways to contribute, but for now, that is the only item we are prepared to make public."

Declan scribbled furiously on his notepad.

She motioned toward the cub reporter. "I met this resourceful young man waiting to speak with Mrs. Stanhope." Declan stood a little straighter at her compliment. "He is a reporter with the *Brockton Enterprise,* and I'd like him to write a press release for the newspaper to help spread the word. Would you be so kind as to coordinate with him to verify his article meets the standards of the mayor's office?"

Declan gave her the side-eye. She hadn't meant to insult him, but the mayor did specifically ask for the copy to be run by Miss Lehr.

"Absolutely. May I contact local funeral directors and pastoral staff who will likely be in contact with the families? They can inform them about available aid for final expenses."

"Wonderful idea." Etta addressed both Miss Lehr and Declan, but her narrowed gaze sharpened on the cub reporter. "I would like to keep the foundation's name out of the press release. Just let people know that funds are available."

Miss Lehr cupped Etta's hand and gently squeezed. "Understood."

Declan tucked his pencil behind his ear. "If that's what you want, Miss Maxwell, but your name in the headline would garner more attention."

"Thank you, young man."

Hopefully, Declan would respect her request. Through her work with the Maxwell Foundation, she'd learned it was often difficult for folks to accept charity, especially hardworking people who found themselves a little short from time to time.

Although it may prove useful to have Declan indebted to her, she didn't desire the same for Brockton's grieving families.

ONE HUNDRED MISSING AFTER BLAZING INFERNO FEARED INCINERATED

Incinerated? Leo folded the broadsheet and tossed it onto the table in the station's break room. How could Etta write a story with such a provocative headline?

Last night she'd spoken with such empathy about the disaster. Didn't it matter to her that the survivors and families of the deceased would read this? Just when he'd been thinking perhaps Etta might be the woman for him. He blew a heavy breath from his lungs, but it did nothing to relieve the weight pressing against his chest. Nor did it stop the throbbing vein in his neck. *Let it go, Leo.*

"What's eating you?"

He'd forgotten Pops sat across from him, sipping his coffee and eating overcooked toast. Without the Drake's cook to prepare their breakfast, they'd been caught with a bare pantry. Sure, there were other diners in Campello, but none of the Erikssons were eager to find a new one yet. By ten o'clock this morning, starvation had driven them to the station to forage through the break room, where they'd found nothing but coffee and stale bread.

"The headline for Henry Mason's article in the *Enterprise*?"

"I hadn't noticed. I was too busy looking at your brother's photographs. Right there on the front page. Who'd have ever thought?"

"Yeah. I'm proud of him." Leo cleared his throat. "Pops, have you considered giving Jens your blessing to leave the family business and pursue photography? We both know he's not cut out for the devastation and loss that's an inevitable part of the job."

"I suppose you're right. I love having all my sons here at the station with me, but Jens is different. He's an artist, as his photographs show. The weight of this job will crush his spirit if he stays too long."

Leo stood and cupped his father's shoulder. "Thanks, Pops."

He took another swig of his coffee. "I'm gonna head over to the excavation site and give Gunnar and the others a hand."

"About that. Seems we have plenty of volunteers, and the overnight team made excellent progress." Pops removed a clipboard from a hook on the wall. "I need you to survey the damage on Calmar, Denton, and Main Street and file an official report. You'll need to determine if any buildings should be condemned."

"I'll need to interview property owners and note the extent of the damage both internally and externally." Leo massaged his temple. "That could take weeks."

"Yes, that's why I would like you to get started as soon as possible. Take Jens with you. This is a good task for him. He can photograph any buildings that need to be demolished."

"Why not just let Jens and Leif do it?" Leo asked. "Then I could help Gunnar with the search for remains?"

"Because neither of them has your attention to detail," Pops said, sliding the clipboard in front of Leo. "Plus, if Jens decides to leave the department, he won't be here to follow up with any questions or claims."

Both statements were true. Pops routinely followed up on Leif's inventory reports and adjusted the figures. And Jens couldn't find a pair of matching socks in his own drawer if his life depended on it. He was a complete train wreck when it came to detail—unless he was behind the lens of his camera.

Normally, this task would fall to Pops as the incident commander, but the scale of the disaster and the breadth of the wreckage made it impossible for him to complete the task in a reasonable amount of time. Occupants would be displaced from their dwellings and businesses would remain closed until the buildings deemed safe to reopen were certified. Those with insurance wouldn't be able to make a claim without verification from the fire department. Whether he liked the paperwork part of firefighting or not, Leo couldn't argue that Brockton citizens needed the inspections completed.

He glanced at his father. Pops' bloodshot eyes bore witness that Leo hadn't been the only Eriksson who'd endured a restless night. Although his father's faith was strong, this incident must be taking a toll on him. And now, instead of stepping up and helping out, Leo was making the situation more difficult for him.

"Sure, Pops. You can count on me to do whatever needs done."

"Thanks, Son."

Leif popped his head inside the break room. "Henry Mason is outside to speak with you, Leo."

The muscles in his shoulders tightened at the sound of Etta's moniker. That headline rankled him. And he owed it to Etta and their budding friendship to let her know.

CHAPTER 11

Etta paced outside the firehouse. Although a former vaudeville actor designed her costume, her nerves tended to catapult around the men in Engine Company No.1. She worried that, with time, her vocabulary and mannerisms would give her away as a woman in disguise.

Leif opened the door. "He's coming. You're welcome to wait inside, you know. You don't have to sneak around."

"I guess all the undercover work on the arson story has made me a little paranoid."

Leif's eyes narrowed. "Para-what?"

"Overly cautious."

He gave a tight nod of his head. "You comin'?"

"Nah, I'll wait here."

"Suit yourself." The door swung closed behind him.

She untucked the gold watch from her pocket and checked the time—11:15. After the meeting with the mayor earlier, she'd stopped by several neighborhood delicatessens and arranged for sandwiches, lemonade, and coffee to be delivered to the Campello station so search crews could be fed without leaving the site. Not wanting to impede on the business of the firehouse, the shopkeepers agreed to bring tables to set up the food and drinks outside the station.

Even on short notice, they'd been eager to be useful in the wake of yesterday's catastrophe. Wishing to remain anonymous, she arranged for the owner of the Brockton Diner to contact the station to let them know of the arrangements and to learn how much they should prepare.

Etta stared at the factory's gutted remains. Search-and-recovery crews had worked through the night. Hopefully, Leo could provide updated information about how the remains were handled and where they were taken once extracted from the rubble. After speaking with him, she planned to return to city hall and see what Henry Mason, ace reporter, could fish from city aldermen that she didn't already know.

Leo and his father stepped outside. "I hope you don't mind me tagging along," Chief Eriksson said. "When Leif told us you were waiting to speak with Leo, I wanted to express my appreciation for your excellent article on yesterday's tragedy. You displayed your usual keen understanding of the topics you write about."

She rarely received such praise from a member of the public, and Chief Eriksson's words lightened the weight she'd been carrying. She'd meticulously researched her article, double-checking—even triple-checking—every detail.

"I appreciate how you stuck to the facts as we know them at this time and conveyed to your readers that information may change as the investigation progresses. We'll know more in the coming days."

"Thanks, Chief Eriksson. Jens' picture sold the story to my editor."

"Yes, he appears to have a real talent and passion for photography. Good day, Henry."

"Good day, sir."

An overwhelming desire to squeal with delight rose within her. However, such behavior would be incongruous with a tough-as-nails reporter for the *Enterprise,* so she stuffed her hands into the pockets of her tweed knickerbockers and rocked on her heels instead.

"Did you have a chance to read my article, Leo? The Associated Press picked up the story and reprinted it in almost every major daily on the East Coast. With that kind of exposure, this story could be the one that finally gets Henrietta Maxwell a byline."

"I'm happy for you, Etta."

Leo's tone contradicted his words. Perhaps he still struggled with the aftermath of the fire and the decision to halt rescue operations. "You okay?"

"Can I speak frankly?"

Instinctively she inched away. "Of. . .course."

He rubbed the back of his neck. "Do me a favor. Remember that *this* story, the one that might earn you a byline, is a human tragedy. Dozens are still unaccounted for, and recovery crews are excavating bodies that aren't recognizable as male or female."

"I don't mean to seem uncaring. I've been working hard for years and haven't received the same credit male journalists would've earned a long time ago."

"Well, *that* kind of reporting should take you a long way to achieving your goal."

What was he saying? Was he praising her article the way his father had? Or did he find the story lacking? "I'm not sure what you mean. What kind of reporting?"

"No sympathy. No voice for the victims. Just straight-forward-details-and-numbers kind of reporting."

"That's good journalism, Leo. Stick to the facts, no embellishing."

"Is that why you used a sensationalist headline like 'One Hundred Missing After Blazing Inferno Feared Incinerated'?"

Was he attacking her? She lifted her palms. "I don't always get to title the articles I submit. The editor makes the final call. As an employee of the *Enterprise*, my stories are the property of the newspaper." She shrugged. "Like it or not, headlines sell papers—and the more sensational, the better. That's the newspaper business."

He shook his head. "But your reporting didn't mention the human tragedy involved."

"Not mention?" Her voice rose, and she reminded herself not to be offended. She paused and inhaled deeply, steadying her nerves. It was a fair question from a friend, one whose knowledge of the newspaper business wasn't as in-depth as her own. "I did include an estimate of the missing, wounded, and deceased."

He stretched his arms wide. "Again, cold numbers and facts. There was no human face to the article, making it relatable. Where was the mention of the young woman who sacrificed her life to save her child?"

"Leo, I—"

"Or my friend, Dora Clark." He patted his chest. "*I* recommended her for the position." His voice softened, and pain filled the space between his words. "Yesterday was her first day."

She sucked in a breath. "Oh heavens, that poor dear." She wanted to hold his hand and comfort him, but Henry Mason couldn't do such a thing.

"I don't expect you to understand."

"But—"

"Never mind, *Henry*. Go chase your byline. See ya around." He spun on his heel and reentered the firehouse.

Etta stood there, blinking. What in the world had just happened?

She regretted that her article and its headline aroused Leo's remorse over losing his friend. Her last wish was to cause anyone pain—especially Leo.

But she'd written a good, clean piece—one that was picked up by the national wire. Why didn't he understand that she'd done her job and done it well? Or that she had little control over the headlines chosen by her editor.

Not if she wanted that byline.

Armed with a tablet and fountain pen, Leo stepped into the breezy, overcast day, ready to begin the tedious task of assessing nearby property for safety and fire damage. He needed to stop by a hardware store and purchase a can of paint and a broad brush. Condemned buildings would receive a large "C" somewhere visible, denoting the structure as unsafe and slated for demolition.

A group of sooty-faced firemen gathered around two tables laden with sandwiches. Pops mentioned an anonymous donor wanted to feed the men excavating the disaster site. Refreshments would be provided around the clock with heartier fare arriving every six hours each day until the recovery operation ceased.

He suspected the Maxwell Foundation furnished the grub. Etta was a mystery to him. On the one hand, she was a thoughtful and generous benefactress to the Brockton Fire Department. She'd anticipated this need and made provision for it. On the other, she was a hardened reporter with no interest in conveying the personal stories of heroism or tragedy from yesterday's disaster in her articles. No two ways about it, Etta Maxwell was a walking conundrum.

He grabbed an egg salad sandwich and joined his brothers by the wrought iron railing separating the firehouse from the alley and the adjoining Bonner Brothers Insurance Company. The spot where Etta literally fell back into his life.

Guilt pricked his conscience. He'd been too harsh with her earlier. What did he know about being a journalist? He knew even less about being female. By all accounts, she was an excellent reporter. She must be frustrated to receive accolades for her writing but no credit merely because she wore petticoats instead of knickerbockers.

Leo shook his head. He'd been a real jerk. He'd need to apologize the next time he saw her.

"Good sandwich," Jens said, before shoving the last quarter in his mouth.

"Yep, it's good enough to rival Trude's," Gunnar said. "But if you tell her I said that, I'll flat out deny it."

Jens wiped his mouth. "I'm gonna get another sandwich, then I'll be ready to go, Leo."

Leo swallowed a bite of his sandwich. "This is good. All I've eaten today is a piece of burnt toast."

Gunnar shook his head. "You three bachelors are gonna waste away. Hey, you should ask the sandwich guy where his restaurant is. Nothing will ever replace the Drake, but at least you won't starve."

Leo punched his brother's arm. "Ya know, for a lughead, every now and then you have a good idea."

Gunnar laughed. "I heard you whined your way out of the search-and-recovery operation."

"Hardly. Pops made a special request. I'd rather be doing my part at the site."

"Pops has a lot on his plate but seems to be handling it well so far."

"I think it eases all our minds, knowing Jens won't be assisting with that gruesome job. No one wants to see him revisit the malaise he experienced after Patrick's death."

"Hey, Jens," Gunnar called, alerting Leo their brother was coming. "I told Leo maybe y'all should visit the egg salad guy's diner."

"We were hoping Trude would take pity on us, weren't we, Leo?"

"Brilliant idea, Jens."

"Don't bet on it," Gunnar said. "At least not regularly enough to avoid starvation. The kids keep her pretty busy."

Leo tossed his napkin in the trash. "See ya later, Gunnar."

Jens grabbed another sandwich from the tray on their way out. "These are great. Where's your place?" he asked the fella behind the table.

"The Brockton Diner. We're beside Hastings Bakery. Got a big, green-checkered awning."

"You'll be seeing more of us," Jens said. "Thanks again."

Leo slapped his brother's back. "What's that, four sandwiches? You're a bottomless pit."

"You're just jealous because you can't eat like that without getting fat, old man."

Leo tousled his brother's hair. Man, he loved this kid. There was nothing he wouldn't do for either of his brothers, and he didn't doubt they felt the same about him.

He eyed Jens, who was staring at the factory's blackened smokestack. Although his brother appeared to be handling the disaster in stride, Leo saw the tiny worry lines at the corners of his eyes. Laughter was a good distraction, but he'd remain vigilant for signs of melancholy.

"You're using the Brownie Box today?" he asked, pointing to the camera hanging around his brother's neck.

"Yeah. I'll need to take the camera to an Eastman Kodak developer in Boston, but it'll be faster and more efficient than setting up and tearing down the dark box at each location."

Leo rubbed his hands together. "Let's ease our way into this project and start with St. Margaret's and the Churchill & Alden Shoe Factory."

They crossed the street in front of the station and turned right. Leo picked up the pace as they passed the excavation site, trying his best to keep Jens engaged in conversation.

They stopped in front of the church. "We should probably speak with the parish secretary," Leo said. "She'll most likely know what damage the building received."

"You go on inside." Jens sat on the church step and stared at the burned-out factory. "I'll wait here."

Now what? His brilliant plan to keep his brother from drifting into melancholy hadn't been so brilliant after all.

"We didn't lose one firefighter yesterday." A hint of sadness tinted his voice. "Yet Patrick died in a much smaller fire."

Leo nudged his brother's arm. "I need you to come with me."

"It's okay," he said, refusing to budge. "I appreciate how the family wants to protect me. I really do." He scratched the stubble on his cheeks. "Truthfully, yesterday was difficult." He shuddered. "But I'm better today, and I'm confident I've made peace with Patrick's death. I don't blame myself, you, or God any longer."

Leo lowered himself onto the step beside his brother. "Yeah?"

"Yeah. No firemen died yesterday because Pops made the right call and the men listened." He jabbed Leo with his elbow. "Whether they wanted to or not. Patrick died because he chose to risk his life rather than follow the rules and disappoint that little girl. If he hadn't wanted to be her hero, he'd still be alive." His voice shook, and he wiped his nose on his sleeve. "God gives us the freedom to make our own choices. Patrick made his, and I've made peace with that."

"That's a hard truth to accept, little brother."

Jens nodded. He dabbed his moisture-laden eyes with his palms. A few minutes passed before he spoke again. "Ya know what's an even harder truth?"

"What's that?"

"The job calls us to protect and serve, but we can't save everyone."

"That's the hardest truth of all." Leo recalled his chat with Etta the night before. A truth he still grappled with.

Jens knocked Leo's arm with his shoulder. "I'm sorry I was mad at you for preventing me from saving Patrick. That wasn't fair. You did your job, and because you did, I'm alive."

"I have no regrets, even if you never forgave me."

"Thanks." Jens shoved a heavy breath from his lungs. "Pops talked with me today."

"Yeah, what about?"

"He's proud my picture made the front page. He said God has given me a gift to help others understand the world through my camera and I shouldn't waste it." Jens leaned forward and rested his elbows on his knees. "Bottom line, he'll support me if I want to work for the *Enterprise*."

"Have they offered you a job?"

"Not yet, but Henry said my photograph showing the boiler smashed into Mrs. Pratt's house was a huge reason why the wire picked up the story. He thinks it's a foregone conclusion that Littleton will press the editor-in-chief to hire me."

"So it sounds like we're gonna have the first Eriksson in the newspaper business."

"Yeah, maybe." Jens interlaced his fingers. "You think Gunnar will be okay with that choice?"

"Gunnar? Definitely. Use the gifts God's given you to glorify Him, Jens. I think Gunnar would agree with that."

"Thanks."

He meant every word he'd just spoken to his younger brother, even if they were somewhat hypocritical. After all, he didn't possess any special gifts that made him a perfect fit for firefighting, like Jens with photography.

Leo had never wanted to be anything but a fireman alongside Pops and his granddad, but did that equate to a "calling"? Or was firefighting a noble but generic aspiration that anyone insane enough to battle a fire could pursue? Had he simply chosen a career, without seeking God's direction?

Perhaps it was time to question his own choices. If he'd been willing to entertain that notion sooner, he might still be engaged to Annika.

CHAPTER 12

Etta turned onto the street in front of City Theater where Mayor Keith intended to hold a press conference that afternoon. She'd chosen to take the trolley, as she often did to get a feel for the city's mood.

Somberness permeated the air. No women gathered on the corners gossiping as they walked their children to school. People who normally greeted one another stumbled past their neighbors in a malaise of shock and grief. Stores and homeowners had draped black fabric over railings and banisters, around streetlights and door knockers.

Mrs. Hemingway had insisted that Etta tie a black armband around her tweed jacket sleeve, and she noticed most of the men she passed had donned one as well. With Brockton being home to more than ninety shoe manufacturing plants, nearly everyone in town had a connection to the industry, and the entire community mourned the tragic loss of life whether they had a personal affiliation with the Grover factory or not.

She arrived thirty minutes early, hoping she'd be able to throw a few questions at the mayor's staffers. Getting a sense of what the briefing would entail allowed her to have quality questions prepared for the mayor.

Two men in dark blue coveralls positioned the podium on the sidewalk underneath the theater's canopy. Frances Lehr placed a megaphone on the podium. She looked smart in her pinstripe shirt and narrow tie. Perhaps she could provide Etta with a hint or two about what the mayor planned to share today.

"Pardon me, I'm Henry Mason, a reporter for the *Brockton Enterprise*. May I ask you a few questions?"

"I'm not supposed to speak with the press," Frances said.

Hmm. Etta would need to try another approach. "Not even about your take on yesterday's events? Your reaction. Did you know anyone who was lost in the explosion?"

Miss Lehr faced Etta. "I suppose that would be fine. I didn't know anyone personally who worked at Grover Shoes. You may want to speak to Antonio." She pointed to a man with a dark mustache setting up chairs on either side of the podium. "His neighbor was missing for a time."

"*Was* missing?"

"Yeah, you should ask him the details, but apparently the man was able to crawl from beneath the rubble unscathed. Instead of going home, he walked across the street and applied for a job at the Churchill & Alden factory. Can you beat that?"

"That sounds like an interesting story." Although perhaps a bit more fluff than she'd prefer to include, it was unique and worth asking about. "Thank you, Miss Lehr."

Her head jerked. "How do you know my name?"

"Didn't you just introduce yourself as the mayor's assistant?"

She folded her arms over her chest. "No."

"Hmm, I suppose it's my familiarity with the mayor's staff and a very lucky guess."

Doubt flitted over Miss Lehr's face, and Etta decided to make a clean getaway before the young woman peppered the reporter with questions for a change.

"Thanks again for the lead."

"Mr. Mason?"

Stay calm, Etta. It was a minor mistake. Certainly nothing that would lead Miss Lehr to suspect Henry Mason isn't who he says he is. "Yes?"

Miss Lehr looked over her shoulder. "The press conference will discuss details of how the bodies are being handled, the formation of a relief fund, and an official day of mourning for Brockton."

Etta touched her cap. "Thanks."

She jotted her moniker, Henry Mason, at the bottom of her tablet paper along with her phone number at the boardinghouse. "If you ever have any information you want to share with a member of the press, feel free to contact me here. I'll keep your name out of it unless you give me permission to use it."

Miss Lehr tucked the slip of paper into her skirt pocket.

Etta checked the time. Fifteen minutes before the press conference was scheduled to begin. Why not speak to Antonio about his friend's story? It had the potential for a great human-interest piece—*if* she ever got around to writing that kind of thing.

She approached the workman. "Antonio?"

He faced her. "*Sì*, I'm Antonio Mancini," he said, his speech thick with an Italian accent.

Etta nodded. "Henry Mason. Reporter for the *Brockton Enterprise*. Miss Lehr mentioned your neighbor survived the blast then left the scene and sought new employment. Could you elaborate?"

"I do not know this word, elaborate?"

"Can you share his story with me?"

Antonio grinned, and his shoulders shook with a hearty laugh. "*Sì*, Salvatore. He say to me, 'Many people will be looking for work now, so I decide to get new job before all are taken.'" He held up his thumb and index finger with a narrow space between them. "He even have a *piccolo*. . .how you say—" He dragged his finger along his temple.

"A small cut?"

"*Sì*, *sì*, small cut. Everyone else find doctor, or look for loved ones and friends." He chuckled to himself. "Not Salvatore. He go gets new job."

Etta hated to admit it, but Salvatore's story truly was remarkable and unique, making it exactly the type of story Leo had encouraged her to include in her articles—the human face of the tragedy. If she opted not to include it in one of her columns, she could always toss it to Declan.

"If I wanted to follow up with Salvatore, where would I find him?" She jotted the address he gave her in her tablet. Normally she relied on her memory for story details, but addresses needed to be precise.

"Thank you for your time."

Antonio touched the brim of his cap. *"Prego, signore."*

"Hey, Mason." Declan peered over her shoulder, eyeing her scribblings.

She snapped the notepad closed. "I'm covering the press conference for the *Enterprise*."

He backed away, palms raised. "Relax, Mason. Littleton got a tip from the mayor's office that tomorrow will be 'a day of mourning.' He sent me here to gauge public reaction and to hopefully find more firsthand survivor accounts." He snickered. "You know, the kind of pathetic, sentimental stories that readers love."

He leaned closer and shielded his mouth with his hand. "But watch your back, Mason. I don't plan to write this drivel for long."

Declan had some nerve. While she'd suspected the kid was gunning for her job, she hadn't realized the depth of his cynicism, making him a larger threat than she'd thought.

A small crowd had gathered while she'd spoken with Antonio, including members of rival newspapers. She spied a few women gathered at the rear of the assembly, handkerchiefs to their noses. Several clutched the hands of little children. Widows, perhaps?

She untucked the watch from her vest pocket and checked the time again. Half past three, and the mayor wasn't in sight. With a little time to kill, she decided to see if any of the women would speak to her. A few more stories like Salvatore's, and she might just write that human-interest piece after all—if for no other reason than to beat Declan at his own game.

"Hello, ladies. I'm Henry Mason from the *Brockton Enterprise*. I'm covering the factory explosion and was wondering if you could tell me your stories. Did you know anyone who was injured or is missing?"

"My Wallace never came home last night."

Etta's heart shredded. Maybe this was why she shied away from these stories. Her instinct was to comfort this young woman, but a male reporter would never cross that line.

"I'm sorry to hear that, ma'am. And you are?"

"Jennie Ambercrombie."

The young woman hiccupped a sob. She couldn't be much more than twenty years old, and from the looks of her round stomach, she was carrying her missing husband's child. How would she endure such heartbreaking loss, let alone pay her rent or put food on her table?

"Did you check with St. Margaret's? Survivors were supposed to report there."

Jennie accepted the handkerchief a silver-haired woman standing nearby offered her. "Wallace wasn't on the list. I've already been to City Hospital and the Campello Police Station. No one has a record of him."

"There, there," a young woman beside Jennie said. "He'll turn up. You know Wallace, he's a fighter."

"May I have your attention, please?" The crowd turned as one toward the speaker standing on the platform.

"Thank you, Jennie." Etta made a mental note to find out what she could about Wallace Ambercrombie so this woman could have some degree of resolution regarding her husband's fate.

A large man in a pinstripe suit shouted through a megaphone at the sizable crowd to quiet down. "Let us open with a word of prayer. Gracious Lord, we come to You with heavy hearts as we grieve the loss of so many friends, neighbors, and family members. Please show each of us how we can comfort and assist those who mourn. By the power of Your Holy Spirit, unite the citizens of Brockton in this effort and let no need go unmet. Amen."

"Amen," the crowd responded in whispered unison.

"Please welcome Mayor Keith."

The mayor stepped to the podium. He refused the offered megaphone, choosing instead to project his voice to the crowd.

"Thank you, Reverend Rae, for opening these proceedings with such a heartfelt prayer." The crowd applauded, which Etta thought an interesting response.

"First, let me commend the brave men of the Brockton Fire Department, especially Engine Company No.1, who sacrificially responded to the call for help." The mayor waved a hand toward Leo's father, who stood behind him. "And for those passersby, who—without thought for their own safety—instinctively responded to aid those trapped in the rubble.

"An event of this magnitude affects the entire city, and I want to assure those who have lost friends and loved ones that you do not grieve alone. To that end, Thursday, May 23, will be a town-wide day of mourning. All city offices will close and services will be suspended, including our public schools. It is our hope that shops and businesses will follow suit and stand in solidarity with our neighbors."

The mayor grasped the lectern and leaned toward his audience. "The city is planning two public services honoring the dead: one here at City Theater and the other at Porter Congregational Church. Following the services, there will be a processional to carry the deceased to Melrose Cemetery. Additional details will be provided to the press following my remarks."

He shuffled a few pages, tapped them against the lectern, and continued his address.

"The city has received several unsolicited donations to assist those affected by the disaster. The town council has established a relief fund for the collection and distribution of all donations."

Etta shot a hand in the air. The mayor leaned toward Miss Lehr, who whispered something in his ear. "Please hold all questions until the end of the press conference. Mr. Mason, you will have the first question."

Etta broadened her stance. She hoped Declan noticed she'd secured the first question. She had years of experience on the kid and wouldn't give up her position without a fight.

"Now where was I? Oh yes, the committee will consist of members from the city council, the business community, city benefactors, and representatives from the Boot and Shoe Worker's Union. Information on how and where to donate will be forthcoming."

She'd make sure to include the information about the committee collecting subscriptions in her article. The black buntings and armbands indicated that folks wanted to show their compassion for the victims' families and survivors of the disaster and would most likely want to give whatever they could spare to assist their neighbors.

"Finally, I've appointed Petter Eriksson, a twenty-six-year veteran of the Brockton Fire Department and the battalion chief of Engine Company No.1, to head up the investigation into the cause of the fire in conjunction with the Hartford Steam Boiler Inspection and Insurance Company, who will conduct an independent inquest. Chief Eriksson will update you on the search-and-recovery operation."

Leo's dad stepped to the podium. "Thank you. Mayor Keith has asked me to update you on the search for survivors. After speaking with Grover employees, we believe approximately 360 people were inside when the boiler exploded. At this time, we have accounted for 304 living souls and 20 identifiable victims recovered at the site. We have several victims who, as of yet, the coroner hasn't been able to identify."

Chief Eriksson paused his remarks and cleared his throat, an action Etta had come to recognize often preceded information that city officials thought the public would find difficult to hear.

"Following an extensive twenty-four-hour around-the-clock excavation of the site, we believe that all human remains have been located, thus completing our recovery operation."

A collective gasp erupted from the crowd. Etta glanced at Jennie, whose face was buried in the older woman's shoulder, and her stomach roiled.

"Ya can't be quittin'," a woman cradling an infant shouted.

"How can you be certain?" a man in a tweed cap asked. "It's a large area with a massive amount of debris to dig through."

"You can't be lettin' them stop, Mayor," the young mother called out a second time. "Would ya be callin' off their searchin' if it was your loved one gone missin'?"

Mayor Keith returned to the podium and motioned for the crowd to simmer down. "I understand your frustration, but we must rely on the knowledge and expertise of the fire department in these matters. However, we will take your concerns under advisement."

Chief Eriksson straightened and clasped his hands together.

"I'll take questions now," the mayor said. "Mr. Mason, you're first."

She'd only get one question, maybe two if she was lucky, so she decided to ask the trickiest one first. "Thank you, Mr. Mayor. It's my understanding the preliminary investigation points to a faulty boiler as the cause of the initial explosion. Do you have any information regarding the source of the second blast—the one that sent the flaming debris over the factory and resulted in the fire department suspending their rescue operation?"

Chief Eriksson whispered to the mayor. "Not at this time," Mayor Keith said.

Every time she asked about the second explosion she received no tangible information, which only raised her curiosity. But, since she only had a gut feeling as the basis for her question, she decided to go a different route.

"If the investigation shows negligence on the part of the factory engineer, David Rockwell, or Robbins Grover, would you be in favor of bringing charges? And second, do you know if the factory was insured?"

"Let's not get ahead of ourselves. Let's stick to the facts as they develop."

She wasn't about to let him pass off her question that easily. "But if negligence is to blame, wouldn't you want accountability on Grover's part?"

"*If* negligence is determined, it will be up to the district attorney to file charges. As to your second question, you'll need to ask Grover about insurance. I have no knowledge about that."

"Where is Grover?" Etta shouted before the mayor called on another reporter. "No one has seen him."

"I guess you'll need to discover that yourself, Mr. Mason. Isn't that what you reporters do? Investigate?"

The crowd laughed. Heat raced up her neck at the sight of Declan grinning in her direction. She'd gotten cocky after receiving the first question and sneaking in a second. That was a sloppy mistake, very unlike Henry Mason.

One she couldn't afford to repeat. Not with Declan Gibney itching for her job.

CHAPTER 13

Leo squinted against the sunlight reflecting off the firehouse's glass door. Bone tired, he reached for the door handle and winced as sharp, stabbing pain rippled down his shoulder blades. He should probably go straight home, get a bath, and crawl into bed, but his weary body wanted to be fed and caffeinated.

He poured coffee into his mug and flopped into a chair across from Jens at the break room table. He hadn't expected his brother to be awake and at the station reading the newspaper by seven a.m. Maybe if he just sipped his coffee, Jens wouldn't pay much attention to him.

"Look here," Jens said, sliding the newspaper across the table.

So much for that theory.

"One of my photographs made the front page—two days in a row." Jens tapped his finger on the image. "Look, Pops is in this one."

His brother had snapped a picture of the press conference the day before. Their father stood behind the mayor, sporting his dress uniform adorned with ribbons and medals earned from his storied service to the community.

He could hardly blame the kid for being excited about that. "That's great, Jens. Mind if I keep this?"

"Nah, go ahead."

Leo scanned the headlines, looking for Henry Mason's articles.

MAYOR KEITH CALLS FOR CITY-WIDE DAY OF MOURNING

RELIEF FUND ESTABLISHED FOR VICTIMS OF DISASTER

OVER THIRTY BODIES TAGGED 'UNIDENTIFIED' FOLLOWING GROVER EXPLOSION

She had three stories in the morning's edition. Very impressive. He skimmed each one. None, however, evoked an ounce of empathy. At least most of today's headlines were less sensational than the day before.

An article in smaller typeface at the bottom of the broadsheet caught his attention.

MAYOR PRESSES FIRE DEPARTMENT TO RESUME SEARCH FOR REMAINS

This was definitely not news to Leo. He'd been up all night searching for more victims when his father had already declared the scene to be cleared of human remains. Leo understood the mayor felt pressure from the missing victims' families to continue the search for their loved ones, but his decision to personally oversee the probe felt like a slap in his father's face. How could it be otherwise?

True to his character, Pops hadn't argued. He simply did what the mayor requested. Although Leo empathized with those hoping to find something of their loved ones to bury, Pops had been vindicated when the search proved fruitless. For that, Leo was thankful.

Jens stood and pushed in his chair. "I'm starving. I'm gonna check out the Brockton Diner. I was hoping you'd join me but. . ."

Perhaps no one at the firehouse would think twice about the dirt beneath Leo's nails or the soot that surely swathed his cheeks like rouge, but he was in no presentable state to eat in a restaurant. "I'm bushed. Think I'll drink my coffee then go home."

The swinging door to the break room swooshed open, and Gunnar bounded in. "Howdy, boys." He raised a white box tied with red and white baker's twine. "Compliments of Trude."

Jens reached for the box. "God bless Trude." He cut the twine with his pocketknife then lifted the lid.

The scent of warm, cinnamony goodness stirred Leo's stomach to life. He rubbed his midsection, though it did little to curb the voracious growling. He slid the container closer. Using a butter knife, he separated the buns into six pieces, each smothered in white icing.

Leo's mouth watered with anticipation as he lifted the coveted center roll to his lips. "I don't think I knew how hungry I was until I smelled these."

"I hope you can survive a few more minutes." Jens said, snatching the yeasty treat from Leo's hand. "'Cause the center one is mine." He unhinged his jaw and stuffed half the bun in his mouth.

"Jens!" Leo sprang from his seat.

"Bery tasthy," Jens said, scurrying behind Gunnar and out of Leo's reach. "Want the rest?" he asked, licking the white icing from the remaining portion.

Five rolls remained in the box. "Ahh, just keep it." He grabbed the container. "I'll take these. It's the only way to make sure Pops and I get any."

Satisfaction rippled through Leo. He rarely outflanked his brother's snatch-and-grab maneuvers, and today, he'd come out on the winning side.

"Hey, that's not fair," Jens said. "I only had one." He reached for the box. "C'mon, Leo. You made your point."

Gunnar chuckled. "Next time I'll have Trude package them individually."

Leo grabbed a roll before handing the box to his brother. "Only one more. Two of those are for Pops."

Jens clutched the box, but Leo didn't release his hold. "Promise?"

"I promise already."

Gunnar shook his head. "Pops won't see any of those, will he?"

"Highly doubtful," Leo said. He washed down a bite of his cinnamon roll with a swig of coffee.

"Pops isn't back yet?"

"No, they were wrapping up the excavation site when I left ten minutes ago. You know Pops won't leave until every man and piece of equipment has left the scene. Then he'll put on a fresh shirt and report to the mayor."

"Did you find any other remains?"

"Only a tooth, bits of charred fabric, and a woman's shoe."

Gunnar sighed. "The mayor should've let Pops' decision stand. We'd done a thorough search. All that did was give false hope to the victims' families."

Gunnar swiped the newspaper from the table. He scanned the main section then turned the page. "Looks like Brockton's heiress has come through again."

Leo hadn't seen Brockton's heiress since yesterday morning when he'd nearly bit Henry Mason's head off. "Oh yeah, what's she been up to?"

"There's an article in here about funds being available for caskets and other funeral-related expenses."

"What makes you think that was Etta. . .er, uh. . .Miss Maxwell?"

Gunnar's lips parted into a broad smile. "Etta, is it?"

"You can wipe that ridiculous grin off your face. It was a simple mistake. I'm tired."

"When are you gonna admit you're attracted to her?"

Where on earth would his brother get an idea like that? Not that there wasn't any truth to the matter, but could Gunnar be as perceptive as their father had been? No, certainly not. "What gives you a foolish notion like that?"

"We all saw you at the dance last year. You lit up like a glowworm in summertime."

Leo pushed in his chair. "That's ridiculous."

Not the part about his attraction to Etta, because he had a definite inclination toward the lady. However, if Gunnar thought Leo had a snowball's chance in August of her returning his affections, he was sorely mistaken.

Besides, there was the whole Henry Mason persona he still grappled with. How could a woman as compassionate as Etta Maxwell write articles devoid of any feeling about a tragedy on the scale of the Grover Shoe Factory? He'd been harsh with her the day before, but it still bewildered him. Either way, it was a convenient excuse to keep her at arm's length.

Gunnar raised his brows, and doggone it if heat didn't creep up Leo's neck and splatter onto his face.

"Thank Trude for the cinnamon rolls. She's a saint. How she ended up with a sinner like you, I'll never understand."

Gunnar laughed. "God blessed me there, no doubt about it."

God certainly had blessed his brother. Trude was not only beautiful, but he'd be hard-pressed to find a gentler soul.

"I'll walk out with you." Gunnar folded the newspaper and tucked it under his arm. "I'm gonna check on Pops. See if he needs anything."

They weren't two steps out the door before a feminine voice called Leo's name. He turned, and Etta waved. "I was hoping to speak with you," she said. "Do you have a minute to spare?"

"Good morning, Miss Maxwell," Gunnar said, poking Leo in the ribs with his elbow. "We were just talking about you. Weren't we, Leo?"

Leo pressed his lips together and smiled in a way he hoped didn't give away his plan to pummel his brother the next time they were alone.

"Really?" She angled her head. "Perhaps I shouldn't ask."

"Leo and I were commenting on your generosity in aiding victims' families with funeral expenses."

"Oh, that. Well, we all must do what we can to aid the suffering of others. I'm grateful to have the means to be of assistance."

The three of them stood in awkward silence. Gunnar rocked on his heels as if he enjoyed the uneasiness filling every inch of their uncomfortable triangle.

"Weren't you heading over to the site to check on Pops?" Leo asked him.

"Right." He swatted Leo on the arm with the newspaper. "You two have a lovely day."

"You. . .too, Mr. Eriksson," Etta said, uncertainty punctuating her words.

She must find the whole lot of them absolutely absurd. "Don't mind him," Leo said. "It's nice to see you, Etta."

It was nice to see *her*, and not Henry Mason. Her feminine tailored skirt and blouse recommended her trim figure much more than Henry's tweed blazer. Oh, brother. Wasn't he just reminding himself to keep Etta at arm's length?

"Be careful, Etta." He touched her elbow and guided her away from the firehouse wall. "Step toward me a little. Those bricks are still extremely hot from the fire on Monday."

"Two days later?"

"Yep. Take off your glove, but don't touch the bricks. Just hold your hand about an inch away from the surface, and you'll feel the heat radiating from the wall."

She removed her glove but hesitated.

"Allow me." He gently lifted her hand closer to the brick wall. "Feel the heat?"

With her mouth agape, Etta nodded, and he released her hand.

"Is that common after a fire?" she asked, slipping her glove back on.

"No, we've never seen that before. That's a true testament to how hot the flames were."

"Fascinating. I'm going to include that in my next article."

"I'm on my way home to clean up and get some rest, but you wanted to speak with me about something first?"

"Oh, I don't want to keep you, but I did want to say— Actually, may I walk with you?"

"You want to walk with me?"

"If you don't mind."

He opened his arms wide and stared down at his soot-stained dungarees. "I'm filthy."

"You're a hardworking man who served the community in a rather grim task. It's an honor to be seen with you."

He was tired. Dead tired. But if she didn't mind being seen with an overworked, dirty fireman, who was he to complain?

CHAPTER 14

Leo's pulse thrummed in his veins. He should apologize to Etta for the way he'd spoken to her the day before. He wiped his sweaty palm on his dirty uniform.

"Miss Maxwell—"

"Eh, eh. Please call me Etta. We made a deal, remember?"

He remembered. A person didn't typically forget being tackled by an eccentric heiress hurtling from a tree.

"Before we continue, Etta, I want to apologize for criticizing your articles about the disaster. You have every right to cover the story the way you think is best. I might disagree with your choice, but it is *your* choice, and I should've respected that. I hope you won't hold it against me."

"Hold it against you?" She brought her hand to her chest. "Certainly not. I'm rather accustomed to ruffling feathers. I truly haven't given it another thought."

"Thank you," he said. "What did you want to ask me?"

"Is there anything the fire department needs? How can I be of assistance?"

"My father would know better than I do, but from where I stand, you've done a lot already. Providing refreshments not only fueled the recovery effort but was a kindness that acknowledged the arduous work and sacrifice of our professional firefighters as well as our volunteers."

"Oh. You figured that out, did you?"

"Well, not too many folks have the means for that level of generosity."

"Just be thankful I didn't make the food."

"What, Brockton's heiress doesn't cook?"

She grinned. "Not at all."

A breeze lifted the auburn hair that framed Etta's face, and she wrapped her shawl a bit more snugly against the chill.

"I'm not very fond of the word *heiress*. The description doesn't suit me. While it's factually true, people tend to jump to conclusions about who I am and how I think. Plus, it sounds so. . .pompous. I'm just a girl from Brockton."

"A girl from Brockton whose father made it big selling business machines."

"True. But I'll never forget where I was raised."

Although they lived in two very different worlds, Etta's determination to keep one foot grounded in the roots of her upbringing made her relatable. A woman of real substance who understood that everyone had dignity regardless of the size of their bank account. In Leo's estimation, that was one of her most endearing traits.

"Are you behind the relief fund mentioned in the paper?"

"Actually, the mayor was already thinking along those same lines when I visited him yesterday. But I offered to be a part of the committee. I think in the days ahead, many pressing needs for both the grieving victims' and survivors' families will come to light."

They paused at the corner. Leo looked in both directions then gently touched her elbow and guided her across the street. Warmth spread through his chest followed by a sting of sadness when he released her.

Oh, Lord, help me. Despite his best efforts to tamp down his interest, he liked this woman.

He searched his mind for something to say. "Would you consider donating the funds from this year's charity ball to the relief fund?"

"That's a lovely idea, but I–I'm thinking of forgoing the charity ball this year."

"Really?"

She turned to face him, her green eyes searching his. "I'm still planning to hold a fundraiser for the fire department, but a ball seems too gay with so much solemnity in the air, sort of a blatant disregard for the suffering the community has experienced. But I do think a silent auction with a plated dinner might be perfect. What do you think?"

Leo shrugged. "I'm not sure what a silent auction is."

They resumed their stroll and turned the corner onto Hamilton Avenue. The small white bungalow he'd called home his entire life came into view.

"My committee and I would solicit donations to be auctioned off during the evening. For example, a restaurant might donate a dinner for two, or the grocer may donate a month's worth of eggs. Families can also participate by offering a pair of cinema tickets or perhaps a handsewn quilt."

Leo scrubbed a hand over his neck. "But why doesn't the grocer just donate the cost of a month's worth of eggs and save all the rigamarole?"

"Ah," she said. "That's where the fun comes in. Because it's a benefit auction, people try to outbid one another, all in the name of charity. In the end, we hope that what is donated for that month's worth of eggs will be double or even triple its real value."

"People actually do that?"

"You'd be surprised. I mean, it's really no different than paying fifty dollars for a pair of tickets to the Fireman's Ball."

His jaw flopped open. *Fifty dollars.* He had no idea those tickets sold for so much.

"The wealthy will come. Not only to aid those in need but also because it will be promoted as part of the Maxwell Foundation. They'll want to see and be seen. Perhaps get their name in the newspaper. The foundation will cover the cost of all overhead—the venue, the decorations, advertising, and, of course, the finest menu at any charity function this season. My mother always sees to that."

They stopped in front of his house. He yawned. "My apologies, Etta. I've had a long night."

"One more thing, then I'll let you go. I want to set up another interview between you, your father, and Henry Mason."

"Sure, we can arrange that. Where? In the park to keep a low profile?"

"I think if you and Henry are spotted together now, people will most likely assume you're working on the fire investigation."

"Good point." He covered his mouth and yawned again. "Perhaps early next week? We'll have our hands full with the Grover factory for the next month, but we'll have a handle on the situation by then."

"That'll work."

"All right. Stop by the firehouse when you have time. But ask for me like it's a spontaneous meeting and you're just looking for information, not that we had an appointment."

"Very smart, Leo." She cleared her throat. "My parents and I will be attending the funeral service at City Theater tomorrow. Will you be there? Would you like to sit with us?"

"Miss Maxwell," a man yelled, crossing the street toward them. A second man followed behind, a camera strapped around his neck. "You sure have been difficult to locate." He held out his hand. "I'm Chip Farnsworth from *The Brockton Times*. I wanted to speak with you about your appointment to the Relief Fund Committee."

The reporter glanced at Leo and waved his hand between him and Etta. "You two know each other?"

Leo's throat went dry. "We. . . Uh. . ."

"This is Leo Eriksson. He's a fireman from Engine Company No. 1. We met at the Fireman's Ball last spring. He was one of the first rescuers on the scene of the Grover disaster on Monday."

"As in Chief Eriksson?"

Leo nodded. "He's my father."

A gleeful grin inched the reporter's lips higher. "This is gonna be great. Step closer to Miss Maxwell, please," he said.

Leo obliged.

"Hold still," the cameraman said. "This will only take a few seconds."

What? He wasn't dressed for a photograph in the newspaper beside Henrietta Maxwell. "No," he said.

Click. "Got it, Chip."

"Excellent," Farnsworth said.

Wonderful. Not only did he have a disheveled appearance, but his mouth probably hung open as well.

As the reporter peppered him with questions, all Leo could think about was a hot bath and crawling into bed—that, and how another interaction with Etta Maxwell had turned his life upside down.

Etta covered her mouth in a vain attempt to stifle the grin spreading across her face. She'd not meant to throw poor Leo to the wolves. Merely to introduce him and let them know of his bravery. She'd really gotten quite adept at diverting attention from herself when reporters cornered her.

Although he resembled a deer caught in a hunter's sights, Leo adeptly answered the reporter's questions without putting on airs about his or any other fireman's heroics two days prior. She liked that about Leo. He was down-to-earth. If he had any hidden vanity, surely this attention from the press would find him out.

Something warm and delightful tingled in her chest. Something she hadn't felt since the Fireman's Ball last year—until she and Leo had reconnected a week ago. With his thick mass of wavy blond hair, umber eyes, and a stellar smile, Etta was in trouble. There was no getting around it, Leo Eriksson was a very attractive man, even with a sooty face and black fingernails.

Perhaps she should rethink her decision to cancel her signature fundraiser. Then again, what were the odds that he would be selected as the fireman to open the dance with her? Slim to none, more than likely.

Just like the odds of Leo taking a romantic interest in her. If it wasn't bad enough that she was about two inches taller than him, half their time together she masqueraded as a male reporter. Could a decent, honorable man like Leo Eriksson fall for a woman with her own career aspirations? Or was his heart searching for a more traditional, hearth-and-home kind of woman?

She brushed the thought aside. Men were usually put off by her independent nature. Not even her father's money had convinced the sons of Boston's most elite families to pursue her. She couldn't really blame them. If her height wasn't enough to chase them away, there was her glasses. If she weren't less adept than a mole above ground without them, she'd hazard to leave them behind. But somehow, she wasn't convinced bumping into furniture and tripping over cats would draw the kind of attention from Leo her heart desired.

Her money didn't seem to interest Leo either. But she wouldn't want him if it did.

Her chest, which had only moments ago felt a type of euphoria, now pinched like a new shoe against her small toe. *Stop thinking about things that can't be, Etta, and focus on your career.*

She swallowed, and the pain of her reality pricked against her throat. She hated feeling sorry for herself. She'd been given a wonderful life and, as she'd told Leo, the means to make others' lives better. That was no small thing, and something in which she found great joy.

"All right, gentlemen. I think that's enough," Etta said. "Mr. Eriksson was up all night at the recovery site and would like to get some rest."

Leo glanced her way and mouthed, "Thank you."

"One more question?" Mr. Farnsworth asked, although he didn't wait for permission. "Seems like you two are pretty chummy. Does Brockton's heiress have a beau?"

Heat flashed over her cheeks. Had her musings about Leo given her away?

Leo cleared his throat. "Miss Maxwell and I are acquaintances. We met at the Fireman's Ball last spring."

"Well acquainted enough that you escorted her to *your* home?"

Crimson darkened Leo's neck. Was he embarrassed about the implication that he might be interested in her? Neither of them had been prepared for this line of questioning.

He held up his palms. "Miss Maxwell, as I'm sure you're aware, is a generous benefactress of the Brockton Fire Department. Since we were already acquainted, she stopped by the firehouse as I was leaving to inquire about any needs the department may have that the Maxwell Foundation could supply."

The reporter jotted down the notes. "May I quote you on that, Mr. Eriksson?"

Leo nodded.

"Wonderful. Thanks for your time."

Mr. Farnsworth and the cameraman hurried to the opposite side of the street where a car with *The Brockton Times* painted on the driver's side door waited. They climbed in and sped off.

"I'm sorry about that, Leo."

"Do you get accosted by reporters often?"

"Unfortunately. I'm a bit of an oddity, but the foundation usually benefits in the end, so I tolerate it."

"You'll be all right to see yourself wherever it is you're going next?"

"Certainly. Just point me in the direction of the nearest trolley."

He arched a brow. "Etta Maxwell rides the trolley?"

"She certainly does. I'm a curiosity, remember?"

He chuckled, and the sound aroused a multitude of butterflies in her stomach.

"Go straight and turn right at the corner. The trolley will be at the next cross street."

"Thank you. Rest well, Leo."

Etta walked in the direction Leo had indicated, but her heart wanted to stay and fan the flames of attraction sparking inside her every time she visited with the dashing fireman. If she were bold enough to flirt with Leo Eriksson, would he douse the fire with water—or an accelerant?

The better question was, could she be brave enough to find out?

CHAPTER 15

Etta pushed through the throng swarming Main Street. Mercy, what a crowd. Had the entire state of Massachusetts come to pay their respects? She really shouldn't be so surprised since Brockton itself was home to more than ninety-one shoe assembly plants. Clearly the disaster had struck a chord with a community so intertwined with the shoe-manufacturing industry.

Etta didn't know a soul who'd been lost or injured in the tragedy, yet she felt the pressing desire to pay tribute to those who perished and a willingness to stand alongside their families and friends who must pick up the pieces of their shattered lives and forge ahead.

The Brockton City Council's resolution marking March 23 as a day of mourning had brought the entire town together to pray, grieve, and pay their last respects for those lost in the Grover Shoe Factory tragedy—and especially for the thirty-six victims who remained unidentified. As the mayor had requested, shops, businesses, and schools were closed.

City Theater came into view. Multitudes waited outside for access. The mayor would host the service there while other city dignitaries and clergy would speak at Porter Congregational Church. Based on the crowd assembled in the streets, two locations wouldn't begin to accommodate the number of people who'd come out to honor those who perished.

The mayor's office had reserved seats inside City Theater for Etta and her parents, *if* she could press her way to the doors. She'd also requested a ticket for Leo but hadn't been able to let him know, since they'd been interrupted by the reporter. Father had offered to collect her in the Pierce Arrow, but she'd chosen to walk, hoping the blue skies and some prayer would prepare her heart for the service. If she was having trouble navigating the streets, she couldn't imagine a motorcar having greater success.

The momentum of the crowd seemed to give it a life of its own. People pressed in all around her, carrying her forward. If she wasn't careful, they'd knock her to her knees and trample her.

"Excuse me," she said, hoping those nearest her would part and grant her access to the sidewalk. *No such luck.*

"Miss Maxwell."

Etta looked about but couldn't find the source of the salutation.

"Miss Maxwell."

Miss Lehr called to her through a large megaphone. Then she turned and spoke to a man in blue coveralls and pointed at Etta. *Antonio.* He and another similarly outfitted gentleman pushed through the masses, parting the crowd like Joshua at the River Jordan, and escorted her to the theater's entrance.

"Thank you, Antonio."

"*Prego, Signora* Maxwell." He pointed to her other rescuer. "This my friend, Matteo. His English not so good."

"Neither is my Italian."

Antonio chuckled. "You say, *grazie*."

She smiled at Matteo. "Grazie."

The men assisted Miss Lehr onto a wooden crate. Using her megaphone, she addressed the assembly. "All seats are filled. I repeat. All seats are filled."

Murmurings of disappointment rose among the crowd.

"There are additional services being held at First Congregational Church, St. Paul's Episcopal Church, and Canton Hall. Please make your way to one of those locations. Thank you."

The protestations simmered down as the assembly dissolved in different directions.

Frances stepped from her crate. "Can you believe this crowd?"

"It's wonderful that so many wanted to participate that you needed additional venues."

"We anticipated a large turnout, so Mrs. Stanhope coordinated the second service at Porter Congregational Church, but even she hadn't anticipated this kind of response. We've been scrambling for the last hour to secure auxiliary locations and speakers using identical programs."

Warmth spread through Etta's chest. She was proud Brockton rallied around the victims and grieving families. "A true testament to the effect the disaster had on the community."

"You'd better take your seat. Your parents are already inside, and they've been asking for you. They're in the second row on the right."

"Thank you."

Etta stepped inside the crowded theater and easily spotted her parents as Mayor Keith approached the lectern. Leo stood behind him, looking smart in his ceremonial uniform. No time to think about that now. She hurried down the center aisle and squeezed into the pew beside her father.

"I thought you'd abandoned ship." Father kissed her cheek.

Mother leaned forward. "You're late."

Etta sighed.

Mother's gaze dropped to Etta's dress, and a broad smile spread over her face. "But you look lovely."

Sometimes her mother thought Etta's unconventionality should not be reined in and other times she described her daughter as charming and unique. Although Etta was quite certain the *grandes dames* of Boston's highest social echelons didn't necessarily agree, Mother didn't seem to care. To her way of thinking, the *nouveau riche*, as families like hers were called, would soon be making all the rules. However, it was apparent to Etta that at least a few of the old rules would remain intact—attire and punctuality among them.

A prayer and a hymn followed the mayor's opening remarks. When the piano ceased its reverent melody, Leo read a list of those who'd perished in the disaster. Several badges and medals adorned the left side of his dark blue jacket. What had he done to earn those? She had so much to learn about this man who intrigued her.

Snap out of it, Etta. This is not the time or place to feed your delusion about Leo.

Instead, she made mental notes of all in attendance, including Governor Douglas himself, born and raised in Brockton, as well as city aldermen, representatives from the Shoe and Boot Worker's Union, and clergy from both Protestant and Catholic congregations.

Declan would write the piece about the funeral services today. While she doubted her *Gilded Gown* readers would find interest in a working man's disaster in Brockton, she planned to pen a small column about the funeral and the procession. To that end she continued committing to memory details about the attendees, the flowers, and those being recognized for outstanding heroism following the service.

If nothing else, the exercise proved an excellent distraction from a certain dashing fireman.

Or did it?

Leo stood on the dais, shoulder-to-shoulder with his father, Gunnar, and the other men from Engine Company No. 1 who were receiving the Meritorious Service Award following the memorial service for their bravery at the scene of the Grover disaster. While all the men who battled the fire that day would receive a commendation, Engine Company No. 1 was the first on the scene and had taken charge of the short-lived rescue operation as well as the search-and-recovery mission.

His heart nearly skipped a beat when Etta rushed down the aisle in her stunning dark green gown. What was it about this woman? How did her mere presence intrigue him?

He sensed her watching him, but Leo couldn't afford to make eye contact without the risk of becoming lost in her green gaze when the mayor called his name to step forward and be pinned with his medal. Instead, he lifted his chin and focused his gaze straight ahead.

Mayor Keith began reading the names of all those receiving recognition. He wanted to clap along with the audience for his father and brother, but protocol dictated discipline.

"Leo Eriksson."

Arms stiff at his side, he stepped forward. Mayor Keith pinned the Meritorious Service Medal to his uniform, a new recognition the city created following the Grover disaster for rescue workers and civilians alike.

After the service concluded, the mayor finished his remarks with a request for the audience to disperse and await the beginning of the funeral procession. He then directed the award recipients to remain near the altar for photographs with the mayor and city council.

Jens organized the men into groups for their pictures.

Etta lingered at the rear of the church. When their gazes met, she waved goodbye.

"Look at the camera, gentlemen."

Leo shifted his attention to the camera box. Nearly twenty people remained inside the theater, but a deep sense of loneliness overtook him. He'd not spoken a word to Etta, yet her presence brought a sense of contentedness.

He longed for her company.

That knowledge filled him with trepidation. But not as much as the revelation that there was little he could do about it.

The Erikssons' tiny kitchen smelled of burnt toast and stale coffee. Now that the memorial service and funeral procession were behind them, Leo's number-one priority was to find a new restaurant for the three bachelors to claim as their new second home before they all wasted away to nothing.

Leo and his fellow firemen from all over the city had marched in the cavalcade from Ward Street through the heart of Brockton all the way to Melrose Cemetery yesterday, and he looked forward to a restful day off. He unfolded the morning edition of the *Enterprise* and glanced at Henry Mason's headline.

HEARSES WITH FIRE VICTIMS LINE BELMONT STREET

Jens peered over his shoulder. "Isn't that a sharp photograph?"

"Yeah, yeah. Stop fishing for compliments."

"You did a great job," Pops said. "You captured the funeral wagons and the altar boys. So many details."

"Thanks, Pops." Jens poured himself a cup of coffee, sniffed it, and then poured it down the drain. "That's it. We're all getting out of this house today and eating at the Brockton Diner. I'm telling you, it's as good as the Drake."

Somehow Leo doubted that, but anything was better than nothing. He continued skimming the story about the processional. "This says nearly twenty-five hundred men marched in the cortege."

"That sounds right," Pops said. "Our group had about eight hundred men between the band members, hearse drivers, altar boys, police and firemen, union workers, clergy, and the carriage drivers conveying the victims' families."

"It was very moving to see the Grover employees walking beside the caissons carrying their former coworkers to their final resting place," Jens said.

Pops scooted his chair closer to the table. "And the boy in the Liberty Band carrying David Rockwell's clarinet on the pillow. That even made this hardened old man tear up."

Who did Pops think he was kidding? He may be brave enough to rescue someone trapped in a burning building, but his heart was as tender as it was wise.

Leo's eyes homed in on a few lines in Etta's article. *There was no creed, no color line, no hostility of capital and labor; the common strifes of men were forgotten, and all were brought closer together in the beautiful harmony of the universal brotherhood. Sorrow, the great leveler, the great arbiter, had done its work.*

Etta certainly possessed a gift for crafting words. He considered the quote he'd just read. She was right. No matter whether rich or poor, businessman or factory worker—all loved and lost equally.

But did loving equally mean people as different as him and Etta, a fireman and an heiress, could find happiness?

An engine rumbled to a stop outside. Jens shoved the curtain aside. "It's Henrietta Maxwell."

Leo jerked upright.

Pops gave him a knowing grin that Leo tried to negate with a stern gaze.

"You know her, Leo?" Jens asked.

"We all know her, dunderhead." He thunked his brother on the head. "She's the fire department's benefactress. What makes you think she's here to see me?" The rise in his pitch gave away the anticipation he'd failed to mask. "She probably wants to talk to Pops about ways her foundation can assist the department."

"If you think a dame like that came to our house in her fancy automobile to talk to Pops, your brain has shrunk to the size of a walnut."

"Very funny."

Her knuckles rapped on the front door.

He hadn't a clue why the heiress to the Maxwell fortune came to his home in a working-class neighborhood of Brockton, but he was about to find out.

CHAPTER 16

Etta climbed the stairs to the small white bungalow Leo shared with his father and younger brother. She shoved a heavy breath from her lungs as she reconsidered the idea of paying a call on Leo.

It wasn't really paying a call, was it? It was just one friend visiting with another friend, right? Or was that paying a call?

Ugh.

Whatever she called it, Etta had never shown up at a man's residence without an escort or an invitation. She straightened her satin sash. She was merely checking on a friend.

The fact that her friend was also a handsome young firefighter hadn't factored into her decision in the slightest. Leo could be as homely as the rear end of a bulldog, and Etta would still be standing on his porch ready to add some cheer to his day. The fact that he was anything but homely was a bonus she didn't mind enjoying.

She smoothed her dress. Ah, she'd just done that. *C'mon, Etta. You can do this. You are a smart, independent woman.* She lifted her gloved hand and paused. Did the curtain move?

No turning back now. Hurry and knock before you lose your courage.

Leo opened the door. His eyes narrowed. "Etta?" His tone gave away his surprise. "What brings you by?"

"Hello, Leo. I hope you don't mind this intrusion on your privacy, but you appeared so sullen on the dais—probably just the solemnity of the occasion—but since I didn't have a chance to speak with you following the ceremony, I thought I'd check on you."

There, she'd spit it out. Sure, she'd prattled on without taking a breath, but she'd done it.

"*Etta*, is it?"

Someone snickered inside. Was that Jens? Heat rushed over her cheeks. She should have realized Leo wouldn't be alone. "Um, I—I shouldn't have come. Sorry to have bothered you."

Confident her face displayed ten shades of crimson, she turned on her heel. Her heart pounded so fiercely her head spun. All she needed to do was navigate about five steps without falling and sprint to the motorcar. Then she could die of embarrassment. The latter she had no doubt she would accomplish in stunning fashion.

Leo reached for her wrist. "Wait. Why did you come?"

"I thought maybe you'd like to go for a walk."

"You came across town to see if I wanted to go for a walk?"

Jens stepped into the doorway. "Hello, Miss Maxwell. I'm Leo's younger brother, Jens. We met at the Fireman's Ball last year."

She forced her breathing to remain even. Would he draw any similarities in her appearance to Henry Mason? "I remember."

"Leo mentioned a few minutes ago that he wanted to get outside and get some fresh air today." Jens shoved a jacket and cap against Leo's chest, pushed him over the threshold, and closed the door behind him.

He stumbled forward. Now, just inches from her face, he froze. They stared awkwardly at each other.

Think, Etta. Remember why you came here? She stepped to the side. "We could visit that little park across the way."

He angled his head, and his eyes widened. "Is that your car?"

She nodded. "I've not learned how to drive it, but we could take a ride rather than a walk if you prefer."

"You wouldn't mind?"

Mind that he was more interested in her father's automobile than her? Story of her life. "Not at all," she replied, hoping to convince herself as well as Leo.

He scooted around her and hustled down the stairs, Etta trailing after him like a lovesick puppy. She needed to check her emotions before this man inadvertently broke her heart.

Leo leaned into the open window and whistled. "Isn't she a beauty."

Their chauffeur stood beside the motorcar. "This is Mitchell, our driver. He can tell you all you want to know about the vehicle."

Leo walked around the car, a schoolboy grin lighting his face. "This sure is a spiffy automobile."

"It's a 1905 Pierce Arrow," Mitchell said, as proudly as if the motorcar were his own.

The two men chatted about the car's tires, steering, brakes, and headlamps then moved on to other bits and pieces, none of which interested Etta.

After a few minutes, she interrupted. "Mitchell, why don't you take Mr. Eriksson and me for a drive?"

"Where to, Miss Maxwell?"

"I know the perfect place," Leo said. "Are you up for an adventure?"

Delighted to be included in the conversation again, she agreed.

He faced Mitchell. "Do you know where Carver's Pond is?"

"I'm afraid not, sir. Most of my driving is in and around Boston and occasional trips to the Cape."

"I can give you directions."

"Very well, sir."

Rather than sit in the rear with Etta, as was the custom for most chauffeured vehicle occupants, Leo hopped in the front passenger seat while Mitchell cranked the engine.

This was not the seating arrangement she'd envisioned when she'd suggested they take a drive. She pushed a breath from her lungs. Nothing was coming along the way she'd envisioned.

Perhaps she and Leo as a couple were not part of God's plan. She must learn to quit striving, quit trying to make her life turn out just as she hoped, and put more trust in God's plan for her life.

So far, she'd found that easier said than done.

She adjusted her pins so the wind wouldn't blow her new hat away and resolved to enjoy the fact that she'd accomplished her main goal. Leo's spirits had clearly been lifted even though hers had taken a back seat.

Before long, they'd reached the outskirts of Bridgewater, and Leo directed Mitchell where to park the car.

He stepped from the vehicle, opened Etta's door, and offered her his hand. She slipped her gloved hand into his palm, stirring the usual frisson of pleasure at his touch. "Thank you."

"Shall I wait here, miss?"

"That will be fine, Mitchell."

A lovely wooded expanse stood before them, and a variety of birds sang a welcoming greeting. "Where is the pond?"

"There's a path straight ahead."

He guided Etta by the elbow. The trail opened on the bank of a large pond. Their arrival prompted a mama goose and her goslings to scurry for the safety of the water's edge. Leo stopped at a large flat rock beside the water.

"This is one of my favorite places," he said. "My parents would bring us ice skating here as children."

"It's beautiful, Leo. It reminds me of the places where my father would go fishing. I would tramp along after him, carrying his pole and a picnic basket."

"Somehow I find it hard to imagine you tramping through the woods."

"That's probably one of the least surprising things about me, wouldn't you agree?"

"True. That's nothing compared to you masquerading as Henry Mason."

"Exactly."

Leo moved toward the water's edge.

Spying the muddy embankment, Etta hesitated. Why hadn't she worn her split skirt and sensible shoes? Because she wanted to look attractive for Leo.

He offered her his hand. Oh, how she wanted to take it, but the soggy ground was a risk she wasn't prepared to take. Her vanity made her hesitant to be by his side, which was exactly where she desired to be.

"C'mon," he said, waggling his fingers.

The temptation was too great to resist. *Please, Lord, don't let me slip.*

"All right, but I'll require a bit of help." She stepped cautiously. "This narrow skirt is much more restricting than Mr. Mason's knickerbockers."

He laughed.

Did he find her amusing, or ridiculous? She didn't have time to unwrap that mystery at the moment. She needed to concentrate on her footing. What could go wrong when a broad-shouldered fireman assisted her?

Her palm slid over Leo's, and his thumb braced her hand. She stepped lightly on the balls of her feet.

"Easy does it."

After a few paces, her confidence grew, and she relaxed into a normal stride. With her next step, however, her left heel sank into the mud.

As momentum thrust her toward an unavoidable reckoning with silt and goose droppings, her scripture reading that morning came to mind.

Pride goeth before destruction, and a haughty spirit before a fall.

Too bad she hadn't recollected that verse when she'd chosen her attire.

Leo relished the feel of Etta's gloved hand in his palm as he moved closer to the pond's edge. Part of him wanted to be as bold as Etta when she visited him unannounced, but his pragmatic nature reminded him he was playing with fire. Something a trained firefighter should never do.

Etta's hand jerked from his hold, and her body hurled forward.

Without hesitation, he lunged in front of her, onto his knees. He grabbed her waist, lifted her in the air, and slung her over his shoulder.

"Oof," she said, her body bouncing when her abdomen landed on his collarbone.

He secured her legs snugly to his chest with one arm and used the other to propel himself up the slope. "I've got you, Etta."

"What are you doing?"

"I'm keeping you from falling into the mud."

Her fists pounded his shoulder blades. "Put me down."

He doubted she wanted him to drop her right then and there, so he continued trudging up the small embankment. "This would be easier if you stopped fighting me." He drew a ragged breath. "I'll put you on that large rock near the footpath to the car."

Leo eased her onto the rock's smooth surface. He scanned her appearance and adjusted her hat perched off-kilter atop her reddish-brown waves. One stockinged foot poked from beneath her mud-stained hem.

He glanced toward the water. "One minute." He jogged to the pond and freed her fancy shoe from the sodden ground.

"I found it."

She looked away sheepishly.

"I can turn my back while you put it on."

"That's not necessary." She pursed her lips. "I'm sorry I hit you. If you hadn't acted so quickly, I would be caked in mud right now. Thank you, Leo."

"You're really not upset with me?"

"No. I apologize for overreacting."

Her tongue slid into the pocket of her cheek. Was she nervous?

She moistened her lips. "I guess whenever I've daydreamed about a handsome man rescuing me, he's never tossed me over his shoulder like a sack of flour."

"My apologies, Etta. Years of firefighting training kicked in."

What a complete and total idiot he was. A lovely woman he not only found fascinating but who also made his pulse spike showed up unexpectedly at his door dressed for a stroll in the park, and where did he take her? To a muddy pond. If that wasn't bad enough, he'd promised to see her safely to the water, and he'd managed to screw that up too. If Gunnar learned of this, he'd never hear the end of it.

Wait. What did she say? A lovely shade of pink danced on her cheeks. "So you think I'm handsome, huh?"

"I'm sorry." She gently turned her head from side to side. "I shouldn't have said that."

"So, you don't think I'm handsome?"

"Ugh. I meant I shouldn't have spoken it aloud." She hid her face in her hands. "Just forget I said anything."

He lifted her chin with his forefinger. "Now why on earth would I want to do that?"

CHAPTER 17

Etta dared not breathe lest she break the spell Leo's brown-eyed gaze cast over her. He leaned closer, and his lips caressed her cheek. The butterflies that previously fluttered in her midsection now somersaulted gleefully.

"I've wanted to do that ever since we danced last spring," he whispered.

His warm breath tickled her skin. He examined her face. While a hint of a smile nudged his lips, the emotion didn't reach his eyes. Was that hesitation she saw? Was he guarding his heart, or did he already regret the intimate gesture?

Children's laughter rang out from the footpath.

Leo offered her a halfhearted shrug and tapped his index finger on her nose before straightening to his full height.

Several boys raced down the embankment, each carrying a wooden sailboat. "Boys," a woman called after them, "wait for us."

"So tell me, Henrietta Maxwell, why does an heiress from Beacon Hill reside in a boardinghouse in Brockton?"

She looked away from him and fiddled with a loose thread on her bodice. Would he understand, or would he be like so many others who dismissed her cares away? "I needed a purpose."

"You?" He sat on the edge of the rock, one foot remaining on the ground. "Your foundation changes so many people's lives. Isn't that purpose enough?"

"Please don't misunderstand me. The foundation is extremely important to me, and I receive great joy from the work we do, but Father created the foundation for me to manage. I didn't earn it. It's not truly mine." She tugged on her lip. "Does that make sense?"

"Absolutely. It would be like me becoming the fire chief my first day on the job because Pops is battalion chief."

He did understand. "But even the success I've enjoyed writing for the *Enterprise* isn't mine, it's Henry's. His name is on every article I've written and on every recognition I've received." She pulled her knees close and wrapped her arms around her legs. "It's very hard to pretend to be someone else most of the time when all you want to be is yourself."

"Your boss must see how talented you are, Etta."

"He does, but he also believes if others know I'm a woman I'll be—"

"You'll be shut out?"

"Exactly." How did he know that? "From clubs, boardrooms, and town council meetings—all the places where men discuss business and make decisions."

"Ah, I can see that."

"It's very frustrating to be limited in what you can achieve for reasons completely beyond your control."

"I understand how you feel."

His tone conveyed such empathy, but how could he understand? What doors were closed to him? She scoffed. "No offense, Leo, but as a man, you don't have the same limitations I experience as a woman."

"True. I don't have the *same* limitations, but I do have different ones."

She studied him, trying to imagine how a bright, strong man like Leo Eriksson could ever be the victim of the same kind of prejudice she endured daily simply for wearing petticoats instead of breeches.

"You don't believe me?"

She shook her head.

"My limitations aren't based on my sex but on my bank account. Fortunately for me, I wanted to be a fireman and work in the family business, as it were, but if I'd wanted to be a lawyer or physician, I wouldn't have possessed the funds to attend university. There are clubs and organizations I'm not allowed to join because I'm not part of the right social circles. And sometimes I feel unwelcome in certain places or events, like the Fireman's Ball."

She swung her legs over the side of the rock. "But the Fireman's Ball was created to benefit the firemen of this city."

"And it does. But last year I was aware of the judgmental eyes on me because I wore my Sunday suit instead of tails like all the wealthy men in attendance."

She touched his arm. "I apologize if anyone made you feel unwelcome. That is not why your station was invited to represent the Brockton Fire Department."

"I know that. I've never felt that way around you, Etta. Only other members of the wealthier class." Her shoe fell from her lap, and he stooped to pick it up. "That's why I support your desire to see the name Henrietta Maxwell attached to one of your articles. And you can count on me to cheer you on every step of the way."

He held her shoe in one hand and nodded to her stockinged foot. "May I?"

She nodded and pushed her glasses higher on her nose. "You don't find that off-putting?"

"What?" He grinned. "Assisting you with your shoe, or that you desire to be the first female journalist for the *Enterprise*?"

"The journalist bit."

"Not in the slightest. You're an excellent reporter, Etta. A reliable voice that people trust for factual information about what's happening in and around Brockton. I look forward to the day when I'll be able to read a story credited to Henrietta Maxwell, because you've earned it."

"Thanks, Leo." The tenderness in his gaze sent those butterflies fluttering again. She'd never met a man like Leo Eriksson. One who saw her as smart and competent—one who wasn't threatened by her goals. She couldn't ignore the lightness in her chest. Her feelings could easily entangle themselves with a man like this. If they hadn't already.

"Now, about this shoe." He cupped her ankle in his left hand and slid the shoe over her foot. Resting the heel against his leg, he tugged the ribbons taut and tied a lopsided bow. He scratched his cheek. "I think that's the best this rookie is gonna be able to do."

They watched the children playing along the edge of the pond and tossing pebbles into the water seeing who could throw the farthest.

"You never answered my question," Leo said. "Why do you live in a boardinghouse in Brockton instead of in Beacon Hill with your family?"

"As I said, the best way to distribute the Maxwell Foundation funds is to understand the people I'm helping."

His brows lifted. "That's not the only reason, is it?"

Why did he have to be so perceptive? He already knew about her double life, but they were creeping closer and closer to the things that truly mattered, things of the heart. Everything in her gut said she could trust him.

"My. . .uh. . .my parents don't know I'm a reporter for the *Enterprise*. They don't know I'm Henry Mason."

Leo's jaw slackened.

The glint in her eye revealed his surprise hadn't gone unnoticed, and he quickly snapped his mouth closed. She'd said that only a few people knew Henry Mason was, in actuality, Henrietta Maxwell, but he'd never considered her own family wasn't among them. Or that she'd not been able to share her challenges and successes with anyone close to her.

"That must be very difficult. . .and lonely?"

Etta glanced away. "At times."

The light spring breeze lifted a loose tendril from her neck. The fugitive strand proved to be a huge distraction. He forced himself to participate in the conversation and stop wondering what it would be like to wrap the wavy lock around his finger.

She turned her face to his again and caught him staring. For the second time in just a few minutes, he'd been treated to that lovely shade of pink splashing over her cheeks.

Leo's pulse quickened. He couldn't be falling in love with Etta Maxwell, could he? He shoved that thought away. He'd promised himself not to pursue her, but somehow, spending time with her shattered that pledge into a hundred little pieces, each sharp enough to pierce his heart.

"They are very understanding of my column in *The Gilded Gown*, as well as my choice to live closer to the people we help through our foundation, but if Mother knew I wore men's breeches and paraded around Brockton as Henry Mason or that I'd climbed a tree chasing a story, Father would most likely need to commit her to the Boston Insane Hospital."

He laughed, and Etta joined in. He liked her laugh. *He liked her.*

"How will they react when you achieve your goal and Henrietta Maxwell has her own byline in the *Enterprise*? Will they ship you across the Atlantic to marry British aristocracy like so many in your circle are doing?"

"Hardly. Mama wants her only daughter close by. If I can pull off the byline without being discovered first, I think my parents will be very proud—after the initial shock, of course." She tucked the wayward lock behind her ear. "Father had to break a few societal rules to create his business."

"Do you have any other dreams?"

"Me?" She paused. "Not really."

"So, there is something."

She reached for his hand and then slid from the rock. "Enough about me. You've hardly told me anything about yourself."

"If you tell me your dreams, I'll tell you anything you want to know."

She narrowed her gaze. "Anything?"

"Anything."

"All right. Even though I'm not the most traditional woman in the greater Boston area, I would like to have a family."

"You're young. You can still have children."

"True, but it's difficult for most men to see past my independent nature; and few, I fear, would tolerate my investigative journalism, let alone keep my secret as you have."

Their gazes connected, and Leo's heart raced faster than a speeding automobile charging toward the finish line of the Vanderbilt Cup. He shouldn't have kissed her cheek. Wasn't he supposed to be keeping her at bay? He had a sinking feeling his heart had already lost that battle, but his head just didn't know it yet.

"Enough about me," she said, smoothing her skirts. "I'll blather all day if you let me."

He narrowed his eyes. "Blather?"

"Prattle on, chatter away, ramble. . .just like I'm doing now. We should probably be heading back to the motorcar before Mitchell sends out a search party. He's very protective of me."

A pair of squirrels scurried across their path. "How about you, Leo? Do you have any secret dreams?"

"I'm generally content with my choice of vocation."

"Vocation. That's not a word one often hears outside the clergy."

"Pops raised us to consider firefighting a calling. We train for a life-and-death mission—to serve and protect our community. So, yes, I consider it a vocation."

She angled her head, contemplating his words. Was that pride reflecting in her gaze?

"That's very noble."

"But?"

She shrugged.

"C'mon, Etta. Out with it."

"You said, and I quote, 'I'm "generally" content with my choice of vocation.'"

Losing Annika had made him sometimes doubt whether or not firefighting was his calling, but only when the loneliness set in. It had never been the deep-in-the-bones kind of questioning that would make him seriously contemplate walking away. He'd made his choice—bachelorhood and the department—even if regret occasionally niggled at the corner of his thoughts. "That's true."

"Sure. But 'generally' implies there's something you're *not* happy about."

It was his turn to shrug now. "I think you would understand better than most that not everyone in our lives will agree with the choices we make and that those choices have consequences. That's why you haven't told your parents you're Henry Mason, right?"

She nodded. "But since your parents and siblings are supportive of your choice to be a fireman, I'm guessing this person was a woman."

How in the world did she deduce that? He both marveled at her intuitiveness and feared her perceptiveness. Maybe if he remained mute on the subject they could move on to another topic of conversation.

They walked in quiet for a few moments before Etta broke the silence. "Whoever she was, you must have loved her very much."

Well, that tactic backfired. What was the use in holding back any longer? This afternoon proved their mutual attraction. Etta was a smart, fetching, independent woman. If he had any chance at lasting happiness with her, he needed to bare his soul and pray that whatever the future held for them, she would tread lightly on his wounded heart.

"Her name is Annika."

Annika.

That could explain why such a kindhearted, attractive man like Leo Eriksson was unattached. The forlorn look in his eyes that remained even after he kissed her cheek certainly sparked her curiosity.

"If you want to tell me about her, I'm happy to listen."

He studied her for a moment, most likely pondering whether it was safe to tell one woman about another who, for at least a time, had captured his heart.

"We were engaged."

Etta swallowed hard. *Engaged.* This wasn't a woman from his past. She was *the* woman—at least Leo once thought she'd been.

"We grew up together. Her father is a policeman in Campello. She's friends with my brother's wife, Trude, and her sister was married to another firefighter friend of ours, Patrick Donavan."

He swiped a stray lock of blond hair off his forehead and sighed. "Patrick died battling a fire three years ago. He disobeyed orders and went back for a family pet. Jens wanted to go after him, but I physically restrained him. Annika's sister lost her husband and Jens, his best friend. My brother nosedived into melancholia."

"I'm so sorry."

He paused and stared at something in the distance. "Seeing her widowed sister's grief and their child without a father, Annika begged me to quit the job." He shook his head. "She asked me to give up who I am, who God created me to be."

"That must have been a very difficult and painful decision."

His gaze latched onto hers, his pain seeking understanding.

"I understand her fear, but not every woman feels the same as Annika," Etta said. "Your mother and Trude were able to accept the risk that loving a firefighter brings to marriage if it meant sharing their lives with the man they love."

His brows peaked, encouraging her to continue.

"Loving someone means embracing the person God has made them to be. If we hold on to them too tightly, we risk suffocating them and crushing their spirit. I think it best to love fully, with our entire being for a short time, rather than safely, and bear the pain of regret for our entire lives."

"Is your wisdom born from heartache?"

He cupped her hands inside his, and his thumbs grazed her skin, making it difficult for her to concentrate.

Oh, she'd known her fair share of heartache, but not the kind Leo encountered. Would he think her an utter fool when he discovered she'd been spouting off about the love between a man and a woman when her experience had been limited to familial affection?

"Not in the least." She glanced away, unable to withstand the pitiful look sure to follow her next declaration. "I've never known the pleasure of a man's affections."

He shuffled back a step. "I find that hard to believe."

She hunched her shoulders and wrapped her arms around her waist. If only she could disappear. But what would that accomplish? If there was any chance he could ever see her as a woman worthy of his heart, she needed to make herself vulnerable.

"It's true." And she bore the scars to prove it. "But I know how I would want to be loved. I want to be cherished as I am, my faults and my shortcomings as well as my strengths. I desire a husband who will help me become the woman God has destined me to be—one who will hold my hand as we forge a new path together."

Tears pricked behind her eyes. She must sound so foolish. "So you see, Leo, I have accepted that my unrealistic expectations mean I will most likely never marry, and for me, that would be the better choice rather than give up the essence of who I am."

He lifted her hand to his lips then brushed her tears away. "I don't think you need to worry about that."

CHAPTER 18

Etta stretched and threw off the covers. When her toes touched the cool floorboards, she shivered. She peeked between the drapes. Despite spring's arrival earlier in the week, a light frost covered the ground, but she didn't mind.

There could've been a raging thunderstorm outside, but it wouldn't dampen Etta's fine mood. Not after her romantic afternoon with Leo yesterday. A pleasant tingle shimmied down her arms. He'd kissed her hand *and* her cheek, and he'd wiped her tears.

None of that compared to him encouraging her to pursue a byline under her own name. There weren't many men in Brockton, or anywhere else for that matter, who would agree with him. And it hadn't gone unnoticed that he'd said *when*, not *if* she earned the recognition she craved.

Don't put the horse before the cart, Etta. One romantic afternoon doesn't equal a lifetime of being cherished.

But it certainly was a good start.

She washed and dressed quickly then stared at her reflection in the handheld mirror and smoothed her mustache. She'd applied the hairpiece above her lip with plenty of adhesive ever since her mishap when she fell from the tree and Leo discovered her ruse due to a misaligned eyebrow.

She couldn't afford a similar calamity today. No, today was too important for mistakes. She planned to be the first reporter to snap up an interview with Robbins Grover.

Local reporters had left Grover alone since the disaster. There'd been sort of an unspoken code to let the man heal and have some privacy. But now that the citywide memorial was over, the gloves would come off. The boiler failure needed to be investigated.

"Etta," Mrs. Hemingway called as she tapped the door, "I have your breakfast."

Her landlady allowed Etta to eat in her room to provide as little contact with the other boarders as possible, thereby reducing the risk of anyone discovering Henrietta Maxwell and Henry Mason as one and the same.

"Come in."

Mrs. Hemingway set the tray on the table beside Etta's typewriter. She untucked the morning editions of both the *Enterprise* and the *Times* from beneath her arm and set them on the chair.

"How do I look?" Etta asked

Her landlady stepped closer and lifted her chin, first examining Etta's eyebrows then her mustache. "You look fine to me."

"Thank you. I can't afford another mistake like the one a couple of weeks ago."

Mrs. Hemingway grabbed an empty coffee mug from the dresser and left the room.

Etta scanned the front page of the *Enterprise* while she ate her oatmeal and toast. Declan's piece on the Meritorious Service Award ceremony snagged her attention. To be more precise, it was the photograph of the recipients recognized for heroic acts during the aftermath of the Grover disaster that caught her gaze. She recognized the man in the center, but from where? She glided her finger over the caption. Olaf Helqvist. His name didn't sound familiar.

Her gaze drifted back to the image and the bandage on his hand.

Etta's pulse kicked up a notch. *That's it.*

She returned her jelly toast to the plate and licked her fingers before flipping through her notepad.

Where is it? She thumbed a few more pages. *C'mon, I know you're in here somewhere.*

Aha! March 15—the stocky man guarding the door during the meeting between the Bonner brothers and the Campello ward boss, Anders Bergstrom. Her description of him included the bandage on his left hand.

What connection did Helqvist have with the Bonner brothers? Furthermore, why would a person with character compromised enough to be mixed up in an arson scheme rush into a burning factory to rescue victims?

So many questions she needed answers to, and now she'd found a lead she could work.

She skimmed the article for any details that might hasten her search and then smacked the broadsheet with the back of her hand. *God bless Declan Gibney.* He'd included the address of each recipient in the piece.

Etta dropped her head into her hands. She'd planned to interview Mr. Grover today. Both were important stories. But Olaf Helqvist was an exclusive. Besides, she could get inspection results more quickly than other journalists because of her connection to the lead investigators. Then she could press Mr. Grover, if necessary, with facts in hand.

With the decision made, she glanced at the mantel clock. If she hurried, she might be able to catch Olaf before he left for work.

Although confident the follow-up story on the personal lives of the Meritorious Service Award recipients would be assigned to Declan Gibney, she was equally confident *this* human-interest piece would be one even Henry Mason would find compelling.

Etta hopped off the trolley and checked the address she'd scribbled in her notepad. The tree-lined street sported the loveliest clapboard bungalows. Spotting number 217, she climbed the stairs and knocked on the door.

A lovely woman about Etta's age answered the door. She wiped her hands on her floral apron. *"God morgon?"*

With the influx of Swedish immigrants making Brockton their home, Etta had become familiar with many of their greetings. "Good morning. I'm Henry Mason, a reporter from the *Enterprise.* Is Olaf Helqvist home?"

"Olaf? *Ja*. He eats breakfast." She stepped back and waved Etta inside.

Etta followed her through the tidy home to the kitchen, where Olaf sat with a mile-high stack of griddle cakes. He wiped his mouth. "Who are you?"

"I'm Henry Mason from the *Brockton Enterprise*. I'm writing a follow-up piece on the Meritorious Service Award recipients. May I talk with you while you eat?"

Heavy footsteps pounded against the floorboards. A tall, broad-shouldered man entered the kitchen. The young woman went to him and kissed his cheek. *"God morgon, Farbror."*

Etta's jaw slackened. She snapped her mouth closed, hoping to hide her surprise. Olaf lived with Lars Bonner? The plot had certainly thickened more than Mrs. Hemingway's gravy.

Lars glanced in Etta's direction. "Have we met?"

"Henry Mason from—"

"The *Enterprise*, yes. I recognize the name."

"I'm here to interview Olaf about his Meritorious Service Award."

"My niece's husband is a good man." Lars clamped a hand on Olaf's shoulder. "But I thought your interview was this afternoon, Olaf?"

Olaf shrugged and shoved a forkful of griddle cakes into his mouth while his bandaged left hand rested on the table.

Lars' steely-eyed gaze bore down on Etta. "*Ja*, I'm certain it was half past three. I am also certain it was not with the most renowned journalist in Brockton. That I would remember."

Etta wiped her palm on her tweed knickerbockers and forced her voice to remain even. "Declan won't be able to make it."

He angled his head and smiled, but it failed to light his eyes. "Ah, well then. Have a seat. Sigrid will make you a plate."

"I ate at home, thank you," Etta said.

Lars seated himself beside Olaf. Apparently, he planned to observe their conversation. "Sigrid, bring Mr. Mason a cup of coffee."

"I'm fine. I won't be here long enough—" Before Etta could finish declining the beverage, Sigrid placed a steaming cup and saucer in front of her.

Etta took a polite sip. "Thank you."

Sigrid offered a demure smile. "*Varsågod.*"

"So, let's begin. Olaf, where were you when the explosion happened at the factory?"

"I was on the street, yust passing by, when the large boom makes me cover my ears, and duck as glass fly in air." He extended his hand and waggled his fingers. "Den I run over street and yelp who I can. We use large timber to—" He pumped his arm up and down.

"Like a lever?"

Olaf shrugged, but Lars nodded.

"Did you know anyone who worked at the factory?"

"*Nej.*"

"So, you just sprang into action after the explosion?"

"*Ja.*"

"That was very brave of you. Most people don't rush into a burning building if they don't have a connection to the people who may be inside."

"*Ja*," Olaf said, his chest broadening. "I not dink of myself at dat time. I dink of de workers."

"Remind me again how many people you assisted."

"Two women and one child."

"Why aren't you writing any of this down?" Lars asked, eyes narrowed. "So you don't forget?"

"I prefer to listen and then make my notes after the interview," she explained. "Olaf, did you get any injuries while helping Grover employees escape?"

"*Nej*. I'm fine."

"Okay, thank you for your time." She stood and scooted her chair closer to the table. "Our readers at the *Enterprise* love a good human-interest story."

"Sigrid," Lars called, "please show Mr. Mason to the door."

Etta followed her for a few steps then turned and went back to the kitchen. "If you don't mind, Mr. Helqvist, I thought of one more question I'd like to ask you."

"*Ja*, sure."

"If you didn't get hurt during the heroic measures you undertook at the disaster site, how did you hurt your hand?"

His gaze darted from Lars to Etta then back to Lars, who gave him a slight shake of his head.

"Olaf misspoke, Mr. Mason. He did get hurt that day. Nothing too severe. The doctor said it's healing nicely."

"*Ja*. Lars is right. I get cut when I rescue the women."

"So you sought medical care for the wound?"

"*Ja*, doctor from City Hospital look at it."

Lars stood. "Do you need anything else for your interview, Mr. Mason?"

That was her cue to leave. "Thank you for your time today, Mr. Helqvist." She touched the brim of her cap. "My apologies for interrupting your breakfast."

Sigrid opened the door. "*Adjö.*"

"Goodbye."

Etta could hardly believe her luck. Not only was Olaf married kin to Lars and Karl Bonner, but she'd also caught him in a lie. At least she believed she had.

Next stop, City Hospital.

Etta pushed open the door to the hospital and approached the front desk attendant.

"Good morning. I'm a journalist with the *Brockton Enterprise*. Whom would I speak to about a patient who may have been treated here for an injury?"

"Is it related to the Grover fire?" she asked. "If so, none of those treatment diaries are available yet."

"No, it was about a week prior to the disaster."

"If the person you're inquiring about has been discharged in the last year, then you'd need to speak with someone in the medical records department. That's located downstairs." The woman pointed to a hallway on her left. "Use the stairway at the end of the corridor and then follow the signs."

Etta offered a tight nod and headed in the direction indicated by the receptionist. A single light bulb dangled from the ceiling, illuminating the narrow basement corridor. The close quarters smelled like an odd mixture of nuts and soil.

An older gentleman in coveralls knelt on the wood floor. He glanced up at her. "Watch your step, sir." He poured a pale-yellow, oily substance onto a white cloth. "That's fresh linseed oil, very slippery."

Etta shuddered. The floors of the Grover factory had been treated with linseed oil. A major factor as to why the fire spread so quickly. What if the hospital caught on fire? How many patients would they be able to evacuate before—? She shoved that thought from her mind.

"Thank you, sir."

She glanced at the sign above his head then followed the arrow to the end of the hallway and pushed through the swinging door marked for her destination. A dozen or more bookshelves filled the expansive room, each housing crates stamped with a letter of the alphabet. Several employees bent over a table, sorting documents.

"Excuse me," Etta said.

A gentleman whose salt-and-pepper eyebrows were bushier than her own looked up from his task. "How may I help you, sir?"

"I'm Henry Mason, a reporter with the *Enterprise*. I'm following up on a story and wonder if I could see the treatment diary for Olaf Helqvist. I believe he may have been treated here between the twelfth and fourteenth of this month."

The attendant reached for a sheet of paper and a fountain pen. He laid both on the counter in front of Etta. "Fill this out. Make sure it's legible and the name you want searched is spelled correctly."

Etta quickly completed the brief form, and the gentleman disappeared in search of the document she hoped would blow the arson investigation wide open. She drummed her fingers on the counter then checked the time on her pocket watch.

"Here you are, sir." The attendant placed a folder in front of Etta. "Helqvist, Olaf" was written on the front of its dark green cover. "The documents may not be removed from the office, but you are free to examine them. Leave the file in this tray when you're finished." He pointed to a small black container labeled TO BE FILED.

"Thank you." Clutching the folder, she moved to a small table in the waiting area. She moistened her lips as she opened the file. The thrill of investigative work excited her more than opening gifts on Christmas morning.

She scanned the document, taking in the day and time of his treatment, the attending physician, and the diagnosis: "Patient presented with second-degree burn on left hand."

Just what she suspected. Olaf had been injured prior to the Grover disaster. Her gaze shifted back to the top of the document to verify the admission date once again. March 13, seven o'clock. He'd waited until the day after the fire at Brockton Hardware to see a doctor. Not enough evidence for a conviction, but a solid lead for the arson investigation team.

Her heart raced as she whipped out her notebook and jotted the relevant details on a clean sheet of paper. She hopped to her feet, returned the folder to the tray, and plowed through the swinging door, nearly losing her footing on the slick hall floor. Undeterred, she took the stairs by twos, once again thankful for the ease of movement that her trousers afforded.

First, she'd stop by the firehouse and give Leo an update on the case. Then, she'd speak to her boss and get Declan pulled from the follow-up article for the Meritorious Service Award recipients before the kid blew her cover story.

Because if her hunch was right, she'd just found the Campello arsonist.

Leo slid into the booth at the Brockton Diner. He grabbed a menu from the end of the table and skimmed the lunch specials.

The bell above the door jingled, and Leo glanced up to see who it was.

"Who are you looking for, Leo? Etta?" Jens said with a teasing tone.

"Don't be ridiculous. Why would Henrietta Maxwell come here?"

"I don't know. Maybe the same reason she whisked you away in her fancy automobile yesterday."

Leo rolled his eyes.

When the bell chimed again, Leo fought the urge to see if it could be Etta. A completely ridiculous notion, since she didn't know they were there. He did, however, make a mental note to share the location of their new second home with her—in case she wanted to discuss one of the cases they were working on.

Who was he kidding? He'd barely slept last night, thinking about his afternoon with the spirited heiress. His heartbeat ticked up. Apparently, life with a firefighter wouldn't chase her away. That was helpful information. But what about her father?

Her parents seemed more progressive than most. Clyde Maxwell was a self-made man, so perhaps he wouldn't hold the same prejudices as others did toward Leo's working-class background. Then again, just because they didn't have their sights set on an aristocratic match for their daughter didn't mean they'd give their blessing to a union with a fireman from Brockton.

Marriage? Leo shook his head. *It was one afternoon. Nothing more.*

Yet she awakened something in him, something dormant since Annika broke their engagement—something he'd given up hope of ever feeling again.

"Leo."

"Huh?"

"I need you to scoot over," Gunnar said.

"Don't mind him, Gunnar," Jens said, his eyes peeking over the top of the menu. "He's sported a goofy look on his face ever since—"

"I have not."

"Yes, you have. Ever since you came back from your drive with Miss Maxwell."

The heat creeping up Leo's neck got hotter by the inch.

"*You* and Henrietta Maxwell? I need all the details. If Trude hears about this from anyone else, I'll be in the doghouse."

"Good morning. I'm Ilsa," the waitress said, pouring their coffee.

The woman's timing couldn't have been better. Although she didn't know it, she'd just saved him from extensive embarrassment. He'd be sure to thank her with a nice tip.

Ilsa slid the cream and sugar toward Pops. When he thanked her, she tilted her head and smiled. "Let me know if you need anything."

He nodded his appreciation.

"What was that all about?" Gunnar asked.

Leo furrowed his brows. "What was what all about?"

"You're hopeless, big brother." Jens elbowed Pops. "Looks like the waitress is sweet on you."

Pops glanced at Ilsa, who waited on a customer. "She seems like a nice lady."

"She's pretty, Pops. You should go talk to her after we eat."

"Let's not make a mountain out of a molehill." Pops sipped his coffee. "Pretty smiles are a dime a dozen."

His brothers had noticed Ilsa flirting with their father. Why hadn't he? Perhaps he needed remedial lessons in the art of love and romance. Leo looked from Jens, to Pops, to Gunnar, before settling on the menu again. If these three understood romance better than he did, then maybe what he'd thought were signs of interest on Etta's part were anything but. What if she was only toying with him, a lowly firefighter from Brockton.

That didn't seem like what she'd been doing, nor did it seem like Etta to do such a thing. But he'd also not expected Annika to end their engagement, when she'd known he was a firefighter long before he'd started paying calls on her.

Ugh.

"Let's review what we've learned about the Grover explosion," Pops said. "We need to be prepared for our meeting with the inspectors from Hartford Steam Boiler."

"Hopefully, they'll bring those records we requested," Gunnar said.

Leo glanced up and saw Etta headed their way. How on earth did she find him? "Pops, Henry Mason is coming."

"Good afternoon," she said, her gaze flitting to each person at the table.

"How did you find us?" Leo asked.

She lightly punched his forearm. "I'm an investigative reporter, Eriksson. It's what I do." She chuckled. "I also saw Gunnar at the firehouse. He told me to stop by when I finished my conversation with Leif."

"Speaking of Firefighter Hansen," she said, "he was kind enough to review everything you've learned so far, including confirmation that the boiler triggered the initial explosion and that Rockwell was in his office in the boiler room at the time of the blast."

Etta shoved her hands in her pockets. "He also mentioned something about a phone call made by the plant manager about five minutes beforehand, expressing concern about strange noises coming from the radiators in the factory. Rockwell's assistant gave him the all-clear. Care to elaborate on that, Chief Eriksson?"

Pops sighed. "Leo, remind me to have a conversation with Hansen about speaking with the press."

"Will do, Pops."

"Firefighter Hansen doesn't speak for the Brockton Fire Department or Engine Company No. 1. Got it, Mason?"

"Got it, Chief, as long as I'm the first reporter that gets the scoop once you have verifiable information."

"Of course."

"Would you care to comment on the facts in Hansen's statement?"

"Mason, you're like a dog with a bone, you know that?"

Etta chuckled. "Thank you, sir."

Leo's chest swelled. Etta was very good at what she did. She deserved to have her work recognized under her true identity.

"I need to speak with my editor about another story I'm working." She gave Leo a pointed look. "I just wanted to confirm Leif's statement. I won't interrupt your meal any longer."

That was odd. Why did she look at him that way? Did she want to speak with him privately? Or was she giving him a clue about the piece she was writing?

If he hoped to pursue a relationship with Etta, he needed to learn to read the subtle clues his brothers seemed so adept at deciphering. Otherwise, he might spend the rest of his life in delightful confusion.

CHAPTER 19

Etta knocked on the door to her editor's office. She didn't wait for an answer but poked her head inside. "Got a minute?"

"Why do you even knock, Mason?"

She shrugged. "Courtesy."

Littleton waved her inside. "What's going on?"

"I need a favor."

He reclined in his chair and laced his fingers together over his stomach. "If you gave me a penny every time you asked for a favor, I'd have—"

"A nickel," Etta chimed in.

"More like a dollar." He laughed, amused by his own joke.

"I need you to pull Declan from the biographical sketches of the Meritorious Service Award recipients."

"Why would I do that?"

She stepped inside and closed the door. "I suspect Olaf Helqvist was involved in the arsons in the Campello District."

Littleton straightened in his chair. "Really? What evidence have you got?"

"I interviewed him this morning."

"The kid know that?"

"Not that I'm aware. I had a hunch, so I went over first thing, and I caught him in a lie."

Her boss leaned forward, elbows on his desk. He loved intrigue as much, if not more, than Etta did. "Let me hear it."

"He was wounded prior to rescuing those folks from the rubble. He was the man I saw guarding the door for the meeting with the ward boss and the Bonner brothers on the fifteenth. He had a bandage on his hand then."

"That's circumstantial, Mason. You know that. He could've been hurt a thousand different ways."

"Right, so I followed up with City Hospital where Olaf said he'd been treated following the disaster. Their records show they treated him on March thirteenth for a severe burn to his left hand."

His eyes widened. "That's six days before the factory blew."

"Correct, and it's also the day *after* the fire at the hardware store. And that's not all. Guess where Olaf lives."

Littleton shook his head. "I have no idea."

"With Lars Bonner."

She'd never seen her editor so flabbergasted before. "You're kidding."

"Olaf Helqvist is married to Lars and Karl Bonner's niece, Sigrid."

Littleton stood and paced the small office, all the while rubbing his chin. "We need to get at least one of the business owners in the Campello District to identify Olaf as part of the protection racket."

"Yeah, that's gonna be the tricky part," she said. "They're scared of the Bonners, and so far, they're staying silent. Hopefully, the picture of the award recipients, coupled with the connection between Olaf and Lars, will help loosen their tongues. Seeing that we're close to putting all the pieces together might be enough to nudge one of them to snap the last one in place."

"Excellent work as usual, Mason."

She lifted her chin. "Thanks, boss."

"Call Gibney in. I'll tell him you're taking the sketches. He's not gonna like it."

He was gonna hate it, but there was nothing that could be done. If she didn't follow through with the story, Lars would get suspicious. He already seemed a bit twitchy.

Etta opened the door and called for Declan. "Hey, kid. The boss wants to see you."

He grabbed a tablet and pencil then joined them in Littleton's office.

Declan glanced between Etta and the boss. He seemed as antsy as Lars Bonner. "What's going on?"

"I'm pulling you from the Meritorious Service Award biographies. I need someone to follow up on—"

He stopped short. They should've thought that through before they sent for Declan. Etta scanned her mind for any story she could think of.

"I think you mentioned the Maxwell Foundation fundraiser for the fire department," she said.

Littleton's gaze narrowed. "Right?"

"No," Declan said, planting his hands squarely on his hips. "The piece was assigned to me. I've already interviewed one of the recipients."

"Turns out, your story is related to another feature Mason's been working on."

"What story?"

She exchanged glances with her boss, along with a tight shake of her head.

"We're not prepared to say at this time," Littleton said. "It needs to stay under wraps until we can prove some of the details."

Declan huffed. "So you expect me to just hand over my notes to Mason, then follow a society dame around to write a story about a fancy dance?"

"It's not a dance this year," Etta said. "She's hosting a charity auction instead."

Declan folded his arms over his chest. "And how, exactly, do you know that?"

She'd mentally slapped her palm to her forehead as soon as the words slipped past her lips. "I. . .heard it around." That was a flimsy response.

"You heard it around?"

She nodded.

"This is the assignment, Gibney," Littleton said. "Take it, or pack up your desk."

"Fine," Declan said. "But this is the second time you've violated newsroom rules to my detriment and Mason's gain. If it happens again, I'm going over your head."

He stepped closer to Etta. Now inches apart, he poked a finger in the middle of her chest.

"Oof." She'd tried hard to contain the rush of air careening from her lungs, to take it like a man, but his bony little finger hurt.

"Don't get in my way again, Mason." He stormed out of the office, knocking her shoulder as he passed. She stumbled backward.

She hadn't expected Declan to like being reassigned. If it had been her, she would have blown a gasket. But was there really much difference between biographical sketches of award recipients and a piece on a charity auction? Not to her there wasn't.

Declan was an ambitious journalist, hungry for the next story. In truth, he reminded Etta a lot of herself when she first started at the *Enterprise*. Didn't he understand that none of it was personal? It was just the newspaper business.

Leo waited on the bench in the park. He glanced at his pocket watch. A quarter past eight. Two minutes later than the last time he'd checked. He tapped the envelope containing the arson investigation report against his palm.

He now assumed the pointed look Etta gave him in the diner earlier meant she'd wanted to speak with him about the boiler inspection, especially after she'd learned about the phone call from the plant manager. When the message she'd left at the station earlier said she had a new lead on the arson investigation, he'd been stunned. He'd assumed the Grover story prevented her from pursuing the arson case any further.

He checked the time again—8:19. Etta petitioned for this meeting. Why wasn't she here?

He glanced toward the walkway. Someone hurried down the path. Was that Etta?

She plopped onto the bench beside him. "Sorry I'm late," she said. "I've. . .been all over town today."

"I was getting worried."

"I'm fine," she said, gasping for breath. "It's been. . .a very full news day. I have a scoop you won't believe." She leaned forward, elbows on her knees, and gulped a breath. "First, can. . .you confirm. . .the fires are—"

"How about I talk while you catch your breath."

"Good idea," she huffed.

"After reexamining the first two fire scenes and comparing what we've seen with the third fire at Brockton Hardware, Pops has what he believes is conclusive evidence that all three fires were deliberately set."

She glanced over her shoulder. "I'm listening."

"We have multiple factors across three fire scenes that lead us to believe an accelerant was used. We already knew about the V pattern on the wall, but Pops noticed the windows in all three scenes have irregular cracks in the glass caused by rapid, intense heat. Again, indicating an accelerant.

"Finally, we reexamined the charred wood. If wood burns long and slow, like in your fireplace, it develops overlapping bumpy layers, similar to a reptile's scales. But the wood left behind at each of our suspicious fires is blistered. Blistering is the result of exposure to very high temperatures only achieved from an accelerant, most likely kerosene."

"This is exactly what I wanted to hear. Wait till you hear my update."

He tugged the report from the pocket in the lining of his coat. "This is the only copy."

She reached for the envelope. When her fingers grazed his palm, they both startled, and Leo jerked his hand away.

Would he ever get used to the way her touch made him feel? He needed to ask her on a proper outing. Then he could caress her hand when she wasn't sporting men's breeches.

"Let's meet here Monday. Pops is off tomorrow and Sunday. And Monday the Hartford inspectors are coming. So I'll have plenty of time to return that to his desk. Let's say ten o'clock, sharp?"

"I'll be here." She crossed her heart. "Now, do you want to find out who I suspect is setting those fires?"

~

Etta updated Leo on her discovery that Olaf Helqvist, the Meritorious Service Award recipient, was present during the meeting she'd observed between the Bonner brothers and Campello ward boss Bergstrom, as well as his familial relationship to the Bonners.

"One day next week, I'll visit the arson victims and see if I can get any bites when I show them Olaf's picture. I'm hoping we can convince one of them to break their silence and implicate him and the Bonners in a protection racket."

Leo's brows drew together. "Mind if I tag along? Sounds a bit dangerous, poking around alone."

That wasn't exactly the way she'd hoped to spend time with him, but she'd take it over nothing. She'd been bold and made the first move in their romantic chess game, but now it was up to Leo to advance his pawn.

"I haven't found a connection yet to Bergstrom." She sighed. "He's been in office a long time. Always implicated, never charged."

"If he's involved, then I hope we can nail him this time."

Had he meant to say "we," or was it merely a slip of the tongue? Either way, she liked the sound of that. They did make a good team in her opinion.

"Any idea when your father will file that report with Deputy Commissioner Nilsson?" she asked.

"Later this week, I imagine. However, if the deputy commissioner signs off on arson, I think we can eliminate him and count his presence with Bonner minutes before Bergstrom arrived as happenstance."

"I don't know, Leo. That's an awfully big coincidence. I'd really like to find out if he buys his insurance from Bonner. I need to find an informant in the Bonners' office to confirm if Nilsson has a policy."

She yawned and covered her mouth. "I need to head back to the boardinghouse. I'll see you in the morning, promptly at ten o'clock."

"See you then."

Etta turned in the direction she'd come and hurried to the trolley. She nearly fell asleep during the short ride to the boardinghouse. She wove her way through several alleys and climbed the stairs to Mrs. Hemingway's back porch.

A rustling noise drew her attention to the shrubs that bordered the neighbor's property.

She stilled. Huh. Only silence lingered on the evening air. Most likely Midnight discovered something to chase. She'd not seen the black cat for several days. Now that spring arrived, he had better things to occupy his time than cuddling by the fireplace.

Using the key under the mat, she opened the door and stepped inside. The rambunctious feline darted between her legs and disappeared outside.

If Midnight had been inside, then what had she heard in the yard?

CHAPTER 20

Leo dipped his shaving brush into the soap and swirled the stiff bristles against his cheek. Etta was on his mind the moment he'd opened his eyes. There was something about the woman that inexplicably drew him to her. He chuckled to himself. Especially baffling, considering that most of the time they'd spent together she'd been impersonating a male reporter.

Tightening his cheek, he carefully glided the straight razor over his skin. Perhaps it was her ability to embrace exactly who God made her to be without concern for the approval of others.

He rinsed the razor and meticulously forged a new trail through the shaving soap with his blade. There was a genuineness about her. That was it. Etta was. . .authentic. That was a quality he admired. If he was honest with himself, he felt more than admiration for the clever woman. She was bright, spirited, and definitely attractive.

Whoa boy, slow down. You're falling hard.

He couldn't believe she hadn't been snatched up already. He supposed her willingness to flout convention or her unusual height had something to do with it, but Leo didn't mind that she was a couple of inches taller than him.

He rinsed the streaks of shaving cream from his cheeks, patted his face and neck dry, then dabbed his skin with a splash of bay-rum-and-spice aftershave. Resting his hands on the sink, he stared at his reflection. *She's way out of your league, Leo boy.*

He didn't doubt there was an attraction between him and Etta, or she would have spoken up when he kissed her cheek. But what if what he felt for her was more than she felt in return? Although the circumstances were entirely different, losing Annika had devastated him. His heart had shattered into a million little pieces that all these years later Etta was helping him put back together.

What if he pursued Etta and, like Annika, she determined life with a firefighter wasn't for her? Would he give up his calling for love this time around?

Sure, Gunnar found Trude, but her father was a cop, and she was accustomed to the family breadwinner risking his life. A vastly different scenario than a father who made his fortune selling office machines.

What if Etta was having fun and enjoyed his company but would never commit to going forward? They were, after all, from very different circumstances. What if he was just a dalliance to her? A distraction?

His head ached from all the questions. *Enough, Leo.*

There was only one way to get the answers he craved. He'd have to summon the courage to share his affections, because the only thing worse than getting his heart broken was never knowing if he was a man Etta Maxwell could love in return.

Etta fastened the black cummerbund around her waist. She turned each way in the mirror. The robin's-egg-blue skirt was definitely her favorite. The black piping that trimmed each panel also decorated the hem and coordinated with the eight large buttons framing the center of the garment. Knowing the skirt was five years old if it was a day made her reluctant to wear it to her mother's bridge party. However, finding nothing she liked better in her wardrobe, she resigned herself to the derisive looks she'd undoubtedly garner. She was nothing if not practical.

She fastened a small brooch to the high-necked collar of her white blouse. Surely that would add a smidgen of ornamentation to her otherwise tired costume. She posed a lovely matching hat with a large white feather at an angle on her head and secured it with several large hat pins. Mrs. Hemingway had fashioned Etta's hair in her best attempt at a pompadour, and Etta was pleased enough with her landlady's efforts.

She grabbed the arson report and her parasol and reached for the doorknob. What would Leo think of her appearance? She examined herself in the full-length mirror in the corner of her room and smoothed her skirt. This had to be better than the knickerbockers and flat cap she usually wore in his company.

She dismissed the thought from her mind. The last time she'd tried to impress Leo Eriksson, she'd nearly windmilled face-first into mud. Nope, if he decided to pursue her—and she definitely hoped he did—he'd have to take her and her five-year-old ensemble as a package deal.

She glanced at the mantel. Only nine o'clock. Plenty of time to reach the park before Leo.

Mrs. Hemingway buzzed about the kitchen. "You look lovely."

The taut muscles in Etta's shoulders relaxed. "Thank you. I'm meeting a gentleman friend this morning."

"I've not heard of any young man before."

"If things progress in the direction I hope they will, you'll be hearing about him."

"I look forward to it."

A happy tune flitted through her thoughts as she slipped out the back door and bounded down the steps.

A scurry of squirrels scattered as she approached, leaving bits of peanut shells littering the stone walkway. She examined the rubbish. Where on earth had they found peanuts? More shells lay on the grass by the shrubs in the general vicinity of the noise she'd heard the night before.

Using her parasol, she pushed the bottom sprigs aside. Several crocuses lay in the dirt, severed from their stems. Over them, a boot print showed in the moist soil.

Someone had been there last night. She hadn't imagined it. But who was it, and what did they want?

~

Leo checked his appearance in the small mirror by the front door. Spying his wayward cowlick, he licked his fingers and smoothed the obstinate strands of hair into place.

"Who are you preening for?" Jens asked.

"Taking pride in one's appearance isn't preening." He eyed the prickly dark shadow on his brother's cheeks. "Just because Genevieve is visiting family in Rhode Island doesn't mean you can't bathe and scape a razor over those whiskers."

"I'll take it under advisement."

Leo snatched the morning edition of the *Enterprise* from his brother's grasp and tucked it beneath his arm.

"Hey, I was—"

"Consider it payback for all the bacon you've swiped over the years." Leo plopped his cap on his head and grasped the door latch.

"You might want to take this."

Jens patted the small package wrapped in brown paper and tied with the red and white twine Leo had saved from the box of cinnamon rolls Trude had sent last week.

"Oh, yeah."

Jens shook his head. "For all your organization and punctuality, you're not very good at the courting thing, are you?"

"I'm a little out of practice."

Jens' expression softened. "Sorry." He stood and put his hand on Leo's shoulder. "I shouldn't have teased you. I know Annika did a number on your heart." He glanced at the gift. "What did you get her?"

"A handkerchief Trude made with Etta's initials embroidered in tiny flowers."

"She'll like that."

His brother's tone rang flat. Clearly, he wasn't impressed with Leo's choice. "What?"

Jens shrugged.

"You don't think it's a nice gift, do you?"

"No, I do. It's personal, and I'm sure dainty. Women like that." He rubbed the back of his neck. "You like this woman, right? You'd like to pay calls on her?"

Leo nodded. "That is the end goal."

"Then maybe stop on the way and buy some flowers or chocolates to go with it. Something that says you care for her romantically."

When had his little brother surpassed him in the art of wooing women? "You're brilliant, Jens. I'll do that."

Leo tugged the newspaper free from beneath his arm and tossed it on the table. "Consider that my tip."

He hurried outside and headed for the trolley, hoping he had time to purchase flowers and still arrive before her.

After a quick stop at the florist and a crowded trolley ride, he pulled the string and the driver stopped at the entrance to City Park. He glanced at his pocket watch as he navigated others strolling on the gravel path. 10:03. His muscles stiffened, and he quickened his pace. Silly, really. Etta wouldn't mind if he was a few minutes late.

He rounded the bend and came to a standstill. A woman in a white feathered hat sat on their bench. Her shoulders bobbed. Was she enjoying the antics of the playful chipmunks scurrying up the nearby oak tree?

"Etta?"

She looked his way. With a simple smile, she stole his breath. Etta Maxwell was not only smart and independent but also stunning. A deadly combination.

He should go to her, but he lacked the confidence that his legs wouldn't buckle with his first step.

She scanned her appearance then sent her green-eyed gaze his direction. "Is something wrong?"

No, Etta. Everything is very right.

She angled her head, probably wondering what she saw in Leo.

Okay, Lord, help me not to blow this to smithereens.

"You're late," she said, an air of lighthearted smugness in her voice.

"I plead guilty, Miss Maxwell. On a whim, I stopped to purchase these." He handed her the bouquet.

She sniffed the fragrant flowers. "These are lovely, Leo." Her smile lighted her eyes. "You're forgiven," she teased.

She was completely charming. He'd move heaven and earth to make this woman his own.

Etta sat on the bench, the bouquet across her lap, and patted the space beside her. She handed him the arson investigation report. "This was very helpful. I took copious notes. Thank you for trusting me with it."

He'd never noticed how rosy her lips were.

"Leo?"

Focus, fella. "Oh, sorry. I'm glad it was helpful."

They sat quietly for a few minutes.

Etta fidgeted with her parasol. "I suppose, if there's nothing else, I should be going. I'm playing bridge with Mother and her friends today."

He swiped his hand through his hair. *C'mon, Leo, you're blowing your opportunity.*

"Are you sure everything is okay, Leo? You seem a bit preoccupied this morning."

She had no idea. "Oh, um, I have something altogether different than our investigation I'd like to discuss with you."

He stood and paced several times. *Come on man, buck up.*

She reached for his arm and tugged him back onto the seat beside her. "Something is clearly troubling you. Is there some way I can help?"

God had provided this opportunity to discover if Etta would return his affections, but to find out, he'd have to lay himself bare before her. Had she meant it when she'd said he had a noble calling? Even so, would the heiress to the Maxwell fortune be willing to keep company with a fireman? Honestly, the whole notion was silly, but he'd have no peace unless he heard the rejection from her own lips.

"As a matter of fact, yes. I've really enjoyed working with you on our undercover investigation, and I'm hoping we can extend our partnership."

Her brow quirked. "Partnership? You mean as additional cases arise?"

Partnership? Is that what he'd said? *You're a real Romeo, Leo. That will definitely make her swoon.*

He cleared his throat. "That's not exactly what I meant."

"Oh?"

He was making a mess of everything. Words were not his strong suit, and it didn't help that his tongue had thickened to three times its normal size.

"What I'm trying to say in my own charmingly awkward way is...I'd like to pay calls on you, Henrietta Maxwell. That is, if you'll have me."

There, he'd said it. Although the words had tumbled from his lips in a most ineloquent fashion, he'd managed to spit it out nonetheless. And there'd be no taking it back now.

A broad smile stretched to her cheeks before she hid it behind her gloved hand.

Had she been flattered by the suggestion or appalled that a man of his status would want to pursue her? Either way, he'd sealed his fate, and it wouldn't be long before she revealed it.

Leo Eriksson wanted to pay calls...*on her?*

Etta reined in her smile, trying to curb her enthusiasm and refrain from the utter schoolgirl giddiness that threatened to overtake her. No man had ever asked to pay calls on her before. Sure, she'd had some attention at her cotillion, but mostly from men more interested in her father's money than Etta herself. Leo Eriksson was the first man to be interested in her apart from her family's status.

She fidgeted with the lavender bow securing the flowers he'd given her, and emotion clogged her throat. His nervous smile transformed into a look of sheer panic. Had he changed his mind? Ready or not, she'd better give him an answer before he had time to reconsider his question.

"I'm flattered, Leo. . ." She swallowed. Why did it feel like a wad of cotton clogged her throat?

He resumed his pacing. "But?"

"But what?" she replied.

"Your initial hesitation coupled with your choice of the word *flattered* has led me to conclude that you are declining my proposition."

"I'm sorry, Leo, I didn't mean—"

His downcast eyes pinched her heart.

"It's all right, Etta. Our worlds are just too different."

What? Why did he think. . .? Ugh, never mind. If she didn't speak up, he'd talk them out of a courtship before one ever began.

"Leo," she said kindly but with a firm tone, "I think you mistake the matter."

His head snapped in her direction, questions looming in his eyes.

She smiled. "I believe there's nothing I'd enjoy better than spending more time with you."

His eyes widened, and he shook his head. "You do?"

She chuckled.

"Why are you laughing?"

"You looked surprised at my answer. Didn't you want me to say yes?"

"Of course I did."

Leo sat beside her and tugged her into a short embrace. "I'm glad that's over."

She wriggled free from his hold. "Am I that scary?"

"You have no idea." He gently kissed her forehead then took the small package from his jacket pocket. "I have a gift for you."

"But you already gave me flowers, and I have nothing for you."

"Agreeing to a courtship is the only gift I need."

Tears pricked the back of her eyes. She didn't want to cry. She squeezed his hand and smiled. "This is so thoughtful, Leo."

"It's nothing fancy, just something that made me think of you."

Thankful for a distraction that would prevent those tears from erupting and treating Leo to a red, splotchy face, she grinned and untied the package.

She unfolded the white cotton fabric and unveiled her initials stitched in a chain of black-eyed Susans. "It's lovely. How did you know black-eyed Susans are my favorite flower?"

"I didn't," he said, his chest broadening. "Gunnar's wife, Trude, makes them. She suggested those yellow flowers." He chuckled. "I didn't even know their name until now."

What had she ever done to deserve such a kindhearted man? She leaned forward and kissed his cheek. "I'll treasure it always."

She looped her arm in his. "So, you realize, as my beau, you're obligated to escort me to the trolley."

"I am, am I?"

His steady gaze provoked longing she'd never known. "Most certainly, Mr. Eriksson."

He stood and offered his arm. "I like it better when you call me Leo."

She stood and slipped her arm through the crook of his elbow. "And you don't mind that I'm so tall?"

"Actually, that's one of my favorite things about you."

She scrunched her brows together. "Really?"

Something akin to mischief sparkled in Leo's gaze. "I think it will be an asset that you can climb trees. You never know when that skill might come in handy."

She swatted his arm.

"Miss Maxwell?"

The interruption cut their shared laughter short. She turned, and her jaw slackened. *Declan Gibney?* How had he known where to find her?

His gaze flitted from Etta to Leo. "I'm sorry to interrupt. May I have a moment of your time?"

"Who is this, Etta?"

"Leo Eriksson. . ." She motioned to Leo then to Declan. "This is Declan Gibney. He's a reporter for the *Brockton Enterprise*."

Declan scribbled something in his notebook. Did he jot down Leo's name?

"Aren't you one of the firefighters from Engine Company No. 1 who received the Meritorious Service Award?"

Eyes narrowed, Leo nodded.

"I thought I recognized you from the photograph in the newspaper."

Declan paused then pointed his pencil at Leo. "Are you related to our photographer, Jens Eriksson?"

"Yes, that's my youngest brother."

"And your father is the battalion chief, correct?"

Leo folded his arms over his chest. "That's correct. Why are you asking?"

Declan glanced at the flowers Etta clutched, and shrugged.

He flipped the page in his tablet and scribbled feverishly. Why was he making notations about her and Leo? She didn't know if the whole encounter was a coincidence or not, but she couldn't ignore the uneasy feeling rumbling in her middle.

"How can I help you, Mr. Gibney?" she asked.

"I've been assigned to cover your annual charity event for the fire department. I was hoping to arrange a meeting to discuss the benefit auction, but I'll stop by the foundation's office later this week."

What was he up to?

Declan touched the brim of his cap. "My apologies, Miss Maxwell. I'll leave you to enjoy your assignation."

There it is. He really wanted to find tawdry gossip he could use to diminish the foundation and elevate his prospects at the *Enterprise.*

Leo stepped forward. "How dare you imply—"

She halted Leo with a hand to his chest.

Declan waved his pencil back and forth between her and Leo. "It's just you two, being here together, arm-in-arm, with flowers, raises questions about Miss Maxwell's motives for her benevolence to the fire department. Would you care to comment on that?"

Bearing the Maxwell name had made her no stranger to gossip, but this was beyond the pale. She inhaled deeply and released her breath slowly, calming her spirit. She would react with strength and dignity even though she secretly wished she were clothed as Henry Mason so she could pummel this clod.

"Not at this time," she said as sweetly as possible with gritted teeth.

"So you deny being romantically attached to Mr. Eriksson?"

Oh, she was romantically attached all right, but her personal life wasn't fodder for the newspaper. This was her heart. While some in the Beacon Hill circle enjoyed seeing their relationships advertised in print, she was not among them. And this wasn't a society magazine like *The*

Gilded Gown; this was the *Brockton Enterprise*—a prominent local newspaper. Declan's unfounded accusations could hinder donations to the foundation.

Leo's hand slid to the small of her back. "Miss Maxwell has been fundraising for the fire department long before we became acquainted. If you have any further questions about our relationship, you can address them to me. Otherwise, keep your inquiries strictly related to the good work the Maxwell Foundation does in our community. Is that understood, Mr. Gibney?"

"So noted." He glanced at Etta. "I'll see you later this week, Miss Maxwell."

The tension drained from Etta's shoulders. She'd always prided herself on being a strong, independent woman, but that had been out of necessity. She may not *need* a man to provide for her, but she certainly longed for companionship and someone to share life's burdens with—and God had blessed her with Leo.

Leo waited for Declan to leave then slipped his arm around her waist. "I'm sorry if I overstepped my bounds."

"Don't apologize. That's your protective nature, and I adore that about you."

That glimmer returned to his eye. "Perhaps I could give Gibney a title for his article."

She narrowed her gaze. "I'm afraid to ask."

"Sparks Fly Between Maxwell Heiress and Local Fireman."

This man. How had he turned a nasty encounter with Declan into something that made her laugh? "Very nice. You know, you might have a second career writing headlines for the *Enterprise*."

He grinned. "I'll leave the headlines to you."

Warmth settled in Etta's chest. She'd longed for this very thing, to feel the genuine affection of an amiable, God-fearing man.

Did Leo have any idea of the headline he'd actually written that day—*Local Fireman Rescues Heart of Maxwell Heiress.*

That was one story she looked forward to investigating.

CHAPTER 21

Etta stopped on the street outside Robbins Grover's house. The place looked deserted. Although he hadn't sat for an interview with any newspaper that she'd seen, he had been cooperating with the fire department's investigation. Perhaps after the memorial service, he'd retreated to the home of family or friends and was keeping a low profile. Very understandable.

But she hadn't come across town for nothing. Over years of reporting the news, she'd found household staff easy to pry information from with the proper inducement. Today's encouragement was courtesy of Hastings Bakery. A loose-lipped neighbor had shared Grover's partiality to the bakery's raisin pies. Hopefully, the pie would offer the same incentive to Grover's housekeeper if he wasn't at home.

She smoothed her mustache and eyebrows. Confident they were secure, she climbed the stairs and banged the lion-head knocker three times against the Grovers' front door.

Someone swished the curtain aside and peered out the window. She lifted the bakery box and offered a friendly wave. That must have done the trick, because the latch clicked.

"Robbins Grover?"

His body shielded a view of the interior. "Who wants to know?"

"Henry Mason. I'm a journalist with—"

Grover looked as if he hadn't slept in months. Dark circles underlined his eyes, and his face bore the grief of every worker lost or injured in the explosion. If she could only pick one word to describe his disheveled appearance, she'd choose *weary*.

He swiped his hand over sallow cheeks. "I know who you are. I'm surprised it's taken you this long to come by. The other wolves have come and gone."

If other journalists had been granted interviews, why hadn't she seen their articles in print?

"It didn't seem appropriate, sir. I thought you needed time to assist with the investigation. And to grieve."

Grover looked away, but she'd already taken notice of the moisture pooling in his eyes. He dabbed it away with the palms of his hands. "That's why I refuse to speak with those other vultures. If anyone will treat me fairly, it will be you."

"Thank you, sir." Etta offered him the bakery box.

"What's that?"

"Raisin pie. It's yours whether or not you grant me an interview."

He shook his head. "How in heaven's name did you find out I like raisin pie?"

"Do you doubt my investigative skills?"

He chuckled.

She leaned forward and put a hand to her mouth as if what she was about to share was extremely confidential. "Your neighbor's housekeeper is partial to honey."

A full chortle erupted, and Grover's eyes sparkled.

"Thank you, son. That's the first good laugh I've had in a very long week." He stepped back and opened the door wider. "You've got as long as it takes me to eat a piece of this pie."

She followed him to the kitchen. "Take a seat, Mason," he said.

He sliced the pie and sat across from Etta. "What do you want to know?"

"It's my understanding that a new boiler was installed two years ago when the additional floor was added to the factory. Is that right?"

Grover used his fork to sever the point. He nodded. "You've done your homework. Some of those other dunderheads haven't researched anything."

"If the new boiler was only two years old, why wasn't it operating on the morning of the explosion?"

He swallowed the bite and then wiped his mouth. "The new boiler had been working hard all winter. According to our engineer, it needed routine maintenance. Rockwell seemed to have the situation in hand and fired up the old boiler Sunday evening so the plant would be warm when employees arrived the next day. Even Rockwell's assistant stated that the gauges showed the old boiler had enough water. He's prepared to testify Rockwell had been monitoring the boiler regularly and keeping it under capacity just to be safe."

"Testify? Are the police pressing charges?"

He scrubbed his wiry beard. "None that I'm aware of at this time, but that many people aren't injured or killed without a coroner's inquest or trial of some kind."

"Let's return to the day of the incident. Did you approve using the old boiler?" she asked.

"I don't get involved in those decisions," he said, forking a second bite of pie. "I'm a businessman, Mason. I hired a certified level-two engineer. Rockwell had at least twelve years of experience. Decisions about the boiler, its operation, and maintenance were made at his discretion in conjunction with the guidelines established by the Hartford Steam Boiler Inspection and Insurance Company."

"Sources in the fire department said the plant manager phoned Rockwell about strange noises in the radiator about five minutes before the explosion. Can you confirm that, Mr. Grover?"

He waved his fork at Etta. "That's supposed to be confidential. Did you ply another source with honey?"

"That *is* confidential."

"Rockwell had stepped out of the boiler room when that call came in. Again, his assistant engineer stated that the boiler's gauges were well within established safe ranges."

Grover swallowed his third bite. "Anything else?"

Etta nodded. "I have a few more questions. The fire department has confirmed the boiler as the cause of the explosion that severed a main support beam as well as knocked down the water tower, which flattened the rear quarter of the building. Do you know the cause of the second explosion? The one that halted the rescue operation?"

His fork clinked against his plate. "You're referring to the naphtha in the shed behind the boiler house?"

Having no clue what naphtha was but wanting to hear whatever he would say, she kept her expression even. He'd most likely answer his own question if she remained silent, and she wouldn't have to lie.

"It looks like hot coals tossed in the air after the initial blast landed on the shed and ignited the solvent we use to make shoe polish."

"I imagine this naphtha is at every shoe plant in Brockton," she said.

Grover nodded then poked his fork into the pie. "It's very commonly used in the industry." He swallowed another bite. "It was unfortunate that the coals ignited the storage shed. I think many more people would've survived if that hadn't happened." His voice choked with emotion. He stared at the wall above Etta's head. "If I had to do it all over again..."

She imagined Robbins Grover would carry many regrets with him for the remainder of his days.

"Are you insured, Mr. Grover? And if so, who with?"

He shoved his plate away with at least two bites remaining. "What are you implying?"

"Nothing, sir, just curious if you have insurance. And if so, who the carrier is."

He eyed Etta. "Yes, I have a policy on the plant, but it's not enough to cover my losses."

"So you have no plans to rebuild?"

"That will be unlikely, since I'll doubtless go bankrupt."

Although she didn't believe the Bonners had anything to do with the explosion, she wanted a definitive answer. She pressed him again. "And who is that policy with?"

"Everything is through Hartford Steam Boiler."

"May I have your permission to verify your policy amount with them?"

"Do you need it?"

"Your permission? Probably not, but I'd like it all the same."

He pinched the bridge of his nose. "Sure. If that's what it takes for people to know that I didn't sabotage my own factory and kill my own employees, then please check the records." He stood and tossed his napkin on the table. "Put all the insurance information on the front page if you like. It makes no never mind to me."

She'd done her best to conduct a fair and impartial interview, but she'd clearly struck a nerve. "My apologies, sir. I didn't mean to impugn your character."

"The interview is over. It's time for you to go, Mason."

Although he still had pie remaining on his plate, Etta didn't push the matter. She stood and walked with him to the foyer. "What plans do you have to aid the survivors' and victims' families."

"No specifics yet, but I've tasked my accountant to determine what can be done to aid my employees."

"When you're ready, you may wish to reach out to Henrietta Maxwell. She may be willing to partner with you to make sure your employees have what they need."

She touched the brim of her cap. "God's peace to you, sir."

Although she'd been wrong before, her gut instincts told her Grover had been open and honest. She sensed an underlying distrust toward her as a journalist, but that was to be expected. No one liked to have their decisions questioned or their shortcomings plastered all over the front page.

Etta prided herself on being fair and thorough. She'd check into those boiler inspection records and his policy with Hartford. Although a discrepancy would make a better story, in this case, she hoped his version of events would play out—for Grover, the dead and wounded, and their families.

Leo inhaled the savory scent of gravy and mashed potatoes, and his stomach roared to life. As much as it made his mouth water, the meat loaf Pops had chosen looked a bit more appetizing than the grayish slice of roast beef on his own plate.

They sat in companionable silence, each perusing a different section of the *Enterprise*. He squinted to read his brother's name in the small print beneath the photograph. This was his second to make the front page in less than three days. Several other images had also been used in the paper's interior articles as well. Jens was well on his way to shedding his firefighter's uniform in exchange for his box camera and a press pass. He'd never seen his brother happier.

He skimmed an article by that Gibney fellow regarding the relief fund receiving $24,000 in subscriptions already. That money should go a long way in assisting the victims and their families.

"We should make a donation to the relief fund," Leo said. "Maybe take up a collection at the station."

Pops paused, his fork halfway to his mouth. "That's a good idea. Every penny will be helpful."

"Henry's coming," Leo said.

Pops laughed under his breath. "Since he spends so much time with us, maybe we should adopt him into the family."

If Pops only knew that Leo was working on a similar idea.

"Hi, fellas," she said. "May I join you?"

"Sure, Henry." Leo scooted over to make room for her. "Have a seat."

"I have an update on my investigation into the arson suspects, but first I'm hoping to confirm some information about the Grover disaster."

Leo nodded. "We'll help if we can."

"Excellent." Etta flipped her notebook open but kept it close to her lap, out of Pops' line of sight. "I have a source who said that naphtha was stored in a shed behind the boiler house. This naphtha is highly flammable and was most likely ignited by burning coals when the boiler exploded. Can you corroborate that information, Chief Eriksson?"

Pops lowered his coffee cup. "Did Hansen tell you that?"

"Hansen wasn't my source. It was Robbins Grover."

"Grover?" Pops shook his head. "We told him not to speak to reporters."

Her brows spiked. "He likes raisin pie."

"And how do you know that?"

With both hands palms up, Etta shrugged. "That's a source I can't name."

Pops smirked.

The waitress returned with a cup of coffee for Etta and a bashful smile for Pops. "Would you fellas like a refill?" she asked.

Leo slid his cup forward.

"You read my mind," Pops said, his grin overly broad for a coffee refill.

Holy smoke. Gunnar and Jens were onto something where Pops and Ilsa were concerned.

She glanced at Etta. "Can I get you anything, sir?"

"No thanks."

Ilsa's gaze returned to Pops. "You fellas let me know if you need *anything* else."

Etta waited until Ilsa had moved a few tables away before returning to her unanswered question. "Can you confirm the information Grover relayed about the naphtha being the source of the secondary explosion, the one that halted rescue efforts? If so, did he handle the solvent properly?"

"That depends on whether you intend to mention the shed in tomorrow's article."

"If we're talking about an exclusive, I'll hold back," she said.

"You know we can't withhold information from other reporters."

"Correct me if I'm wrong, Chief, but I believe you can decide to share information *first* with members of the press you deem the most responsible to report the facts accurately."

Leo shook his head. Etta was a force to be reckoned with.

Pops sighed. "Then yes, Mr. Mason, it looks like the solvent was the cause of the secondary explosion. We don't know if any regulations were violated regarding where and how the naphtha was stored. The Hartford inspectors will have the final word on that matter. Once the determination is made, you'll be the first to know."

The edges of her lips lifted in satisfaction. She was a good negotiator.

"If proper guidelines were not followed regarding the storage of the naphtha, could charges be filed against Grover and his plant manager?"

"I would imagine so, but if I see one hint of that in your paper before a determination is made, you'll be persona non grata at the fire station. Understood, Mason?"

His voice was firm yet respectful. Leo knew that tone well. When he was a child, it had signaled the end of the discussion and that any additional pushback would yield consequences he and his siblings wouldn't appreciate. Would his father's response appease her? If not, he was certain Pops would end the interview.

"A few more questions."

Leo winced, hoping she wasn't returning to the solvent again. He sensed Pops was finished with that line of questioning.

"When are you anticipating a meeting with the Hartford inspectors?"

"Tomorrow morning, but it may be a week or more before we know the official cause of the boiler malfunction and come to a resolution on the naphtha storage issue."

He thought back to his conversation with Etta yesterday. It was hard to believe the woman he was attracted to was hiding under the men's clothing and fake hair and mustache. Her mannerisms were so different, even the way she walked and sat. How had she learned those masculine traits?

"You've inspected the boiler, Chief. What do you think?"

"Off the record?"

She nodded.

"I think the boiler was old and just gave out, but we'll know more after the inspection. I don't think Grover will be liable."

"How can he not be liable if he was using such an old boiler?"

"If the company can produce records showing the engineer had stuck to the recommended maintenance schedule and passed its most recent inspection, then Grover did his due diligence."

Pops cut his meat loaf and dipped it into his gravy. "Unfortunately, Mr. Mason, accidents do happen, and as much as we may want to find someone to blame, the fire at Grover Shoes may very well have been just that—an unfortunate accident."

"What if the Hartford inquest produces disparate results, or if they differ from what Grover has said? Then what?"

"We'll cross that bridge when we come to it, but, needless to say, things will get very difficult for Robbins Grover."

Leo shoved his plate aside, having only eaten the potatoes and gravy. The roast beef had been as tasteless as it had appeared. Taking a play out of his youngest brother's book, he forked a piece of Pops' meat loaf. Now, that was delicious.

"While I have you here, any more updates on the arson investigation?" Etta asked.

Pops sipped his coffee. "Not at this time. We gave our information to the police, who are conducting the criminal side of the investigation. From this point forward, the case is in their hands—unless there are more suspicious fires."

"So, no leads?"

"Look, Mason, I just said—"

Etta waved her palm. "I'm only doing my job, sir. I should go." She gulped the coffee that no longer had steam rising from the cup. "I know when I've overstayed my welcome."

She dug in her pocket and placed a few coins on the table. "That should cover my coffee. And thank you, Chief, for taking my questions while you ate."

She touched the brim of her cap and left the diner. Had she been satisfied with her interview? Had she gleaned enough information to write a piece about Grover for the *Enterprise*?

He understood the investigative reporter part of her wanted to unearth the cause of the explosion. Based on her previous articles, he believed her writing was fair, accurate, and unbiased. However, he also knew that scandal created those sensationalist headlines he despised.

They were used to sell newspapers, and her editor could probably find a way to hyperbolize Grover's due diligence if necessary. She'd said it was her boss' s prerogative to change those headlines, but did Etta ever consider that Henry Mason's name and reputation might enable her to push for less exaggeration and more facts in the titles of her articles?

That might be the perfect solution to the only hesitation he had about a future with the tough-as-nails reporter.

CHAPTER 22

Etta placed the last of the food items she'd purchased from the corner deli into the basket. She hesitated. Would Leo be disappointed that she hadn't prepared the meal herself?

Did he know she was a domestic disaster? She'd never cooked anything. Although she had successfully boiled water for coffee or tea, she was fairly confident that didn't count. Perhaps she should purchase a cookbook or ask Mrs. Hemingway for a few lessons.

Even if she knew how to cook, she'd been so busy since the factory fire, she hadn't had time to prepare something herself. Besides, why spend time doing something that someone else had already done and done much better?

The doorbell rang. "I'll get that, Mrs. Hemingway. I'm expecting Mitchell."

She grabbed the basket and headed for the door.

Mitchell greeted her with his customary smile and well wishes then reached for the basket.

"I'll be right there," she said, positioning a large-brimmed hat on top of her pompadour.

"Fine, miss. I'll be waiting by the automobile."

She secured the hat with several large pins, grabbed her parasol, and hurried out the door and down the stairs.

Mitchell opened the rear door. After he cranked the engine, he slid behind the large black steering wheel. "Are we headed to your young gentleman's house?"

"If you mean Mr. Eriksson's, then yes, that is our destination. But what makes you think he's my young gentleman?"

"I may be an old man now, miss, but I remember love's first light well enough."

Although he hadn't been in her family's employ a long time, Mitchell had endeared himself to Etta in short order.

As he wound the automobile through the streets of Brockton, a bit of trepidation roiled in her stomach. Would Leo think her brazen to show up outside his cottage and ask him to spend the afternoon with her for a second time? Surely it couldn't be as shocking this go-around.

Although Thursday was an unusual day for an outing, Leo had the overnight shift at the fire department this evening, so she hoped to surprise him just as he'd done for her with the flowers and lovely handsewn handkerchief. She glanced at the overcast sky threatening to hinder her plans and prayed the rain would hold off.

Mitchell steered the vehicle to the curb in front of the Erikssons' bungalow.

He opened her door, and she stepped out. "Wait here, please, while I invite Mr. Eriksson to join me for a picnic."

Someone tugged back the curtain at the front window. Before she reached his porch, Leo had stepped outside. His father and Jens filled the doorway behind him.

Hands on his hips, Leo shook his head. His initial puzzled expression melted into a delightful grin that sparkled in his eyes.

"I've come to take you on a picnic, and you're not allowed to say no."

His gaze drifted to the darkening clouds. "A picnic? Today? Looks like we might get rained on."

"Where's your sense of adventure? Besides, our destination has a gazebo we can use if it rains."

Jens gave him a little shove. "What are you waiting for?"

"Nothing," he said, laughing as he descended the steps. "Is the news business so slow you need to create your own headline—'Heiress Kidnaps Local Fireman'?"

She grinned. "I like it. I'll make a first-rate reporter out of you yet, Eriksson."

"I'm sorry, Etta, I forgot you don't like the title heiress, and here I am, teasing you."

"I actually don't mind when you use it. You see all of me, not just a title."

He lifted her hand to his lips. Gooseflesh rippled over her arms with his tender caress. Heat flooded her cheeks when she remembered they had an audience.

Mitchell reached for the handle.

"I'll do that," Leo said.

"Very good, sir."

Leo assisted her into the back seat then slid in beside her and closed the door. His leg brushed hers. Although there was plenty of room, she didn't say a word. She liked having him near.

"So where are we headed today?" he asked.

"Do you have an aversion to surprises?"

"Not good ones."

"Where does being kidnapped by Brockton's heiress stand?"

He angled his head and matched her gaze. "About as delightful as they come."

"You're a smooth talker, Mr. Eriksson. I imagine you've practiced on a myriad of young ladies over the years."

"Hardly," he said, his tone playful. "But I'm blessed that God has brought another remarkable woman into my life."

She remembered what he'd told her about Annika. "I'm sorry to bring up old ghosts. That was careless of me."

He cupped her hand in his and caressed her skin with his thumb. "I have a feeling you're just what I need to be rid of them for good."

Leo stared at the red and white awnings hanging above the shops on Main Street as they rode by. Etta's hand felt good in his, as if it had been designed by God to be a perfect fit.

Minutes went by without either one saying anything, and then she squeezed his hand. When he looked her way, she smiled and shifted her attention to the scenery passing by now that they'd left the city.

He stroked the back of her hand. What a refreshing change. He didn't need to mask his emotions, nor did he feel the need to explain them any more than he already had. For now, he'd enjoy the comfortable silence and the warmth of her hand inside his.

Mitchell slowed and turned left into the Massachusetts Automobile Club entrance. Leo jerked his head in her direction.

"What do you say, Mr. Eriksson? Care to give the Pierce Arrow a drive around a course? Then we can have our picnic."

"Really?" He felt like a kid on Christmas morning.

"Yes, I asked Father, and he agreed that as long as you go around the track several times with Mitchell giving you a few tips first."

Leo rubbed his hands together in eager expectation. He'd had a fascination with automobiles for a while now, but he'd never had the pleasure of driving one. She'd put a lot of thought into this gesture. "Thank you, Etta. This is a terrific surprise."

She beamed. "You're welcome."

Mitchell paid the fee at the attendant's booth. "All right, sir, we're just about set," he said, steering the car toward the track marked *Novice.*

He parked near a grandstand perfectly situated for viewers to observe the course then stepped from the motorcar. "Mr. Maxwell has asked Etta to forgo staying in the Pierce Arrow during our first passes around the track," Mitchell said, opening Etta's door.

"I have something for you, Leo." Etta waited while Mitchell fetched the picnic hamper from the rear of the motorcar. Then she handed Leo a thin gray box she removed from the basket.

"For me?"

"It isn't much. Very practical, really."

He opened the box and unfolded the tissue paper, revealing a pair of brown leather driving gloves. "Etta, you shouldn't have gone to this expense."

"Now you'll be outfitted properly."

He tugged the gloves onto his hands then opened and closed his fists. "They fit perfectly." He stared into those endless green eyes of hers. Just as perfectly as the woman herself seemed to fit into every part of his life. "Thank you."

She held his gaze and nodded.

Mitchell cleared his throat. "Shall we proceed, sir?"

Proceed? While Mitchell may have meant proceeding with the driving lesson, Leo had a whole other thing on his mind he wanted to pursue. And she was standing directly in front of him. "I'm ready," he said. "More ready than I've ever been."

CHAPTER 23

After Mitchell demonstrated the proper way to crank the engine, Leo hopped behind the wheel and followed his instructions to enter the track. After a dozen or so hard stops, he got the hang of easing onto the brake. An accomplishment that should remove any future potential for railway spine injuries.

He kept both hands on the wheel and maneuvered the vehicle around the large oval track. Even at this slow pace, the tires kicked up dirt that ricocheted off the windshield. How did drivers manage in less expensive models without a roof?

On his third pass around the track, Etta shot to her feet and waved. Not only had she arranged this opportunity for him to drive her father's Pierce Arrow, but she appeared engaged in his efforts to learn.

Leo kept his hands on the wheel and his eyes on the course. "Think I'm ready to drive Miss Maxwell around?"

"You seem to have gathered the knack of it quite well, sir," Mitchell said. "I think she'll be delighted."

Leo maneuvered the motorcar near the viewing stand where Etta stood, and set the brake. "How about I take you for a ride around the track?"

Mitchell exited the vehicle then assisted Etta into the front passenger seat and closed the door. "I believe you're ready for your first solo trip, sir."

Etta's eyes sparkled. "What did you think?"

"Marvelous. What an amazing automobile. And a thoughtful surprise, Etta. Thank you." He leaned toward her and placed a lingering kiss on her cheek.

"Ahem," Mitchell said, clearing his throat.

"I, for one, want to see if the fellow can drive this motorcar." She glanced at the sky. "Preferably before the rain sets in."

"I'll crank the engine, sir."

Once the motorcar rumbled to life, Leo eased his foot onto the gas pedal and entered the course. After several trips around the track, he parked the car near the bleachers where Mitchell waited patiently.

She slid her hand over his. "Well done, Leo. You're a natural."

Mitchell opened her door. "Would you prefer to eat in the clubhouse, miss?"

"No, I think we'll take advantage of the gazebo where we can enjoy our basket lunch."

"Very well, I'll take the car to the garage and return for you in one and a half hours."

Leo grabbed the picnic basket in one hand and Etta's in the other, and hurried toward the gazebo's shelter as the first droplets fell from the sky.

"That was exhilarating," she said, catching her breath. "Too bad the rain had to spoil our fun."

"I'm rather fond of rainy days," Leo said. "There's something cleansing about them. It's like you have a fresh new beginning when the sun comes out."

She eyed him, but he didn't feel uncomfortable under her scrutiny. "I've always considered them quite dreary and limiting," she said. "But that's a lovely way to think about a rainy day. I think I'll try to adopt that attitude. See what a wonderful influence you are on me?"

Water droplets spotted her glasses. She removed them and stared at her dress. How would she dry them?

"May, I?" Leo asked.

She nodded.

He untucked the hem of his shirt and reached for her spectacles. After he rubbed his shirttail over her lenses, he leaned forward and secured the tips over her ears. His fingers brushed her earlobes, sending that familiar spark coursing through her. "You have lovely eyes, Etta."

She held his gaze. "Thank you, Leo."

"My pleasure."

"I. . .uh. . .I suppose we should eat. You must be famished." She looked back over her shoulder in the direction Mitchell had driven the Pierce Arrow. "I'm afraid I left the blanket in the motorcar."

"I can help with that." He unbuttoned his sweater and spread it over the wood planking of the gazebo floor. "Your throne, madam," he said, assisting her to the ground.

He settled beside her as she unpacked the basket of chicken salad, rolls, and pickled eggs with beets.

"Have you ever considered learning to drive, Etta?"

She cut a roll, filled it with chicken salad, and handed it to Leo. "I've always wanted to learn, but it's one of the few things Father has explicitly forbidden me to do. At least in *his* automobile. He says women don't have the temperament for it. Perhaps one day I'll change his mind."

"Once I get more experience, I'll teach you if you want."

She licked chicken salad from her thumb. "Really? Mitchell said the club has rentals." Her gaze softened. "Thank you, Leo."

"For offering to teach you how to drive?"

"That too, but mostly for not looking at my femininity as a negative. For not thinking that being a woman isn't in and of itself a limitation."

Her femininity was definitely *not* a negative from Leo's perspective. "I don't think you have to worry about that."

He skimmed her cheek with the back of his knuckles. When he opened his hand, she nuzzled her cheek into his palm. How in the world did such a unique and charismatic woman like Henrietta Maxwell find him interesting?

Only God could engineer his meeting a woman who could rival his emotion for Annika. Leo had resigned himself to a loveless bachelorhood, living out the rest of his days with Pops. But Etta made him feel alive again, invincible even.

His gaze drifted to her lips, slightly parted as she enjoyed the touch of his hand against her face. *Whoa there, boy.* His thumb caressed her soft skin one last time.

She opened her eyes when he slid his hand away. Her gaze sent a thrill skittering down his spine.

He'd have to wait a bit longer to be certain, but he was growing more confident by the minute that God had answered an unspoken prayer to bring love back into his life.

Etta relished the warm tingle that Leo's touch had sent cascading over her shoulders. Did he have any idea how his presence affected her?

Perhaps it was a bit wanton, but she'd desperately wanted him to kiss her. Although she had no idea how to kiss a man, Leo seemed like the right person to share in that experiment.

Experiment? She wasn't a scientist in a laboratory, for heaven's sake. For a journalist, *experiment* had been a poor word choice. That wasn't what this was at all—at least not for Etta. That made it sound like her feelings weren't serious where Leo was concerned, and nothing could be further from the truth.

She'd given up on marriage and a family, and then God brought Leo into her life when she'd least expected it. Wasn't that so like Him? The fact she'd played so little a part in their introduction raised her confidence that Leo was, indeed, a gift from the Almighty. If it had been up to her, she certainly wouldn't have orchestrated their reintroduction by crushing him into a fresh patch of manure.

She giggled.

"What's so funny?" Leo asked.

"I was reminiscing about how I plunged from the tree and flattened you."

Leo chuckled. "That will be a story for the ages. Can you imagine someday when you don't have to hide behind your Henry Mason moniker, sharing that story with our chil—?"

Etta pursed her lips, willing herself not to blush, but that did little to stop the heat flooding her cheeks. *Children?* So, he contemplated a future—with *her*.

Leo shook his head. "I suppose the cat is finally out of the proverbial bag." He reached for her hand. "You've mentioned desiring marriage and children someday, but how do you see that fitting into your life as a reporter for the *Enterprise*?"

She held his gaze. She wasn't prepared for this conversation, yet here it was—and with a man she desired a future with. How much to say? What if she was honest and it scared him away? Didn't he deserve honesty? Especially after the way Annika hurt him?

She fidgeted with the pleats in her skirt and avoided his gaze. "I'd like nothing more than to have a family someday. I'm just not sure what that looks like, Leo. I don't want to give up my position at the *Enterprise*, but who in their right mind would be married to a woman who parades around town as a man? How would I raise children and write for a newspaper?"

Oh, heaven help her. Why hadn't she thought any of this through before accepting his invitation to court her? She'd acted only on what her heart wanted and had given little consideration to Leo's. And now it seemed as though she was poised to shatter his heart all over again.

He squeezed her hand. "Maybe we don't need to know all the answers yet. Maybe with prayer, we can figure them out as we go along."

He was right. If God intended them to be joined as husband and wife, He'd either provide a way for her to be a journalist and a mother, or He'd change the desires of her heart.

Leo stood and brushed his trousers. "But for now, may I have this dance?"

She crinkled her nose. "There's no music."

Mischief danced in his eyes as he waggled his hand, encouraging her to stand with him.

Once on her feet, he tugged her close. She inhaled the crisp scent of his aftershave. With their cheeks side by side, his warm breath tickled her skin as he softly sang a sweet melody.

"In the shade of the old apple tree,
Where the love in your eyes I could see,
When the voice that I heard, like the song of the bird,
Seemed to whisper sweet music to me."

Rain spattered off the tin roof, and Etta lost herself in his nearness.

"I could hear the dull buzz of the bee,
In the blossoms as you said to me,
With a heart that is true, I'll be waiting for you,
In the shade of the old apple tree."

The heavens released a heavy downpour that cascaded like a waterfall over the side of the gazebo's domed roof. The effect was magical. At that moment, Etta knew that no matter what transpired between her and Leo, she'd cherish this dance until her dying breath.

Leo hummed the melody a few more times, relishing the feel of Etta in his arms, her soft cheek next to his, and the smell of milk and honey in her hair. But it was also her keen mind and her sense of adventure that endeared her to him.

As the rain subsided, he slowed their steps until they no longer swayed as one.

"You've been a breath of fresh air in my life," she said. Her sultry voice quickened the pounding of his pulse.

"One I've desperately needed." Etta caressed his cheek with her thumb. "I'm afraid with each minute we spend together, my heart becomes less my own."

Her eyes glistened. Was that love staring back at him? Heaven help him. He loved her too. Admitting that truth both frightened and exhilarated him at the same time.

He slid her palm to his chest. "Can you feel my heart beating wildly?"

She nodded. When her mouth parted slightly, Leo leaned forward and pressed his lips to hers. They were so soft, so tender.

But were they his to have in this way? He pulled back and gazed into her lovely green eyes. When he saw no censure, he inched closer. This time he cradled her face in his palms. "I didn't think it would ever be possible, but you've captured my heart."

"No ghosts?" she whispered.

"No ghosts."

He lowered his mouth to hers and tenderly expressed all he felt for her. She relaxed into his embrace and returned his affection. His arms slid around her and pulled her closer. She wrapped her arms around his neck. Her fingers stroked his hair.

The sound of gentle rain drops vanished, and the gazebo disappeared. Arms entwined, only he and Etta existed at that moment, and he deepened their kiss.

The tiny trail of feathery kisses Leo forged from her jaw to her earlobe weakened Etta's limbs. If he hadn't been holding her, she surely would have sunk to the gazebo floor like a pat of melted butter.

She angled her head, granting his lips access to the delicate skin on her neck. She shivered as he took the hint.

Too quickly he broke their embrace, leaving her dazed and confused. She blinked at him. He'd aroused feelings she'd never known before, and she wasn't ready for their passionate display of affection to end.

He leaned his forehead against hers. "I shouldn't have kissed you like that, Etta. It wasn't gentlemanly of me."

"I don't have any regrets."

He chuckled and kissed her cheek. "The rain has let up. I think we'd better pack up and find Mitchell," he said.

She nodded and tried to hide her disappointment. She knew he was right, but he'd sparked something in her, something dormant that no one else had ever kindled. From the looks of Leo's disheveled hair and rapid breathing, she'd done the same to him.

They'd ignited a firestorm this afternoon and would need to be careful about lighting that fuse again.

CHAPTER 24

Leo stumbled to the stove. Thank heavens Pops had made a large pot of coffee. Thoughts of Etta and the kiss they'd shared yesterday gave him plenty to think about.

The front door flew open, and Gunnar stormed in, a rolled newspaper in his fist. "Have you read the *Times* this morning? Did you know about this?"

His brother knew Leo didn't read that rag. "Know about what?" he said, struggling to clear the sleepy fog still misting his brain. "I haven't even drunk my first cup of coffee this morning."

Footsteps pounded on the stairs. "Now you've done it," Leo said, stifling a yawn. "You woke Pops."

"What in heaven's name is going on down here? It's not even six o'clock in the morning."

Pops was a kind man—when he had a good night's rest. Years ago, if he'd been on duty overnight, their mom would bundle Leo and his brothers up and send them outside to play during the day so he could sleep.

Leo held up his empty palm. "Don't blame me." He sank into his chair. "It's your middle child who's raising all the ruckus."

"Don't you have a wife and children waiting at home for you after your shift?" Pops grumbled. "Surely Trude will listen to whatever you need to talk about before the sun's up."

"Sorry, this couldn't wait."

Pops harrumphed and poured himself a cup of coffee. "This better be good, Gunnar, or you're going on report."

Leo snickered. When they were children, Pops always threatened to put one of his sons "on report" when they disobeyed. Now Pops glared at Gunnar, apparently not seeing the humor in the fact that his noisy son was twenty-seven years old.

Gunnar unrolled the broadsheet and smacked it on the table between Leo and Pops.

Jaw unhinged, Leo bolted upright from his chair. How could this be? He stared in disbelief at the bold typeface.

UNDERCOVER HEIRESS EXPOSED

HENRIETTA MAXWELL LEADS DOUBLE LIFE AS ESTEEMED JOURNALIST HENRY MASON

BY DECLAN GIBNEY

Beneath the headline, two large side-by-side images told the entire story. One depicted Henrietta Maxwell, Brockton's benevolent heiress. The other, Etta, dressed as Henry Mason.

The muscles in his neck and shoulders corded, but that was nothing compared to the gut-twisting pain in his middle. He felt sucker-punched. Etta would be devastated.

His gaze shifted to the byline. Declan Gibney? That was the fella who showed up in the park when he'd met Etta there. He didn't write for the *Times. That huckster sold her out.* He slumped into his chair, shaking his head. "I can't believe it."

"Leo!"

"What?"

"I've asked you several times," Pops said. "Did you know about this?"

"Yes, sir."

Pops grimaced. "And you never said a word?"

The hurt of his son's deception reflected in his father's eyes. "I'm sorry. Etta begged me to keep her secret. Her editor said he'd fire her if her identity was revealed."

Gunnar shook his head. "And you allowed us to trust a dame with confidential information regarding the arson investigation and the Grover explosion."

"I'm sorry I deceived you, but don't give me this nonsense that Etta couldn't be trusted because she's a woman. We've all relied on every word she's written as Henry Mason. This whole city did."

"I think half the public will feel as betrayed by Henry Mason as I do," Pops said, pouring himself a cup of coffee. "The other half will find it scandalous that she masqueraded as a man and penned investigative news pieces for money. They'll quickly forget the excellent articles she wrote and deem her character flawed. Sadly, her reputation will be severely tarnished."

"That's rich," Leo scoffed. "If society gave her a choice, she'd use her own name on those articles."

Gunnar scrubbed his jaw. "I can't believe she fooled us all."

Jens trudged into the kitchen. "Why is everyone in an uproar? It's barely six o'clock."

Gunnar grabbed the paper and showed the headline to Jens. "That can't be right. Henry Mason, a dame?"

"It's true, Jens," Leo said. "I've known for a while."

Jens skimmed the article then shoved the paper under his arm and headed for the coffeepot. "Gotta hand it to Miss Maxwell though. A woman from her position in society, dressing like a man and conducting undercover investigations. . . She's got pluck. I admire that."

Leo's chest puffed a bit. "She's brave and smart, with a penchant for standing up for good over evil and justice over inequity. She's always standing up for the person who hasn't had the advantages she's had."

"Only time will tell if the public will stand with her," Pops said. He dropped two sugar cubes into his coffee. "That will be the best way for her to keep her position at the *Enterprise*."

Leo's heart pinched. Etta must be heartbroken.

He may not like the sensationalist headlines that were splayed across the front page or the occasional lack of compassion in her articles, but he did understand that this scoop in a rival newspaper would most likely bring her career to a screeching halt.

"I know you just pulled an overnighter, Gunnar," Leo said, "but could you cover my shift for a few hours?"

"Sure. What are you going to do?"

"I'm going to shave and dress, then go find Etta and make sure she's all right."

At least that's what he told his family. In actuality, he was going to find the woman he loved and console her however he could. He was going to make sure she knew she didn't have to weather this storm alone. They would get through it together.

Etta wove her way through the maze of desks in the city room, the fabric of her dress ruffling as it swooshed against metal chairs, the morning edition of *The Brockton Times* folded under her arm. She'd not bothered to dress as Henry Mason. There was no point in furthering that ruse. The jig was up. And if Henry Mason was now a permanent part of her past, then she would hold her head up high and present herself as Henrietta Maxwell. Perhaps her new moniker, "The Undercover Heiress," could carry some clout.

Because it was barely seven a.m., most of the reporters hadn't arrived for the day; but by afternoon, the place would be humming with the clack of Underwood typewriters and the air cloudy with cigarette smoke. Of all the things she'd miss about the city room at the *Enterprise*, the cough-inducing smoke cloud would not be one of them. *Silver linings, Etta. Silver linings.*

Several mouths fell agape at the sight of Henrietta in their newsroom. A fellow reporter for the *Enterprise* approached. "Lewis Foster," he said, dipping his chin. "Can I help you, Miss Maxwell?"

His inquiry told Etta he must not have seen the morning edition of their rival newspaper.

One of the first things she did each day was to compare the front-page coverage between the two papers.

"I'm fine, thank you. I want to speak with Mr. Littleton."

Foster checked his pocket watch. "He's probably in a meeting with his editorial staff."

The editor's door stood ajar. "I think he'll see me."

"Wait, Miss Maxwell. He's asked not to be disturbed."

Etta ignored the man's protests and rapped her knuckles on the beveled glass.

Mr. Littleton glanced up and waved her inside. "I wondered how long it would be before you showed up. Shut the door."

"Nice to see you too, *boss*."

He poured clear liquid into his coffee cup, screwed the lid onto the flask, and tucked the container inside his desk drawer. He took a swig of his doctored coffee. They'd worked many long hours together in the last several years, but she'd never seen her boss looking so. . .unkempt. Between his unbuttoned collar, loose tie, and disheveled hair, he looked more like something Midnight dragged home after a night of hunting than the city editor for the *Brockton Enterprise*.

She tossed the copy of the *Times* onto his desk. "Having a rough morning?"

His bloodshot eyes narrowed. "Aren't you?"

"Yes, but I'm channeling my anger into more productive endeavors."

"Like?"

"Like pummeling Declan Gibney with my parasol for stabbing us in the back and not only outing me but reporting the story in the *Times*."

"Yeah, well yours may not be the only neck on the chopping block."

"What do you mean?"

"Mr. Russell, you remember him, don't you? The owner of this little newspaper that employs us both? Well, he says we've violated the public's trust and ruined the paper's credibility. He's threatening to relegate me to obituaries—*if* he doesn't fire me."

"I'm sorry, William. You stuck your neck out for me, and I've always appreciated that."

"You're welcome. You deserved a shot, and you did great."

While she relished his compliments, they did little to soothe the venom seething in her veins. "It just flat-out burns. There was nothing false about my reporting. I turned in quality stories as good or better than any reporter in the city room."

"I told him that."

"What if I write a piece about being a woman in a man's world? A sort of personal plea saying I used an alias not with the intention to deceive but to chase my dream. Why not go out with a bang?"

"I don't know, Etta. Russell is still weighing his options. If he lets me go, printing a 'bang' like that could keep me from getting hired at any other paper in the Boston area."

She couldn't argue with him there. Actually, she could, and she usually did. "Why not make a stand? For posterity's sake."

His look conveyed that he was more concerned with the roof over his head and food on his table than with taking a stand on women's rights. She switched tactics.

"Okay, what if we pitch a new column to Mr. Russell, one written by

'The Undercover Heiress' herself? Let's try to capitalize on the scuttlebutt and notoriety. This time, people will know who's writing the stories. Who knows? They might find it fascinating to read the news covered from a woman's perspective."

He steepled his fingers in contemplation then sighed. "Men will dismiss it."

"You mean, dismiss me."

"I'm sorry, Etta. You're a good reporter, and you deserve the same shot as any of my male journalists, but we must face the facts. The world's not ready to let women in the boardroom or the back room where decisions are made."

She sighed. "Or the newsroom."

As a general principle, she avoided trading on the Maxwell name, but she was willing to use any weapon in her arsenal if it meant keeping her position at the *Enterprise*. "Perhaps the Maxwell name can persuade him?"

Littleton gulped at whatever concoction he'd made in his mug then wiped his mouth on his sleeve. "Should Russell be expecting a call from your father?"

"I think I've managed to dissuade him from that. I'm fairly sure I took the brunt of his anger last night. But if Russell tosses you out, let me know. I'm sure my father will be happy to advertise elsewhere."

"Last night?"

"Declan confronted my parents when they arrived at the Empire Theater. He asked if they knew their daughter was Henry Mason, a reporter for this newspaper. Needless to say, he was escorted from the theater. And the car was sent to bring me to Beacon Hill."

"Oh, dear." Littleton reached for the mug and took another swig.

"Fortunately, they haven't disowned me. My parents are both on the progressive side of politics and are in favor of women's suffrage in general. But they didn't appreciate being blindsided by that opportunist."

"Despite it only being April, they've decided to depart for our home on the shore for a week or two. They want me to join them, but I'm undecided."

Her boss was quiet for a moment. "The article didn't mention how Gibney figured out you were Henry Mason. Have any leads on that?"

Besides Mrs. Hemingway, who loved and protected her like a mama bear, and her boss, who had his own interests to safeguard, only one other person had known about her alternate identity. Her stomach roiled at the deception.

"Leo Eriksson."

Outrage and indignation had fueled her thoughts and actions ever since she read Declan's piece in the *Times*. It was the best way she knew to combat the pinching pain in her chest that had robbed her of a good night's sleep. The anger staved off the tears she knew would come if she let herself calm down.

She had trouble believing Leo would have sold her out, even if it had only been a slip of the tongue. But she'd trusted him to keep her secret.

An obvious mistake.

Her nose burned as she bit back tears. The grief weighted her limbs, and she sank into the chair across from her editor.

"Leo Eriksson? Your source in Engine Company No. 1? You sure about that?"

Knowing full well any words would reveal what Leo's betrayal cost her, she offered only a tight nod to his question.

"Sorry, kid."

She was sorry too.

She'd lost more than a source; she'd lost her only friend and the man she'd hoped to share her future with.

CHAPTER 25

Leo tapped his pencil against the tablet. He wasn't very good with written words, and the pressure of writing to Etta, a successful journalist, made him doubt his efforts even more. But what choice did he have? He'd searched everywhere he'd known to look for her—the boardinghouse, the Brockton Diner, and the newspaper office.

He'd enjoyed meeting her editor, William Littleton. The man had stuck his neck out for Etta and given her the opportunity to pursue her dreams, if only for a little while. Littleton hadn't seen her since the morning but gave him the address of the boardinghouse.

On a whim, he'd even taken the trolley to her parents' home in Beacon Hill. The streetcar into Boston cost him a pretty penny, but the chance of finding Etta and ensuring she was all right had been worth it.

He only regretted that the family hadn't been home. Their butler, Thomas, said they'd gone to their summer cottage in Hull. If traveling into Boston set him back, there was no way he could afford to go gallivanting off to the southern edge of Boston Harbor. Thomas assured Leo that if he wanted to write a missive, he would see that the family received it.

The man seated beside Leo stood and pulled the cord for the trolley to stop at the next corner. Three more stops, and he'd be at the fire station. He'd asked Gunnar to cover a few hours of his shift, but he'd been so wrecked with worry he'd not contemplated how long the trip to and from Boston would take. His sole mission had been to find Etta.

She must've been pretty shaken up to leave town and head to Hull without saying goodbye. Especially after they'd so tenderly affirmed their affection for one another the day before. That didn't sound like the woman he knew. Then again, he'd never seen her in a personal crisis. Perhaps her parents insisted she join them.

Either way, he'd have to put pen to paper in the hopes his letter would find her. If she needed some time and space to deal with the fallout of Gibney's revelation, he could give her that, no matter how much it hurt that she didn't cling to him during this crisis.

He chided himself for thinking about himself, even for a minute. Etta should be his sole focus.

How could he put all that into words? Not an easy task for a firefighter who'd only completed the eighth grade. He scratched out the few words he'd managed to scribble and closed the notebook, determined to try again once he settled in at the firehouse.

He tugged the cord and hopped off the trolley at the next stop. His stomach rumbled. He'd not eaten all day, but he should relieve Gunnar. Maybe Pops would have pity on him and let him get an order of fried chicken to bring back to the station.

He swung the firehouse door open and saw Pops talking with Leif. His father turned to Leo. "Henrietta was here looking for you."

"What? Her parents' butler said the family went to the shore."

"Not Henrietta."

"Did she say where I could find her?"

"She'll be at the boardinghouse for at least another day, then she might join her parents. She hadn't decided."

"Thanks, Pops." He glanced around the firehouse. "Is Gunnar in the turnout room?"

"He was falling asleep standing up. I sent him home two hours ago."

His shoulders slumped. Great. Now he wouldn't be able to speak with Etta until his shift was over in four hours. How could he be so selfish? Gunnar had done him a huge favor. After all, his family needed him too.

Jens entered the fire station's main room. "Hey, Leo."

"What are you doing here, Jens? Thought you gave up the job."

He smirked. "Pops asked me to cover your shift, since you're trying to find Etta."

"Really, Jens?" His hopes lifted on his brother's kind offer.

"She helped me get my job at the paper. This is my way of saying thank you. Hopefully, you two will be able to get this all straightened out."

Leo narrowed his gaze. "Get what straightened out?"

"Son," Pops said, "before you go charging after Etta, there's a few things you should know. First, a follow-up article made the front page of the *Times'* evening edition. There's a photograph of you and Etta together."

Leo pinched the bridge of his nose. Could things get any worse?

Pops gripped his shoulder. "But the worst of it is, she thinks you're the source for the article in the *Times*—that you betrayed her."

"Me?" He grimaced. "I. . .I would never do that."

"That's what I told her, but she's mad enough to spit tacks." He squeezed Leo's shoulder then stuffed his hand in his pocket. "I, uh, I didn't want you to be blindsided. I'll be praying."

"We'll be praying," Jens added.

Leo's heart plummeted into his gut. He needed to find Etta and clear things up. Let her know he was ready to knock Declan Gibney into the middle of next week and help her pick up the pieces of her shattered dreams—to tell her how much he loved her.

As he raced across town, all he could do was pray. *Lord, I need You. Give me wisdom as I speak with Etta. She's hurting. Give me comforting words, and please, soften her heart. Help her to know that no matter what the situation appears to be, I'd never betray her. May Your will be done. Amen.*

It was all in the hands of the one who held their future, and Leo couldn't think of a better place for his troubles to be.

Cuddled in a blanket, Etta sat on Mrs. Hemingway's back porch, Midnight curled in her lap. He was her only solace after a harrowing day. The spring evening's cool temperatures sent a chill rippling over her skin, but she didn't budge. Exhaustion now followed the anger that had carried her through most of her day.

Alone with her thoughts, she could no longer ignore the fallout from Leo's devastating betrayal. He'd played her for the lovesick fool that she was. Singing and dancing with her just the day before, whispering sweet words about a future together.

She sniffled and wiped her nose with the edge of the blanket. Had he planned to double-cross her all along, or did the opportunity arise recently? What inducement did Declan offer that would turn Leo against her?

The evening edition of the paper displayed the photograph of them together taken outside his house, with another jarring headline.

DETAILS OF HEIRESS' DOUBLE LIFE EMERGE.

Had he sold her out for fame? Perhaps he planned to extort money from her family and Declan jumped the gun by printing the article too early?

What a simpleton she'd been.

The door opened behind her, and Midnight scurried inside. "You have a visitor," Mrs. Hemingway said.

"Hello, Etta."

The sound of Leo's voice gutted her. She lifted her chin, determined to hide the agony his duplicity caused. "I wondered if you'd be brave enough to show yourself. How did you find this address?"

"Littleton gave it to me," he said, his tone gentle but not repentant.

Mrs. Hemingway stepped back inside. "I'll be in the kitchen if you need anything," she said before closing the door.

He squatted beside her and removed his cap. He reached for her hand, a gesture she'd longed for yesterday. Now his touch made her stomach churn, and she jerked away.

Was that disappointment in his eyes? *Some nerve.*

"I've been looking for you all day. I even went to your parents' home in Boston. Why didn't you come to me? I'm so sorry Declan revealed your secret in such a public way. You must be devastated."

Etta kept her gaze focused on the yard and refused to look at him. She wouldn't let him see how much his deceitfulness pained her. "I've endured a full range of emotions today." She bit back the bile burning in her throat. "Devastation. Shock. Anger. But the most detrimental one, the one I'd not prepared my heart for, was betrayal."

"I've had nothing to do with those articles, Etta. Please, believe me."

She stood, and the blanket crumpled to her feet. "You're only digging yourself into a deeper hole, *Mr.* Eriksson."

Whether he cringed at the use of his formal name or the biting tone in which she'd said it, she didn't know. But she'd heard enough excuses, enough lies, and suffered enough heartache to last the remainder of her life.

"I confronted Declan Gibney. He told me his source was someone with intimate knowledge of the situation."

"And he named me specifically?"

"Not by name. No. He wouldn't reveal his source."

"Think, Etta—"

"You can address me as Miss Maxwell going forward."

He pinched his eyes closed briefly then cast a pleading gaze her direction. "There must be someone else."

"The only other people who knew about Henry Mason were my editor, Mr. Littleton, and Mrs. Hemingway, my landlady. Mr. Littleton will most likely lose his position over this fiasco and may never work in the newspaper business again. I think it's fair to rule him out."

She folded her arms over her chest. "And Mrs. Hemingway treats me like a daughter. She's very protective of me and would never speak to a reporter."

She pressed her lips together firmly, willing herself to remain strong. "You're the only other person who knew—the only other person I trusted."

Her voice warbled, and inwardly she chided herself for not controlling her emotions. She needed him to depart before her suppressed tears streamed over her cheeks. She could not let that happen. Not in front of Leo.

"I think it's best you leave."

The pain on Etta's face tore at Leo. He didn't know which was worse, the fact she would believe he could betray her, or the fact he couldn't comfort her when she needed him most.

How could he persuade her to see that she was making a calamitous mistake, one that would affect them both forever? Appealing to her emotions hadn't worked, but perhaps appealing to her intellect would.

"Hear me out, Miss Maxwell. If you wanted to write an article naming Gibney's source, would you print a headline with the accusation 'Heiress Betrayed by Gentleman's Love' without proper evidence? Would you have me tried and convicted with no proof?"

"There was no one else who knew, Mr. Eriksson. There is your proof."

"More than one thing can be true at the same time."

Lips pursed, she eyed him. He had her attention now. *Lord, give me the words to persuade her.*

"It can be true that you are not aware of anyone else who had knowledge that you are Henry Mason, and it can also be true that I didn't reveal your secret. Someone else must have figured out you were Henry Mason, and you are unaware of it."

"That's preposterous."

"Think about it for a minute. Have you slipped up in your appearance or mannerisms? Have you mentioned a fact as Henry that only Henrietta would know, or vice versa?"

She shook her head.

"Has anyone threatened you or followed you during your investigation of the Bonner brothers?"

"No," she said. Her tongue glided over her lips.

"What reason would I have to do such a thing?" he asked, praying the tone of his voice and softness of his eyes conveyed all the love he held in his heart for her.

Instead, her steely gaze sent a chill snaking down his spine. "I don't know what makes men like you do what they do. Perhaps the fame of saying you were my beau or getting your name in the paper. Or maybe you intended to blackmail my father for a large sum of money."

The last accusation sickened him. Did she not know him at all? She may as well have punched him in the gut.

She scoffed. "I should've known you were too good to be true. Men like you don't want women like me, except for our money. I knew to protect my heart from the social climbers in Beacon Hill, but all it took was one dance with a handsome fireman at a charity ball and I let my guard down. You shattered my hopes and dreams—not to mention my heart."

"Etta—"

She stiffened, and he quickly corrected his address. "Miss Maxwell, how can you believe that? I would never. . .not in a thousand years would I. . ." His chest was heavy, as if the weight of a water tanker crushed against him. Her green eyes, which only yesterday held such love and promise, glared back at him, piercing his soul. "You must know in your heart that I'd never betray—"

She stiffened and held up her palm, stopping him midsentence. Tears puddled in her eyes. "Good evening, Mr. Eriksson."

And with that, she swished past him and disappeared into the house, leaving him alone on the porch.

Alone with his thoughts.

Alone with the false accusation still hanging over him.

Alone with all the broken dreams for his future once again.

CHAPTER 26

Hull, Massachusetts
Mid-April, 1905

Etta walked along the shore of Nantasket Beach, the fabric of her skirt bunched in her fist. The overcast sky bade her to leave her parasol at the cottage. White foam loped over her bare toes and then retreated into the ocean. She'd always appreciated the sea and her family's trips to Hull, but never more so than on this occasion.

There was a resilience to the sea that she'd always admired. No matter what obstacles man placed in its way—piers, docks, or ocean liners—the sea adjusted and continued moving. In. Out. In. Out. The waves broke and were swept back into the ocean, only to repeat the process over and over again. In. Out. In. Out.

They were steady. Constant.

And when a storm came, they were a force to be reckoned with. Nothing could restrain them except the mighty hand of God Himself.

To the ocean, obstacles were only temporary diversions. Just like the exposé and subsequent discovery that Leo had betrayed her. She inhaled the sea air and slowly released the breath.

Like the sea, she too needed to find the inner strength to move on and begin the next chapter of her life. The one without her position at the *Enterprise*.

The one without Leo.

To that end, she would return to Brockton and finalize the plans for the charity auction. She'd ventured to the Cape with her parents to lick her wounds, but two weeks had been long enough. She didn't plan to remain sequestered any longer.

Although Mother said people would understand if she canceled the event, she didn't wish to disappoint Brockton's firefighters. They depended on this fundraiser to provide training for their staff and to purchase necessary equipment their budget couldn't cover. With any luck, she'd be able to avoid the Eriksson family, and she'd definitely steer clear of Engine Company No. 1.

To accomplish all that must be done over the next several weeks, she'd written to Frances Lehr, hoping she might be interested in some side employment on Saturdays. The woman was organized and detail-oriented—just what Etta needed on her team if she hoped to make the charity as grand a success as the Fireman's Ball.

Leo's image invaded her thoughts, and her heart cinched tight like the strings on her handbag. He'd sounded so convincing when he'd denied being Declan's source, she'd almost believed him. Almost. But who else could it be?

Mother called to her from beneath her umbrella on the shore. "Let's return to the house. It's nearly time for lunch and bridge with Mrs. Atwater and her daughter."

Etta waved and headed toward her family's cottage.

Somehow, she must summon the strength to move on to where God was leading her next, including a conversation with her father that she hoped would revive at least one of her dreams.

And the sooner the better.

"Sit tight," Leo said. "He'll come."

"How can you be so sure?" Gunnar asked, sprinkling salt and pepper over his chicken and rice soup.

"Because he's a journalist. If he's anything like Etta, he won't be able to resist the temptation for an exclusive."

Would Etta approve of what he was about to do? This was her story, and he was about to give her best lead to her nemesis. What was the worst that could happen? She already believed him guilty of betrayal.

His brother sat at the table nearest the booth Leo occupied. "Just remember the plan," Leo said.

Gunnar gave Leo a tight nod. "You sure you want to do this? She gutted you pretty bad."

In the weeks since Etta accused him of breaking his promise, he'd anguished over losing her. He'd not eaten or slept much at all. Eventually, anger replaced his sadness. She'd jumped to the wrong conclusion and refused to believe him when he denied being Gibney's source. That hurt. Now, he was the one who felt betrayed.

What he was about to do was more about clearing his name than winning the lady back. Although he ached for Etta's company, he'd been hurt too. And as of now, he didn't know if he could trust his heart to her again.

The bell chimed above the door. "That's him," Leo said.

Leo waved. "Mr. Gibney." The reporter smiled in recognition and wound his way through the busy diner. "Have a seat."

Gibney slid into the booth across from Leo. "I was surprised to hear from you after I blew your sweetheart's cover."

Leo squeezed his fist under the table. *Don't let him get your goat.*

"So, your message said you have a scoop on the arsonist."

"I do, but first I want you to tell me who spilled the beans about Henry Mason."

Gibney held up his palms. "No can do, Eriksson. That would be a confidential informant."

Gunnar approached their table, soup in hand. "Hey, big brother, mind if I join you?" He set his bowl on the table and scooted onto the seat beside Gibney, scrunching the journalist against the wall.

"Hey, what's this?"

"Don't mind me. I'm just here to ensure Leo gets the information he needs so you can get the information you need."

"Are you threatening me?"

"Heavens, no," Leo said. "Etta Maxwell told me that with the proper inducement, most people would squawk like chickens."

Leo tugged an envelope from the lining of the jacket. *Forgive me, Etta.*

"What's that?" Gibney asked

"It's your inducement—notes on the arson investigation."

That got the reporter's attention. "Those are Henry Mason's notes?"

"More or less."

"What does that mean."

"Etta and I worked that case together. I was her confidential source inside the fire department. I wrote down everything I know, including the name of the person she believed to be the arsonist and why."

Gibney was practically salivating. He reached for the envelope, and Gunnar grabbed his wrist. "Not so fast."

"Okay, okay, Eriksson. You can call your dog off."

"Mind your manners, Gibney," Leo said. "That particular dog is my little brother."

Gunnar rolled his eyes.

"Tell me who broke Etta's confidence, and the contents are yours." Leo tapped the envelope against his palm. "You can pick up where she left off and get all the front-page glory you ever dreamed of."

"And if I don't?"

Leo held the envelope between his thumbs and forefingers, ready to tear its contents in two. "You're free to leave, without the information you came for."

Gibney massaged the scruff on his cheeks. "I can't give you a name. All I can say is the tipster used to live at her boardinghouse. Talk to the landlady. You'll figure it out."

Leo slid the envelope across the table. "Nice doing business with you."

The Maxwell Home
Boston, Massachusetts
Mid-April, 1905

"So, what do you think?"

Father steepled his fingers, his elbows propped on the supple leather of his desk chair.

As a child, she'd always called this his "thinking position." Although her stomach churned with anticipation, she knew that if he remained in this posture, he hadn't decided against her. Yet.

"It's not been done before, at least not in Brockton, which makes it a bit risky..."

She held her breath. If he said no, she doubted she would find funding elsewhere, even with the name Maxwell.

"...but it also makes it a novel idea."

Etta scooted closer to the edge of her seat. Father was poised to approve her request. Her heart raced. She would be the first woman in

Brockton to own a newspaper.

"You realize the money will come from your trust fund, young lady. If this newspaper fails, I won't be bailing it out."

"Yes, sir."

"I will expect a monthly accounting of expenses."

She nodded. "Word on the street is *The Daily Gazette* is going under. I think I can purchase their presses, office furniture, and lease their space for a song."

"That's my girl. You have not only a nose for the news but a head for business." He opened his desk drawer and retrieved a cigar box. "Promise me you'll put your heart and soul into this upstart, just like I did when I started Maxwell Business Machines. If you can commit to that, not only will I release your funds, I also think you'll be a huge success."

She was ready. She needed to face the future and devote herself to something different—something entirely her own. "I promise."

Father extended his large, beefy hand toward her. "In the business world, Etta, a handshake is as good as a man's word." She grasped his hand. "Always look 'em in the eye and remember you're a Maxwell and a Maxwell always keeps their word."

"I will," she said, shaking his hand with all the strength she could muster. Perhaps she should purchase a small set of barbells.

"One question," she said. "I'd like to have the funds transferred to the Brockton Community Bank. I think it would be valuable to the small bank to have such a large account. That's money that can be reinvested in Brockton."

One of Father's bushy eyebrows quirked. "And enough for you to gain a voting position on their board of directors."

Father selected a panatela from the box and sniffed the slender cigar before snipping the head with his gold cigar cutter.

"I'm hoping that will be the case," she said. "While I don't have plans to use the position to take control of the bank, I would be in excellent standing to encourage prioritizing small business loans for women and working-class folks with solid business plans who would otherwise be passed over."

"That's my girl." He withdrew his sterling silver lighter from his pocket and dipped the head of his cigar into the flame. After a few puffs, he leaned back in his chair and eyed Etta. Was he having second thoughts?

"Something wrong, Father? If you have any doubts, I'd rather you voice them now."

"No doubts. I think you've thought this through. Only time will tell how well the community takes to a female-owned newspaper."

"But there is something?"

He tapped the end of his cigar against the glass ashtray on his desk. "My concerns are of. . .a personal nature."

Where was he going with this? Was he worried she'd be considered even more peculiar in society? Etta didn't think that could be possible. "Please, speak your mind."

"I know you harbor strong feelings for the fireman. What would happen to your newspaper if Mr. Eriksson came calling again?"

Oh. She hadn't seen their conversation taking this turn. While she loved her father dearly and held no reservations regarding his affections for her, they rarely spoke of personal matters, let alone those of a romantic nature.

"I doubt that is going to happen."

"Amuse me, Etta. What if he did? You will have squandered your inheritance."

She straightened in her seat. "My newspaper is my future now. If God sees fit to bring a husband into my life, I suppose he'll need to take me as I am, which will include being the sole proprietor and editor-in-chief of Brockton's newest periodical."

"Even if a child or two came along?"

Heat blossomed on her cheeks. He was relentless. She didn't see a future with Leo, but if a husband was in her future before she passed her childbearing years, she supposed she could hire a nanny who could assist her while the little ones toddled around the shop. Even if that idea wasn't the most practical solution, the image warmed her heart. *Don't ponder what may not be, Etta. Concentrate on what is here in front of you right now.*

"I suppose I'll have to cross that bridge *if* I come to it."

She remained confident, however, that any bridge leading to a certain dashing fireman who'd once promised his heart had burned long before now.

CHAPTER 27

Leo dipped the stiff-bristled brush into the protective wax then vigorously rubbed it onto his rubber boots in a swirling motion. No matter how hard he swished and swiped, he couldn't remove the look of betrayal on Etta's face from his thoughts.

He'd followed up on Gibney's lead and believed with certainty the snitch had been one of Etta's fellow boarders at Mrs. Hemingway's. A retired vaudeville actor, Milton Rhoades, who'd helped Etta create her disguise. No wonder she'd fooled so many people. She had professional help crafting her costume.

According to Mrs. Hemingway, Rhoades disappeared without warning the day before the story broke, leaving no forwarding address. She'd been adamant that Rhoades didn't know Etta was masquerading as Henry Mason, and neither had any of her other boarders. But Leo had his doubts, and it definitely was an alternative theory that Etta should've pursued before leveling such harsh accusations against him.

He'd debated sending a letter detailing his findings to her home in Beacon Hill but then thought better of it. She'd made up her mind about him. Maybe someday he'd share the information with her, but for now he'd keep it close.

He examined the waxing brush. Its bristles now pointed in multiple directions. Ugh, he'd taken his frustration out on the tool.

"Keep that up, and you'll ruin that brush," Gunnar said.

Leo shrugged and picked waxy filament off his boot. "I can't even get any peace in the turnout room."

His brother plopped on the bench beside him. "Have you written Etta yet?"

"No."

"Maybe if you wrote her, shared what you've discovered, you'd find some peace."

Gunnar had practically glued himself to Leo's side since Etta accused him of betraying her. He loved his brother for it, but sometimes he just needed to be alone.

"I want her to come around because she misses me. Because she realizes I'd never do that to her. She shouldn't need evidence."

"C'mon, Leo. You're crazy about her."

Leo stuck his hand inside his other boot and applied sealant to its rubber toe. "I don't deny that. I have no clue how to move past that kind of hurt. She didn't ask me if I told anyone by mistake. She accused me of purposely telling a reporter from a rival newspaper she was Henry Mason. That stings."

Gunnar grabbed his boots and a brush and sat next to him. "I'm sure it does."

"Scripture says, 'Love believeth all things,' right?"

His brother nodded.

"To me that means giving someone the benefit of the doubt until you have conclusive proof they've sinned against you. Etta chucked everything she knew and believed about me, everything we meant to each other, the moment things didn't make sense. That's a deep kind of hurt."

Gunnar swiped his brush in the wax. "Yet you can't get her out of your thoughts, even after she's wronged you, can you?"

Perhaps his brother had missed his calling and should've been a minister. He shared their father's keen insight, which Leo found to be both a blessing and utterly annoying.

"What's wrong with me?" he asked, pausing the application of the sealant. "She trampled all over *my* heart, and I miss *her* fiercely?" He shook his head. "What a chump."

"Nah," Gunnar said. "Loving someone doesn't make you foolish." He knocked his shoulder into Leo's. "You may not like what I'm gonna say, but I think you need to hear it."

Leo's shoulders sagged. He was probably gonna hate it, but in the end, Gunnar was often proven right. Which was also annoying.

"Show Etta you still love her."

"No." His voice rose an octave. "I'm not going to her parents' home in that fancy neighborhood and beg her to take me back when I'm the aggrieved party."

"Whoa there, big brother." Gunnar lifted his hands, his rubber boot covering one arm.

Leo chuckled. "You're ridiculous."

Gunnar shrugged. "No one said anything about begging."

"Then what do you suggest?"

"Forgive her. Love forgives all, Leo. That's also in scripture. Turn the cheek seventy times seven. It's not just for little things but the big things. The painful things."

"What makes you think Etta gives a hoot if I forgive her? As far as she's concerned, she's done nothing to need forgiveness for."

"That doesn't matter either. It's your heart that's at risk of becoming bitter."

"But isn't that about me? How does that show love to her?"

"Etta's a smart woman. Eventually, after she simmers down, she's gonna figure this out. When she does, she'll be back here faster than we roll out to a three-alarm fire. But if you're still angry—or worse, bitter—your heart won't be ready to receive her apology."

Perhaps marriage and fatherhood had transformed Gunnar into a wise sage like Pops. Leo didn't doubt he'd be able to forgive Etta, whether she sought his forgiveness or not. Not only because he loved her but because that's what Jesus taught His disciples to do in all situations.

The real problem ran much deeper. Could he trust her with his heart again?

That was a question only time could answer.

Today was the big day. She would take possession of the defunct *Daily Gazette* and reshape the paper in her vision under its new name, *The Daily Beacon.* Her only regret: Leo wasn't there to share the moment with her.

She still struggled to believe he would betray her. Her chest tightened. That was nothing like the man she'd come to know. His pleading eyes flashed through her mind.

Could she have drawn the wrong conclusion?

He'd made a good point about the lack of evidence, and he'd been correct—she'd never print an accusation like the one she'd leveled at Leo with so little proof pointing to him as the source of Declan's article. But nothing else made sense.

Think Etta. Did you make any mistakes? Did anyone follow you?

She did slip up once. She mentioned the charity auction to Declan before advertising the switch from a ball to an auction. Come to think of it, not long after that he showed up in the park when she met with Leo. Had Declan followed her?

If he had surveilled her, would that help Leo's case or hurt it? Because if Declan came to the park to meet with Leo, that would further implicate him as the reporter's source.

Etta massaged her temple. What was she missing? No matter how many times she contemplated Declan's revelation, it always seemed to lead right back to Leo. None of it made any sense.

She glanced at the clock. Time to wash and dress. Mitchell would be around after breakfast to help her take her belongings to the newspaper office. She'd decided to save money and move into the empty office space upstairs. Eventually, she'd hire a contractor to remodel the entire second floor for her living quarters; but for now, her bed and wardrobe would fit inside one of the rooms. She planned to put every cent her father entrusted to her into making her newspaper profitable.

She chuckled to herself. Maybe from now on she should be known as the "Frugal Heiress" instead of the "Undercover Heiress." Father instilled in her from a young age to save money and to spend it wisely by always seeking God's direction before making any purchase.

Sage advice if ever there was any.

She'd applied that wise counsel already as she'd begun the hiring process. Her staff would be crucial to the *Beacon*'s fortunes. First and foremost, she'd managed to lure Miss Lehr away from the mayor's office. It turned out that Francie, as she preferred to be called, liked the idea of working for a woman, and their time planning the charity auction showed Etta what a valuable employee she could be. Francie was nothing if not organized and efficient. Having someone Etta could trust as the office manager was crucial.

While Etta would retain the title editor-in-chief, she'd hired her old boss, William Littleton, to be her managing editor. Even though he never gave Etta her own byline, the man believed in her. In the end, he'd been right about the consequences of that decision. She could trust William to carry out her vision for the newspaper, which would start as a weekly publication. Then, as subscriptions increased, they'd print a morning edition seven days a week.

Mrs. Hemingway poked her head inside the door. "Have a minute?"

"Yes, come in." Etta added her nightdress to the neatly folded garments in the large steamer trunk her Mother sent over.

"This is for you." Mrs. Hemingway placed a large hamper on the table. "Just a few things to get you started while you settle in. I can't have you wasting away to nothing."

"That is very thoughtful." She hugged her landlady. No, Mrs. Hemingway was much dearer to her than that. She was family. "Thank you."

Moisture pooled in Mrs. Hemingway's eyes. "Don't be a stranger," she said, backing out of the room. "Come by now and then for a chat, you hear?"

"I will."

The older woman tugged a handkerchief from her apron pocket and dabbed her nose. "Oh my, I've been meaning to give you this," she said, retrieving an envelope from the same pocket. "It's from Milton. With all the hullabaloo about the newspapers saying you were Henry Mason and your trip to Hull, I completely forgot."

Etta scanned the front of the envelope. Just her name and address at the boardinghouse. No return address but postmarked from Brockton nearly two weeks ago. How odd. Hopefully, Milton included that information in the enclosed note. She'd enjoy corresponding with him.

She slipped her finger under the edge of the flap and broke the seal.

An engine rumbled outside. She peeked out the window. "There's Mitchell now."

She dropped the letter inside the basket of food Mrs. Hemingway graciously provided, and grabbed the handle. "Shall we go?"

A new adventure awaited her today—the fulfillment of a dream God had planted in her heart a long time ago.

She didn't pretend to understand why some dreams came to fruition and others died a long and painful death. While her heart still pined for Leo and the promise of what might have been, it was time to close that door—at least for now.

Etta took her seat at the head of the large oak table in *The Daily Beacon*'s editorial conference room. She'd be lying to herself if she said she wasn't nervous. Acquiring a defunct newspaper and turning it into a profitable source of reliable information was a huge undertaking. But people would be relying on her for more than just the news. Many would be counting on the *Beacon*'s success as the source of their employment. As her gaze traveled from William to Francie, she was confident she had a dedicated and competent staff to assist her.

The most pressing task on today's agenda was determining what other positions to fill and prioritizing a timeline for those hires so Etta didn't fly through her trust fund and bankrupt the paper in its first year. That meant everyone willing to come on board would need to roll up their sleeves and take on more work than their salaries would compensate them for. Their dedication would be rewarded with generous bonuses at the end of the year *if* the paper was profitable, thereby giving everyone a stake in the *Beacon*'s viability.

Although she did make an exception when she acquired Jens Eriksson to be their one and only staff photographer. As such, he would cover all their front-page stories, stock the darkroom, and develop all the images himself. She'd matched his salary from the *Enterprise*, but he was worth it. And he'd agreed to a two-year contract.

"Have you given any consideration to an accountant, Miss Maxwell?" Francie asked.

"Let's put an advertisement in the *Times* and the *Enterprise*."

Francie jotted the item on her ever-increasing to-do list.

"I've been thinking about our biggest problem as I see it," William said. "We need lots of news covered but don't have the full-time staff or the budget to write the articles we'll need even for a weekly print run."

He motioned between Etta and himself. "You and I will handle the headline stories for now, but I'd like to put the word out that we're looking for independent journalists to submit human-interest and second-tier pieces. If anyone shows particular promise, we could discuss bringing them on board on a part-time basis."

"That's an excellent idea, William. Could you draw up some compensation guidelines?"

He nodded then turned to Francie. "Can you give me a reminder on that tomorrow?"

"Check," she said. "Should I place an ad for the freelance writers too?"

"Yes," Etta added. "Run the copy by William or me before you send it over. And, since we're discussing our writers, we're looking for well-researched, well-written articles. I don't care about anything else. And whoever writes the piece gets the credit. End of story."

William nodded. "I wouldn't expect anything less."

"One more thing," Francie said. "We're going to run those ads in the *Beacon* too, correct?"

How had Etta missed that? There were thousands of details to cover before they launched their first edition, and Francie was already proving her worth to the team. "Yes. Excellent suggestion, Francie."

Etta glanced at her meeting agenda. "William, have you given any thought to an advertising and circulation manager?"

"If you're on board, Etta," he said, "I was thinking of speaking with the assistant manager at the *Enterprise*, Charlie Scott. I think he's champing at the bit for a promotion, but the guy in front of him isn't going anywhere for a long time."

"You trust him?"

"I do. He's a go-getter."

"Excellent." She shuffled her papers. "Okay, last item, and this will be quick. For our first edition, I'm planning a front-page editorial introducing myself as the publisher and editor-in-chief. I want to write my side of the story, explaining why I masqueraded as Henry Mason. I don't plan to hide the fact that a woman runs this newspaper and that women will be writing some of the articles and doing many of the behind-the-scenes jobs that get the *Beacon* to print."

He leaned forward, elbows on his knees. "Do you think that's wise when we're trying to get the paper off the ground? I'm not saying you should hide the fact you're the publisher, but do we need a front-page piece?"

The muscles in her neck stiffened. Was he waffling?

"Look, William, you've been incredibly supportive, and I'm grateful. But I'm not hiding in the shadows anymore. I know my decision may affect initial readership, but I'm willing to be patient and let the quality of the reporting be the selling point of the paper."

She didn't want to lose William, but she wasn't compromising any longer. "Are you still on board?"

He straightened in his chair immediately. "One hundred percent," he said. "No hesitation. Just making sure we all understand what's at stake."

"Thank you, William. You're essential to this team." The tension drained from her shoulders. She didn't want to think about what a setback losing her managing editor would be.

She glanced around the small circle. "Anything else?"

When no one responded, she adjourned the meeting.

Francie grabbed a paper sack. "I'll be back in half an hour," she said, then stepped outside.

William squatted by the hamper Etta had carried in, and opened the lid. "Wowee, where'd you get the grub?"

"My former landlady. She's worried I'll starve."

He foraged through an assortment of cheese, rolls, vegetables, and fruit. "Here's a card addressed to you." He held the envelope over his shoulder.

"Thanks. I'd forgotten about that. It's from Milton Rhoades."

"The fella who helped create Henry Mason's public image."

"One and the same." She leaned against the wall and tugged the paper free from the envelope. She skimmed the short letter then gasped and jerked upright. "I can't believe this."

William moved beside her. "What is it?"

"Would you be surprised to learn the once great Henry Mason got his last story entirely wrong?"

"What are you talking about?"

"It wasn't Leo who blew my cover. It was Milton." Etta waved the letter. "Declan paid him to spy on me."

Leo insisted there must have been someone else who knew. She'd never considered the retired vaudeville actor as the possible culprit, since she'd never disclosed the purpose of her disguise. She shook her head. How could she have made such a colossal mistake?

"Read this. It explains everything." She shoved the missive into William's fumbling hands, and the pages scattered to the floor.

He stooped and picked up the letter. "Did Milton say how Declan found him at the boardinghouse? Something or someone must've tipped him off to go snooping around there."

"No, but it's time I found out."

She grabbed her handbag and hurried to the door.

"Where are you going?"

"To make the most important retraction of my life."

CHAPTER 28

Etta jostled her way through busy streets crowded with pedestrians, wagons, and automobiles. Was everyone in Campello out during the noon hour? She needed to hurry if she wanted to catch Leo at the diner, but her diversion to confront Declan had been well worth her time.

The kid had been none too happy to see her. He originally thought she was there to question him about the arson story in today's edition, but she didn't have time to listen to whatever excuses he spouted about his source for the article. That was not on her list of priorities at the moment.

When she confronted him with Milton's letter, he snickered. If she hadn't been in a hurry to make amends with Leo, she'd have clobbered him right then and there and asked God for forgiveness later.

The truth, as it turned out, was much simpler than she'd imagined. There was no grand conspiracy to blackmail her parents, just an eager reporter who wanted to crush his competition.

Declan's initial hunch was that Henry Mason was romantically involved with the heiress. He decided to tail his rival then staked out the boardinghouse, leaving copious amounts of peanut shells in his wake. Once he discovered that Etta Maxwell lived at the same address, he suspected something tawdry happening between the two of them.

When his surveillance failed to yield any substantial clues, he targeted Milton and made him an offer. Always short on cash, the old vaudeville actor agreed to spy on her, handing Declan a story he'd never anticipated. And all along, Etta had been clueless that Milton had discovered her ruse.

A couple passed her, strolling arm in arm, and her stomach churned. That could've been Leo and her if she hadn't been such a fool. If she hadn't let passion dictate her actions instead of the love and kindness he had always shown her. What a terrible mistake she'd made. How could she have ever doubted him?

She paused outside the diner and inhaled deeply, holding her breath until her lungs ached, then forcefully exhaled. *Lord, please give me the words. I've misjudged Leo terribly. Help him to hear my apology and grant me forgiveness.*

"You going in, lady?" a large man with slicked hair asked.

"Oh yes. My apologies."

He stepped around her and opened the door, allowing Etta to enter first. She spied the Eriksson clan. Leo faced away from her, but her gaze locked with Gunnar's. He wiped his mouth and leaned forward. She didn't need to be a mind reader to deduce that conversation.

No turning back now.

She mustered her courage and approached their table. "Hello, everyone. It's nice to see you all. It's been too long."

"Miss Maxwell," Gunnar said with a stiff formality to his tone.

Chief Eriksson stared straight ahead. Jens acknowledged her presence with a tight nod. What choice did he have as her employee? She'd not only hurt Leo but wounded his entire family.

"No need to be so formal. Please, call me Etta. Everyone I care about does." She glanced at Leo. "Or at least, I hope they still do."

His eyes were soft, and she breathed a sigh of relief. Perhaps there was some hope of reconciliation after all.

Gunnar stood, put his silverware on his plate, and then grabbed his coffee cup and saucer. "We'll move to another table."

"That's not necessary," Leo said, crushing her hopes of a private conversation.

"We insist, don't we, Jens? Pops?"

Reluctantly, the other two men followed suit and joined Gunnar at another table, just out of earshot if she kept her voice low.

Leo stood and, for a moment, she thought he planned to join his brothers and leave her alone beside an empty table in the middle of the crowded diner.

He used his napkin to wipe crumbs from the table and red leather chair where Gunnar sat moments before. "Please have a seat, Miss Maxwell."

She'd requested that he use her proper name, but now it was a chilly reminder of all she'd lost.

"Are you hungry?" he asked. "I can call the waitress over."

She should be hungry. It was noon, after all, but she feared even one bite of food would send her stomach roiling past the point of no return. "No thank you."

Leo pulled apart a large roll. That did look good and might settle her stomach. "Perhaps I might order a roll like that one and a glass of water."

He placed half the roll on a napkin and slid it toward her. "Help yourself. You can have my water as well." He nudged the glass beside the roll. "I'm fine with only coffee."

"Oh, I can't take it from—"

He stopped her with an expression that said "just take the roll," so she thanked him, slathered butter on the warm bread, and waited for it to melt.

The uncomfortable silence stretched between them for what seemed like hours. Leo's gaze concentrated on the meat loaf and side of mashed potatoes and gravy occupying his plate. He'd not looked at her since passing his water glass nor spoken a word since offering his roll.

This was harder than she'd thought it would be. Where was the easy conversation they'd always enjoyed? Oh, right, she'd suffocated it when she'd accused him of stabbing her in the back. Funny how that worked.

Leo broke the silence. "We finally got the results of the Hartford agency's boiler inspection. A crack in a lap joint was to blame."

"And that was never detected in any of the routine maintenance inspections?"

He shook his head. "The crack was hidden in between two overlapping pieces of steel."

"I'm relieved to learn that Mr. Grover won't be held liable. He's been working with the Maxwell Foundation to aid the victims. I fear he'll carry the weight of this accident until his dying breath."

"Yeah, I imagine he will." Leo's attention returned to the uneaten mashed potatoes on his plate.

Etta tore off a piece of bread and popped it into her mouth. She glanced at the Erikssons' table. Gunnar nodded his head toward Leo, apparently encouraging her to get on with it.

He was right. She was the one who'd come there with something to say. She might as well get it over with. Even his rejection would be better than sitting in the uncomfortable quiet hovering over them like gray clouds before a snowstorm.

"Leo, I want to apologize for my behavior. I should never have accused you of betraying me. That is not the man I know you to be. I let my hurt and anger dictate my actions instead of allowing reason to guide me to the truth. You are a kind, honorable, and God-fearing man who would never. . ."

Regret wadded in her throat, making it difficult to swallow. She gulped some water and wiped her mouth. "You've been nothing but supportive of my dreams and ambitions."

She slid her finger over the condensation on the outside of her water glass. "Milton mailed a letter to me at the boardinghouse weeks ago. He confessed everything and asked my forgiveness. Unfortunately, I only received it this morning."

"Good. Mystery solved."

"Please, believe me, Leo. I never imagined Milton had discovered I was Henry Mason. I never told him why I wanted his help with my disguise."

"Yet you had no trouble believing I'd betray your secret."

The pain she'd caused Leo punctuated every syllable he spoke. He still smarted from her accusation, and she couldn't blame him.

He raked his fingers through his hair. "The irony is, I suspected Rhoades before you did."

She straightened in her chair. "You suspected?"

"Yes, but having no definitive proof, I didn't want to make a false accusation and tarnish his reputation."

Like she'd done to him.

"Although you didn't believe me, I knew I was telling the truth. Curious how Declan learned Henry Mason's true identity. I confronted him."

"And he revealed his source?"

"Declan wouldn't talk at first, so I provided some Henry Mason-style inducement." He motioned for the waitress. "Check, please."

The woman nodded. "I'll be right there, Leo."

She arched her brows. "What kind of inducement?"

He unfolded a copy of the *Times*, pushed it toward her, and tapped the headline.

Etta skimmed the bold print at the top of the front page.

POLICE MAKE ARREST IN CAMPELLO ARSONS

EVIDENCE POINTS TO PROTECTION RACKET
BY DECLAN GIBNEY

Her story. The one she'd hoped would earn Henrietta Maxwell a byline was now credited to her nemesis, Declan Gibney. That was what he'd been babbling about when she confronted him earlier. Seeing his name beneath what should've been her headline rankled more than it ought. But what did this have to do with Leo discovering that Milton betrayed her secret?

She narrowed her eyes. "I don't understand."

"I gave Declan everything I knew about the investigation, including what you'd learned about Olaf and his relationship to Lars. Gibney wouldn't give me Milton's name, just that it was someone from the boardinghouse. I'd ruled out Mrs. Hemingway, based on your glowing opinion of her, but over a cup of coffee, I grilled her for information. She gave me the scoop on all of her boarders but remained adamant that no one knew you were Henry Mason. Rhoades seemed like the obvious choice, but again, I didn't have hard proof."

He glanced at the issue of the *Times* splayed between them. "I'm sorry, Etta. I know how much that story meant to you, but I needed to understand why things went so horribly wrong for us."

She leaned back in her chair. *He* was sorry. If she hadn't already realized what a fool she'd been, she'd just been served a heaping plate of humble pie.

"Don't be sorry, Leo. You've done nothing wrong."

"Talking to Gibney felt dishonest. Even though we'd already gone our separate ways, I felt I'd betrayed you."

He pinched his eyes closed for a brief second then focused his gaze on her, his eyes glistening. Did he have regrets too?

"I'm sorry you lost your job, Etta. Maybe in the long run, this will be good for you."

He reached for her hand. And that familiar jolt shot through her, spreading hope of reconciliation between them.

"God gave you a heart to fight injustice and an amazing ability to persuade others with your pen to stand up for what is right. Don't hide your talent. Embrace who He has made you to be so your gifts can glorify the giver."

"Thank you, Leo." Her spirits lifted. Were his gracious words an indication that he still cared for her? That he could forgive her? "I'm so sorry, Leo. I made a huge mistake. Can you forgive me? Can we please start over?"

He squeezed her fingers then slid his hand away, and the temporary hope she'd experienced vanished with his touch. "I'm not a man to hold a grudge, Etta. I forgave you long before you asked."

He sighed. "I'm just not certain I can ever trust you again."

Sleep eluded Etta. She stared at her bedroom ceiling, the morning light poking through the tiny crack between the drapes. Tears welled in her eyes as she recalled Leo's words. *I'm just not certain I can ever trust you again.*

Why had she clammed up? She never lacked for words. Why didn't she fight for the man she loved? If she'd spoken those three powerful words, *I love you*, would it have made any difference?

She'd never uttered those words to any man except her father. Love was an emotion she'd never felt for anyone but her parents. And while her feelings for Leo encompassed the kind of affection she held for her family, it was also much, much more.

She rolled onto her side. Why hadn't she considered, before accusing Leo, that Milton might have seen through her cover story? Why had she blamed him at all? She should've trusted him. Isn't that what it all boiled down to?

Etta flopped on her back again, her arm draped over her eyes. She'd made a real mess of everything. She'd not thought about anyone but herself, always striving to get that byline.

Her head ached from the tears she'd shed during the night. She whispered into the darkness, "Lord, forgive me for my selfishness. Forgive me for striving. Help me, Lord, to remember that it's my job to knock on the doors that come my way and Your job to open them. Help me remember that I can trust Your plan for my life, even when some doors close."

She dabbed her eyes with the embroidered handkerchief Leo had given her. She smoothed her finger over the string of tiny black-eyed Susans forming her initials.

Such a thoughtful gift. One she'd cherish forever.

Abandoning any hope of additional rest, she shoved herself to a sitting position and swung her legs over the side of the bed. There was no point in rehashing what couldn't be changed.

Leo had made his decision, and she must move on with her life. Whether she liked it or not, some things couldn't be fixed with an "I'm sorry." Biting back tears, she swallowed the heartache one more time and determined to lay the past to rest.

CHAPTER 29

Leo wove through the pedestrians crossing Main Street then took a left onto Broad. He reviewed his mental list of items to pick up at the grocer. Although little if any cooking occurred in the Eriksson home, staples like coffee, cream, and butter were a must.

He came to an abrupt halt at the sight of a Pierce Arrow parked outside the Brockton Community Bank. There were not many automobiles rumbling down the streets of Brockton, let alone fancy ones. What were the odds there were two Pierce Arrows in Campello? Not high.

Perhaps he should pivot and stop by the grocer after work. Although he missed Etta terribly, he didn't know what to say to her. Somehow, small talk about the weather would only increase the awkwardness of the moment and the pain of losing her.

"Good afternoon, Leo."

Too late. He should've acted on his instincts. His hesitation would cost him.

"Hello, Etta." Why did she have to look so fetching? He'd tried to forget the depth of her green eyes. They still sparkled behind those lenses at the sight of him, warming his heart.

She waved her hand toward the woman standing beside her. "This is my assistant, Francie Lehr. Francie, this is Leo Eriksson."

He dipped his chin. "Miss Lehr."

"Pleased to meet you, Mr. Eriksson."

Silence stretched between them as taut as the skin on a drum. *Think of something to say, Eriksson.*

Etta's tongue glided over her lips. "I–I've been meaning to stop by the firehouse to see how you're doing," she said, finally breaking the awkward silence.

"Things have slowed with the close of the arson investigation."

She nodded.

He searched his mind for something to say. "Father received a commendation from the mayor for his leadership during the Grover Shoe disaster."

"I read about that in the *Enterprise*. Please pass on my congratulations."

There was no ease to their conversation, no connection. Every word he uttered felt like sandpaper grating against his teeth. He longed for the days their words flowed with ease.

Miss Lehr motioned toward the Pierce Arrow. "I'll wait in the motorcar, Miss Maxwell. Take your time."

"Oh, that won't be necessary, Francie. I'm sure Leo has a busy schedule and I'm not part. . . I mean, he didn't expect to run into an old acquaintance today."

Is that all they were—acquaintances? What else did he expect? The word sounded so cold, considering how much she'd meant to him.

How much she still did.

"Best of luck to you, Leo, and please give my best to your family." She stepped toward the automobile, and Mitchell opened the door. "Goodbye, Leo."

She hadn't uttered the words with any finality, but as the door closed and the automobile merged into the mix of pedestrians, wagons, and carriages clogging Main Street, her words seemed very final.

Why did this upset him? Wasn't this what he wanted? He was the one who'd terminated the "something more" that she'd sought to rekindle.

Etta looked over her shoulder and waved through the rear window as the car pulled away.

He returned the gesture, all the while realizing what an absolute fool he'd been to let a woman like Etta Maxwell drive out of his life.

Francie knocked on Etta's open office door. "The repairman is here to look over the printing press."

"Excellent. Will you show him to the pressroom floor? Please ask William to speak with him. Anything else?"

"A young boy is waiting to speak with you."

"Me?"

"Yes. His name is Noah Desmond. He's looking for work. I told him to come back in a few days when we'd have a better idea how many paper boys we were hiring, but he insisted."

"I suppose the budget can wait a few more minutes." She closed the ledger. "Send him in."

Francie returned a few seconds later, a young boy in tow. "Noah Desmond, this is Miss Henrietta Maxwell, editor-in-chief of *The Daily Beacon*."

The boy's large eyes stared at Etta, a quizzical mix of curiosity and apprehension reflecting in his gaze. "I know who she is. Everyone in Brockton knows the Undercover Heiress."

Warmth spread over her cheeks at the sound of her new moniker.

Noah removed his cap then wiped his hands against his patched knickers and extended it to Etta. His mother had probably advised him on proper interview etiquette.

"Nice to meet you, Miss Maxwell."

"Nice to meet you too, Noah," she said, shaking his hand. "My assistant tells me you're looking for a job."

"Yes, miss. My father died in the Grover fire, and I'm lookin' for work to help support my mother and younger brothers and sisters. I thought since you were setting up shop you might be hiring."

Etta's heart pinched. The boy looked small and much too young to be carrying the burden of supporting his family.

"I'll do anything you need—deliver papers, clean, set type, fetch coal for your furnace. I'm a hard worker, and I won't complain."

The words flew from his lips as if he worried that any delay in stating his purpose might cost him an opportunity. But what struck Etta most was the boy's diction and mannerisms. He sounded educated. "How old are you, Noah?"

He stood straighter and lifted his chin. "I'm ten, but I've completed five years of grammar school. I can read and write. I'm also very good with numbers, according to my teacher, Mrs. Everhart."

Ten? Etta's heart nearly broke. The boy should be in school, not working to provide for his family. "How many siblings do you have, Noah?"

"I'm the eldest of six, miss."

"Well, I will need paper boys to deliver the morning paper. Right now, we're only printing a Sunday edition, but in time, I plan to do a daily run.

You'd need to be here early. Five o'clock."

Noah didn't flinch. "I'll be here. You can count on me. I won't let you down."

She didn't doubt that for one minute. "If you know anyone looking for work, Noah, we'll need more delivery boys and girls. It's a big city to cover."

"Girls?"

She stifled a grin. "Yes, Noah. Girls can deliver newspapers as well as boys can."

"Okay, miss, if you say so. I can find some others."

"Wonderful. Let them know to tell me you sent them. For each delivery person you recruit, I'll give you a nickel."

His eyes widened. "Gee, thanks."

He scrunched his cap between his hands. "I don't mean to sound ungrateful, miss, but do you have any other jobs you need filled? I won't be returning to school and can work for you during the day."

She'd seen this so many times, children earning a living to help their families. Like little Nellie Hurd, the child she'd found in the rubble. Nellie wasn't much older than Noah, and she had worked in the factory to help support her family.

"In the long run, getting an education will serve your family best, Noah."

"I mean no disrespect, Miss Maxwell, but I'm the man of the family now. Schooling won't put food on our table now or keep a roof over our heads. I'm smart. I can learn anything I set my mind to."

He fidgeted from one foot to the other. Apparently, her contemplation made him anxious.

"Please, miss. My mother is counting on me."

She admired his pluck. "I'll tell you what, Noah. You come by before and after school, and I'll find odd jobs for you to do. I'll pay you ten cents per day."

Noah's eyes narrowed. "You're gonna pay me ten cents a day to only work before and after school?" He shook his head. "That doesn't sound right, miss." He straightened his shoulders. "My mama says Desmonds don't take charity."

"No charity. I expect you to attend school and get good grades," she said in a kind but firm tone. "If I find out you're working somewhere else during the day, our deal is off, and I'll only employ you to deliver the morning paper. Understood?"

Noah offered his hand again, and Etta shook it. "Deal," he said.

"Excellent. You start Sunday, five a.m. sharp."

"I'll be here. And I'll be sending kids over to deliver your papers." He plopped his cap on his head and hustled to the door. He halted in the doorway and pivoted on his heel. "Thanks, Miss Maxwell."

Etta grinned. She had a hunch someday the enterprising Noah Desmond could be running *The Daily Beacon*.

CHAPTER 30

Think, Etta. There has to be a story somewhere you've overlooked.

Etta slumped in her desk chair and tapped her pencil on the blotter. If she didn't land on an idea soon, the only piece with her byline would be her editorial about life as a male journalist. She needed more for the first edition—something special.

She'd given William the follow-up on the arson investigation. Surrendering that piece had been difficult, but in the end, she'd made the right decision. Her administrative duties setting up the newspaper required much of her time, even with Francie shouldering a great deal of the burden.

Francie knocked on Etta's open door. "Still no luck?"

"I'm so exhausted, I don't think I can string two words together let alone write an article—even if an idea fell out of the sky and landed right on my desk."

Francie dragged a chair into Etta's office. "Let's put our heads together."

Etta pulled out her notebook and flipped to the section where she had jotted down some ideas.

"There's a new attraction planned for Highland Park," she suggested.

Francie wrinkled her nose.

"There's talk of a strike among the Leather Workers Union members."

"Maybe." Her assistant tapped her finger against her cheek. "Anything else?"

"Just a note about the Ladies Guild at St. Margaret's holding a bake sale with the proceeds going to provide educational scholarships for the children of Grover victims."

"That's it," Francie said, hopping to her feet.

"I appreciate your help, Francie, you know that, but the Ladies Guild of St. Margaret's bake sale, while admirable, isn't exactly front-page news."

"Don't be silly, I know that. But didn't you tell me you uncovered a whole host of stories from survivors and grieving families that you didn't know what to do with?"

Etta's pulse thrummed a little stronger. "I sure did. Where is *that* notebook?" She riffled through her drawer.

"Can you be a little more specific? You have a lot of those."

Etta chuckled. Francie wasn't wrong. "It's about this big," she said, offering a visual representation of the size of the notepad she was hunting. "The cover has bloodstains, and it smells like smoke."

Francie pulled a small basket off the top shelf of the bookcase. "It's most likely in here. I hope you don't mind, but I took the liberty of organizing your old notebooks in date order."

"Mind? I don't know what I'd do without you."

Francie thumbed through the tablets then held one up. "Is this it?"

Etta clapped her hands. "Remind me to give you a big fat bonus." She flipped through the pages, name after name bringing to mind the stories of heartache, devastation, and loss as well as the enduring hope born of a community banding together through adversity.

She handed a fresh notepad to her assistant. "Let's make a list."

"That morning was Dora Clark's first day on the job at Grover Shoes." She paused and glanced at her assistant over her spectacles. "She never even stitched one shoe."

Francie shook her head. "How terrible."

"George E. Smith. He was pinned but helped three others escape before he died. I believe he left a widow and several children behind." She squinted, struggling to decipher her own scribblings. "And the priest from St. Margaret's. I saw him rush into the burning building with my own eyes."

"I like that idea." Francie jotted notes on a sheet of paper Etta tore from her tablet. "Have you considered including heroic stories too?"

"What a brilliant idea, Francie. Thank you."

Her assistant beamed. They made a great team.

Etta skimmed through the pages of the smoky notepad. So many stories. Many more than she could ever do justice to in one article. "I think I'll write an ongoing series. Each week, I can cover one victim's story, one survivor's, and one hero's."

She drummed her fingers on her desk. Hadn't Leo suggested this very idca?

At the time, she'd brushed off his suggestion. Perhaps Henry Mason hadn't been the right person to pen such a tribute, but Etta Maxwell was more than ready. After all she'd been through in the weeks following the Undercover Heiress exposé, she'd learned how suddenly a person's life could change. Sure, it wasn't the same as losing a loved one, but the course she'd charted for her future had radically altered in the blink of an eye.

Maybe hard-hitting, fact-based reporting, coupled with human-interest pieces, would be the hallmark of *The Daily Beacon*. And she had Leo Eriksson to thank for it.

Leo glanced at his watch. Pops and his brothers were late again. Couldn't anyone in his family be on time?

He'd hardly finished the thought before Gunnar slid into the booth across from him and grabbed a piece of Leo's toast.

"Thanks, big brother."

"I ordered the breakfast special for all of you."

"I'm hungry now." Gunnar dipped his toast in the runny yolk of Leo's egg.

"Do you mind?"

"What has you so wound up this morning?"

"Does anything have to be wrong to *not* appreciate someone else dipping *my* toast in *my* eggs?"

Gunnar offered the slice of toasted rye to Leo. "Here. If it's that big a deal, you can have it back."

Leo rolled his eyes.

"What's eating you this morning?"

"Nothing."

Gunnar eyed him in disbelief.

"There's been a lot on my mind lately." He sipped his coffee. "I've had the maintenance schedule for the tanker and ladder trucks to manage, and I haven't been able to fix the alarm box on Broad Street. Just to name a few."

His answer did little to squelch Gunnar's inquiring gaze. "What?" Leo asked, nearly wincing at the sharpness in his voice.

"If I didn't know better, I'd say someone was missing a certain stunning young heiress we both know you're still in love with."

"That's ridiculous."

"Is it?"

Ilsa set Gunnar's breakfast in front of him. "I told the cook to hold the other two orders until Chief Eriksson and Jens arrive," she said. She scanned the dining area. "Do you think they'll be long?"

Gunnar shook his head. "No. But in case you're wondering, Pops likes his coffee with cream and two sugars."

She smiled. "Thanks, I'll remember that."

Gunnar waited till Ilsa moved to another booth before leaning over the table. "I think Pops is taking a liking to Ilsa too."

"Pops and Ilsa, again? When did you become so concerned with everyone's love life?"

"Wouldn't it be great if Dad found a nice woman and didn't have to be alone?"

"He's not alone. He has me and Jens."

Now it was Gunnar's turn to roll his eyes. "That's not the same thing, and you know it. Besides, eventually you and Jens will marry and move out."

Leo sprinkled salt and pepper on his eggs. Jens might, but now that Leo's relationship with Etta had taken an unexpected turn south, he doubted marriage was in his future.

Gunnar cleared his throat. "Have you seen Etta lately?"

Leo lifted his cup and blew on the steaming beverage. "Not since I ran into her outside the bank about a week ago."

"Well, you're about to see her again," his brother said, nodding toward the aisle.

When Leo's gaze landed on Etta, she smiled, and his throat thickened, making it hard to swallow. She looked smart in a tailored skirt with her hair styled loosely over her shoulder.

He briefly contemplated fleeing the scene, but where would he go? With her investigative skills, there was nowhere to hide from Henrietta Maxwell. He shook his head. What a ridiculous notion. He was a grown man after all. Why should he avoid this woman?

Because, despite everything, she still owned his heart, that's why.

"Hello, Leo. Gunnar."

Leo stuffed a large piece of sausage into his mouth.

Gunnar shook his head, his expression telling Leo his brother thought him a complete and utter moron. "Hi, Miss Maxwell."

"Call me Etta, please." She turned to Leo. "I was hoping to find you here this morning. I have some news I want to share, and I want you to hear it from me."

He'd finally chewed that hunk of sausage well enough to swallow then washed it down with a gulp of water. "I don't think that's a good idea, Etta," he said, sawing his meat like it was shoe leather rather than a breakfast sausage. "I wish you well and all, but it's best if we go our separate ways."

No, it wasn't. Not really. But it was easier to believe that so the pain of missing her wouldn't be so overwhelming.

"It will only take a minute. I promise."

Her pleading tone nearly made him change his mind. *Don't look at her, Eriksson. It's your only defense.* "I can't, Etta."

"Oh...all right. I...I understand." Her voice cracked. "I shouldn't have interrupted your breakfast uninvited."

Head down, he cast a sideways glance toward Etta. Her fingers tightened around a scroll of newsprint.

"I...I should be on my way then. Good day." She turned on her heel and made a beeline for the exit.

Gunnar tossed his crumpled napkin across the table. "You're a real class act, Leo."

"What would you know about anything?"

"I know that woman still loves you."

"What makes you so sure?"

"I'm married, aren't I?" He cut a bite of sausage with his fork. "Didn't you see the way her eyes brightened when she was talking to you?"

"No. I...I didn't look at her. But what does that have to do with anything?"

"It has everything to do with everything. I'm telling you, she loves you. You should go after her."

"Go after her?"

Gunnar nodded. "You hurt her feelings. She nearly cried."

"Look, I don't like being unkind to Etta. But don't forget, she's the one who ended things between us. Every time I see her, it rips the scab off my heart, and I hurt all over again. The best way for me to heal is to stay clear of her. The sooner everyone understands that, the better it'll be for all of us."

"Morning." Jens squeezed into the booth beside Leo.

Pops, on the other hand, went straight to the counter to speak with Ilsa. Whatever he said made her laugh. It certainly looked like Gunnar might be right about Pops taking a shine to her. Was it possible his younger brother knew what he was talking about when it came to women? By all accounts, he and Trude were happily married.

"What did we miss?" Jens asked, sticking his fork into one of Leo's sausages.

"Leo gave Etta the brush-off."

"What'd you do that for? She was a perfect match for you," Jens said. "You should go after her."

"Can you both stay out of my social life and eat your *own* breakfast?"

"I've lost my appetite." Gunnar shoved the remainder of his breakfast toward Jens and wiped his mouth.

"Gee, thanks." Jens stuffed an entire sausage link in his mouth.

Gunnar stood and dug some coins from his pocket. "I'll see you at the firehouse."

They didn't understand how much he'd hated sending Etta away. The woman occupied his thoughts during the day and his dreams at night. Maybe he should accept her olive branch and try rebuilding a friendship, see if they could fall back into easy conversation and witty banter, see if he could learn to trust her again.

Memories of their dance in the gazebo and those first tender kisses sprang to mind. He longed for that woman, and he was deluding himself if he thought he could settle for friendship. It just wasn't meant to be. His best defense was to employ the number one rule he'd learned in the fire department: To avoid getting burned, don't play with fire.

CHAPTER 31

Etta trembled as she wove through the tables in the diner. Her stomach churned, and she covered her mouth as her breakfast burned in her throat. Using her hip, she pushed the door open and burst into the sunny spring morning.

She'd misled herself into believing that time could heal all wounds. What a bunch of malarky. Apparently, time had convinced Leo he'd been right to end their relationship.

Refusing to make eye contact with her fellow pedestrians, she strode down the block, reliving the embarrassing scene in her mind. All she'd wanted to do was show him the first edition of *The Daily Beacon*. To let him know she'd taken his advice and was writing a series of pieces each week featuring the stories of the victims, survivors, and heroes of the Grover disaster.

"Etta."

She paused and turned in the direction she'd just come. Gunnar sprinted toward her.

"I'm sorry, Etta. Leo shouldn't have treated you like that."

Her throat thickened, as if she'd swallowed a wad of cotton. She squared her shoulders, hoping to veil her emotions from him. "It's fine, Gunnar. He has every right to eat his breakfast in peace without me barging in unannounced."

"He's a dunderhead, Etta. Don't give up on him."

"I'm the fool, Gunnar. I thought in time, perhaps, he'd miss me. . . possibly want to reconcile. . ." Tears stung her eyes. Oh, she wouldn't cry in front of Leo's brother, would she?

"Hang in there, Etta. I know he loves you. He's still smarting. That's all."

She nodded and checked her emotions. "I just wanted to let him know I'd taken his advice for a story." She handed Gunnar the rolled newspaper. "This is the first edition of my new enterprise, *The Daily Beacon*. Will you see that he gets it?"

Gunnar unrolled the paper and scanned the headlines. "This is *your* newspaper?"

She nodded and pointed to the top of the front page. "See, my name is in the masthead. Editor-in-Chief, Henrietta Maxwell."

"I know my thickheaded brother will be proud of you."

"Thanks, Gunnar."

"Mind what I say, and don't give up on Leo."

"Even if I were brave enough to keep trying, it's obvious your brother has let me go. Love is a two-way street, I'm afraid." She placed her hand on his arm. "God bless you, Gunnar. Blessings on your entire family."

Tears spilled from her eyes as she turned away. She wished with all her might that there was a reason to remain hopeful, but Leo made it clear there was no point in hoping for what would never be.

No, Leo Eriksson had moved on.

And so must she.

Leo knelt beside the tanker truck. Always vigilant, Wilson curled along the wall where he could see both Leo and the horses in their nearby stalls. The dog was better company than he cared to admit.

He removed the coal bin and stuck his fingers beneath the boiler. During their training exercise yesterday, the boiler failed to produce enough steam to force the water through the hose. That kind of failure during a fire could have catastrophic results.

Nothing clogged the opening. That would have been the easiest repair, but it was also the least likely problem. Next he checked to make sure the bolts and screws were tight. The wagon often hit hard ruts that could easily have knocked a connection loose.

Gunnar strode into the garage and shoved a folded newspaper in Leo's face. "You're a complete idiot. Do you know that?"

Leo unrolled the broadsheet. "*The Daily Beacon*? Never heard of it," he said, refolding the paper and shoving it back at his brother. "And for the record, I'm getting tired of everyone telling me I'm a fool." He riffled through the toolbox, looking for a screwdriver.

Gunnar grabbed the paper and swatted Leo's head. "Then stop acting like one."

"What'd you do that for?"

Gunnar stuck the newspaper under Leo's nose again, this time pointing to the large, bold typeface. "Did you even notice the headline *or* who wrote it?"

THE GROVER DISASTER
TRUE STORIES OF FAITH & HOPE IN THE WAKE OF TRAGEDY
BY HENRIETTA MAXWELL

Leo squinted. "Etta wrote this?" He rolled back on his heels. Pride swelled in his chest as he reread her byline. She'd done it. *Good for you, Etta.*

"That's not all, Leo," Gunnar said. "Look at the masthead."

"The what?"

"The masthead," Gunnar said. "I learned it from Etta. That's fancy newspaper talk for the top section of the paper."

His gaze swept to the top of the broadsheet.

EDITOR-IN-CHIEF, HENRIETTA MAXWELL

He handed the newspaper back to Gunnar. "Thanks for letting me know." He removed the hammer from the toolbox and continued rummaging. He glanced at his brother. "Do you know where the smaller flathead screwdriver is?"

Gunnar's eyebrows furrowed. "That's all you have to say?"

Leo shrugged. "What am I supposed to say?"

"You're as dense as they come, you know that?"

Leo removed a set of pliers and placed them on the floor beside the hammer. "Do you know where the screwdriver is or not?"

Gunnar went to the cabinet where the toolbox lived when not in use. "Did you look in here?" He opened a drawer and retrieved the missing screwdriver. "Here. Now for the love of Pete and all that's holy, focus on what I'm telling you."

"I appreciate your concern, Gunnar, I really do. I'm happy for Etta, but I don't know how this changes anything."

"Just hear me out, and I promise, if you don't change your mind, I'll drop it."

He locked eyes with his brother. "For good?"

"For good."

"All right. Then I need to see if I can get this boiler working."

Gunnar dragged two chairs into the wagon shed. "Take a seat. You're a slow learner."

"Thanks," Leo said, straddling the back of the chair.

Gunnar held up his index finger. "Etta came to the diner and apologized, didn't she?"

"Yeah."

He raised a second finger. "She took your advice and wrote a story about the Grover victims."

"I read the headlines." He massaged his temple. "C'mon, Gunnar, get to the point."

"Because you can influence her means she still cares about you. You need to go find her and tell her you love her."

"I can't do that. Accusing me of betraying her confidence cut deep. How could she think that of me? It's like she doesn't know me at all."

"Based on what she knew, it made sense."

"It made sense for her to ask me if I'd let it slip, not to jump to conclusions. Not to accuse me of wanting to blackmail her father."

"She made a mistake—a big one. We all do. But she demonstrated the courage to come and admit she was wrong and ask your forgiveness. That should count for something."

Gunnar was right, but how much should it count? He'd made his peace with her about her accusation, but it still burned. "I'm not holding a grudge, Gunnar. I'm just not sure my heart can take another betrayal like that. I'm not sure it's safe to let her back in my life again."

He swiped a lock of hair from his forehead. "Forgiveness doesn't always mean the restoration of relationships."

"True, but the thing is, Leo, you're not at peace. If you were, you wouldn't have given her the big heave-ho this morning."

"Yeah, that was uncalled for. I need to apologize for that."

Gunnar gripped his shoulder. "Trusting someone with your heart isn't easy. We men try to be tough and not let our emotions show, but we know heartache as deeply as any woman. We just try to muscle through it—ignore it so it won't hurt so badly."

The words resonated, slowly chipping away at the barriers he'd constructed to protect himself after Annika ended their relationship. The same ones he'd reinforced after Etta's accusation.

"I guess you have to figure out which is worse—risking your heart by allowing Etta back in, or the ache of loneliness you'll feel if you don't."

Gunnar not only hit the proverbial nail on the head, he'd hammered it clear through the thick board that was Leo's brain. His brother was absolutely right. Neither choice would guard his heart completely. But one choice did offer hope.

"Okay, you've convinced me."

"That's the spirit. Now what?"

"You got any money I can borrow?"

"Yeah." Gunnar narrowed his gaze. "Why?"

"I need to buy a ticket to that charity auction."

CHAPTER 32

Etta perused the tables where the items for auction were displayed, making sure a bid sheet and a fountain pen were positioned by each one. From the amounts written as preliminary offers, Boston's elite were certainly being generous tonight—just as she'd hoped.

She straightened a few items. Perfect. From the centerpieces to the lovely printed programs, Francie had outdone herself executing Etta's vision for the evening.

The Grand Hotel's ballroom glittered from the chandeliers to the jewelry trimming the necks of the prestigious women in attendance. Etta hadn't taken as much care with her appearance as she most likely should have, choosing to wear a gown from a prior year instead of purchasing a new one as Mother requested.

She'd been looking forward to tonight's event for so long, but now that the time had arrived, she wanted to be anywhere else.

"May I escort you around the ballroom, Miss Maxwell?" The Brockton Fire Department had selected the young fireman from Engine Co. 5, Sean O'Brien, to be her companion this evening. He was a cordial young man but seemed as out of place as a bear in the streets of Boston. Although Leo hadn't come from wealth, he'd managed to charm the entire room last year—including her.

"Thank you, Mr. O'Brien."

She glanced at Francie standing near the stage at the front of the room. When she saw Etta looking at her, she used her index fingers to push her lips up. Her way of telling Etta to paste a smile on her face and mingle.

She approached Maeve's table on Sean's arm, hoping to hide the lonely ache in her heart she feared would erupt into tears if she indulged it in any way.

"Etta, you look so beautiful," Maeve declared, rising to her feet and kissing one cheek then the other. "Something right off the cover of *The Gilded Gown*."

She could always count on Maeve to raise her spirits, even if she was exaggerating. Etta greeted Maeve's husband and parents.

She introduced Sean to the entire table. "This is our honorary fireman for tonight's auction, Sean O'Brien. He serves the city from Engine Company No. 5."

Sean's shoulders straightened. "Nice to meet you."

Maeve extended her gloved hand, expecting a kiss on her knuckles as was the custom among the Beacon Hill set, but Sean shook Maeve's hand so hard Etta thought the pins securing her friend's Gibson Girl coiffure would shake free.

"Thank you for coming." Etta made eye contact with each guest. "The Brockton Fire Department appreciates your support." She steered Sean to another table.

Thirty minutes later, Etta's cheeks ached from the perpetual phony smile plastered on her lips. One she was confident didn't reach her eyes. She believed wholeheartedly in the cause she raised money for this evening, but everywhere she looked reminded her of who was missing: Leo Eriksson.

"I've got my eye on those golf clubs, young lady. And I intend to win them," Mr. Worthington said.

"Best of luck to you, sir, and thank you for supporting the brave men of the Brockton Fire Department."

One of the *grandes dames* of Boston nudged her elbow as she passed. "Etta, dear. This is a lovely event. Your mother must be so proud."

"Thank you, Mrs. Carmichael. We appreciate your generous support." Mrs. Carmichael came from old money, but she'd welcomed the Maxwells into Boston society when the family moved to Beacon Hill.

Francie motioned for Etta and Sean to join her at the front of the ballroom near the dais. Sean bumped into one of the tables, spilling a glass of water. His face reddened. A server quickly sopped up the puddle, and Etta assured him all was well.

"It's time for you to make the announcement for the final silent bidding, Miss Maxwell," Francie said.

With Sean by her side, Etta stepped to the lectern. Someone tinked a fork against a water goblet, and the room grew silent.

"Ladies and gentlemen, welcome to the Spring Fling Charity Auction for the Brockton Fire Department. I'd like to introduce our honorary fireman for the evening, Sean O'Brien. Mr. O'Brien serves with Engine Company No. 5."

Applause filled the room.

Etta stepped aside so Sean could say a few words.

Francie handed him a megaphone then left the dais and walked to the rear of the ballroom.

Sean cleared his throat. "I'm not very good with words, but I just want to thank you for coming tonight. The Brockton Fire Department can't do the work that it does without your generous support. Each of you makes it possible for us to save lives and protect the property of the good citizens of this city. Thank you."

Applause again filled the room as Sean retreated behind Etta.

Etta retook her position at the podium. "Before we begin, I'd like to thank the many people who have worked behind the scenes to make this evening happen. While I may be the public face of this event, I can promise you it wouldn't have come together without the help of my assistant, Miss Frances Lehr." Etta motioned to Francie, who smiled and waved.

"Or the staff of the Grand Hotel."

She paused for another round of applause.

"As many of you know, I began supporting the Brockton Fire Department after my grandfather, Conrad Maxwell, fell through the ice and drowned in a pond near his home in Campello. It was then I learned that had the fire department been able to purchase the right equipment, their efforts to rescue him might have produced a different outcome for my grandfather. I also witnessed firsthand the bravery of these men and how they're willing to risk their lives for their fellow citizens. These are the reasons we're gathered here tonight."

She moistened her lips. "Without further ado, we'll continue with the auction. We have forty-five items up for bid this evening. Following my remarks, everyone will have fifteen additional minutes to finish making your preliminary bids. When we reconvene, Sean will present each item and announce the name and amount of the highest bidder. This will immediately be followed by a one-minute lightning round, where you are highly encouraged to outbid one another."

The audience laughed. "Remember," Etta continued, "you must call out loudly so your bid can be recorded. When time is called, the lady or gentleman with the highest bid will acquire the item. Miss Lehr will give you a slip of paper with your item and the amount of your winning bid. At the end of the evening, you will bring your slips to the cashiers at the rear of the room. Then see Mr. O'Brien and his fellow firefighters from Engine Company No. 5 to arrange—"

Etta paused midsentence. A man entered the rear of the ballroom, carrying something in his hand. What, she couldn't discern, but his build and hair color reminded her of— Her heart skipped a beat, or possibly ten. Was that Leo? She shoved her glasses higher on her nose and squinted. She couldn't be certain from this distance.

Focus, Etta. Why would Leo come to the auction?

"Miss Maxwell?" Sean asked, nudging her elbow. She turned her attention to the fireman. "You all right?"

"Yes, thank you."

She faced the patrons and mustered one more half-hearted smile. "As I was saying, Mr. O'Brien and his fellow firemen of Engine Company No. 1—"

Sean leaned close to her ear. "We're with Engine Company No. 5, miss," he whispered.

"My apologies." She looked over the guests, who were clearly confused by her lack of coherency.

"See Mr. O'Brien to make arrangements for your deliveries."

As attendees rose from their chairs to make their final bids, Etta slipped to the side of the room and avoided eye contact as much as possible, hoping to forestall any conversations that might delay her. She had to know for certain if Leo had come.

"Excuse me." She squeezed between two ladies bidding on a set of ivory hair combs and her heart sank.

The man she'd seen was gone.

Etta bit back the disappointment burning in her throat. Why had she allowed herself to hope?

Leo slipped into the hallway outside the grand ballroom and ducked around the corner. That had been much too close. Etta had noticed him standing near the exit all the way from the dais. She may be as blind as a bat without her glasses, but with them, she had eagle eyes.

Despite the close call, he'd managed to slip his note to Miss Lehr, and now he could only wait to see if Etta's assistant would agree to help him.

Thanks to Trude, he wore a freshly pressed suit. He even finagled a hair trim from his sister-in-law. With little time to prepare what he might say, he would rely on his heavenly Father to give him the words Etta needed to hear. Tonight, he would speak from the heart, whatever it might cost him.

He'd never pictured his father as a romantic, but he'd suggested Leo hire a musician to serenade them. Short on time, Leo asked Jens to make the arrangements.

He cupped his hands together, and his pulse ticked up a notch. He could hardly wait to see the look on Etta's face when he surprised her.

Leo rocked on his heels. Everything was coming together, but his plan ultimately hinged on Miss Lehr's cooperation.

The door from the ballroom swung open, and Miss Lehr entered the hallway.

"Nice to see you again, Mr. Eriksson."

"Same to you, Miss Lehr. Thank you for meeting with me."

"Your note said you wanted to enter a last-minute item into the auction." She shook her head. "I'm afraid that isn't possible, sir. Our patrons are concluding their preliminary bids as we speak."

"If you'll indulge me, Miss Lehr. I'll be the only one bidding on this item."

Her brows crinkled. "I'm afraid I don't understand. You want to supply an item and then be the only person to bid on it?"

"That's exactly what I want to do."

Etta dipped her spoon into the watermelon sorbet. Ever since she'd mistaken the man in the rear of the room for Leo, her mood had grown even more sour. She needed to rally her spirits, but the sorbet wasn't doing the trick.

In a few minutes Etta would return to the dais for the closing remarks. She'd persuaded Sean to assist Francie with the final round of verbal bids. So far, the pair were doing swimmingly without her.

"Why so glum, dear?" her mother asked. "Your event appears very successful. Were you hoping for more?"

Her mother was right. The evening was a triumph. Although she'd not been keeping an exact count, the tally in her head approximated they'd raised over one thousand dollars for the Brockton Fire Department. *Thank you, Father, for such wonderful provision. May it bless the lives of those who serve and those in the city whom they serve.*

"Item forty-five. A pair of tickets to *The Toreador* at the Bowdoin Square Theatre in Boston."

That was the last item on the docket and her signal to make her way to the dais to thank those in attendance for their generosity this evening. She wiped her mouth and excused herself from her parents' table.

Sean slammed the gavel. "Sold for thirteen dollars."

Etta climbed onto the dais. "Thank you, Sean. Francie. You did a wonderful job calling the auction."

She stepped behind the podium and addressed the patrons. "I cannot begin to express my gratitude as well as the gratitude of the men who serve in the Brockton Fire Department. Your generosity this evening has been outstanding."

She looked toward the cashiers in the rear of the ballroom. "We should have a final sum momentarily."

Francie handed Sean a piece of paper. Etta leaned closer to Francie. "I planned to read the total we raised tonight," she said to her assistant.

"It's not the total. We received a last-minute item for the auction."

"That's odd. How will that work if—"

"Just trust me," Francie said.

"One moment, ladies and gentlemen," Etta said. "We appear to have a last-minute item to bid on."

Sean skimmed the information on the bid sheet. His gaze flitted from Francie to Etta.

"Something wrong?" she whispered.

Francie stepped behind Sean. "It's all right, Mr. O'Brien. I've approved it."

Etta tugged on her bottom lip. What on earth was going on? The entire evening had run smoothly, and now a last-minute hiccup threatened to leave their guests with an unflattering image of the Maxwell Foundation. "May I see that, please?"

Francie looped her arm inside Etta's. "Just trust me," she repeated.

Flummoxed, and standing in front of a room filled with the wealthiest and most influential people in Boston, Etta smiled and nodded. Really, what choice did she have?

"Please proceed, Mr. O'Brien," Francie said.

Sean cleared his voice. "The final item for bid, number forty-six—a dance with Miss Henrietta Maxwell."

A collective gasp filled the room as multiple ladies covered their gaping mouths with white-gloved hands.

Etta stared at Francie. "Is this some kind of joke? I didn't authorize this."

Music drifting from the rear of the ballroom drew everyone's attention. A man with a violin slowly wound his way between tables until he reached the center of the room.

A man followed him. Her heart pounded. Leo?

He walked to the front of the dais, dropped to one knee, and extended his hand. "Henrietta Maxwell, I pledge all my worldly goods, my steadfast support, and my undying devotion if you pledge to dance with none other than me for the rest of our lives."

The room fell silent as all eyes shifted to Etta.

He'd come. Her pulse thundered in her ears. He'd come for *her*.

Leo remained on bended knee. "How about it, Miss Maxwell? Are you willing to accept my bid and dance with me now and as long as we both shall live?"

"In front of all these people?"

He waggled his hand. "I love you, Etta. And I don't want to live another day without you in my life."

What was she waiting for? The man she loved had come for her, and she didn't care if every *grande dame* in Boston approved or not. She left the podium and hurried down the stairs. She took his hand, and he stood.

"I love you too, Leo," she whispered. Tears cascaded down her cheeks. "I'm truly sorry I hurt you. I never should have doubted you."

Leo brushed her tears away then tapped his index finger against her lips. "All is forgiven. Now how about that dance?"

He nodded to the violinist and then swept her into his arms. His warm breath tickled her cheek as he softly serenaded her.

"In the shade of the old apple tree,
Where the love in your eyes I could see,
When the voice that I heard, like the song of the bird,
Seemed to whisper sweet music to me."

A deep abiding contentedness washed over Etta as she stared into his umber eyes. Loving Leo Eriksson was easy, but not as easy as being loved by him. There was no striving with Leo. No need to prove herself. He'd always loved her for who she was, even when she didn't know herself.

"So," he whispered, his soft breath tickling her ear. "Do you accept my bid, Miss Maxwell? Will you promise to dance with none but me?"

She did. And she would every day for the rest of their lives.

EPILOGUE

The Daily Beacon
Brockton, Massachusetts
Late Summer, 1907

Etta leaned over her desk, examining the copy she'd be submitting for next Sunday's edition of *The Daily Beacon*. Most likely her last piece for several months.

She examined her headline then made a tweak. She held the document up closer to the light.

GROVER DISASTER LEAVES SAFETY LEGACY
STATE LEGISLATURE ADOPTS STRICTEST STANDARDS IN NATION
BY HENRIETTA MAXWELL ERIKSSON

In response to the horrible explosion and fire at the R.B. Grover Shoe Factory over two years ago, and a similar disaster in Lynn, the Massachusetts State Assembly passed regulations for the use of steam boilers throughout the state. There was already talk of this bill becoming a model for similar legislation in every state in the union. She was proud that *The Daily Beacon* had been at the forefront of the movement to make factories safer for workers when other local papers had shown little interest.

Knuckles rapped on her office door. "The presses are ready to run," William said.

Etta rose and waddled to the print room. She angled her burgeoning belly sideways to scooch close to the large machines.

A little over two years had passed since the *Beacon* began operations, and she still hadn't tired of the thrum of the presses as they churned out copies of her weekly broadsheet. Although the paper had yet to meet her goal of a daily print run, their readership had grown steadily. For now, that was enough.

Leo slipped his hand into hers. "Is that a wrap?"

"That's a wrap," William said. "We can take it from here."

Etta chuckled. "Well, you know where to find me if you need anything."

Although she'd scheduled three months off following the birth of the newest member of the Eriksson family, which according to Dr. Tanner should be any day now, no one believed Etta would be too far removed from the daily operations of the paper. Especially since she, Leo, and the baby would be residing in the renovated apartment above the newspaper offices.

They lived solely off Leo's income from the fire department and any profits *The Daily Beacon* might generate, but that was okay with Etta. She was nothing if not practical. And she enjoyed the Eriksson family's new nickname for her, "The Thrifty Heiress."

Leo led her outside into the warm summer evening. "Do you know what my favorite three words in the English language are?"

"I have no idea."

"That's a wrap."

She grinned. "Why is that, Mr. Eriksson?"

He slipped his arms around her waist, or least what portion he could, and nuzzled his nose against her neck. "Because that means you've put your paper to bed, and you're all mine for the next few months."

Etta trailed her finger along Leo's cheek. She'd waited a long time to find a man who would not only love her but who'd encourage her to embrace the woman God created her to be, eccentricities and all.

Her pulse skittered at the gleam in his eyes. "What do you have planned for us this evening?"

"I thought we'd start with a little bit of this." His eyes gazed lovingly into hers as his nimble fingers unbuttoned her cuff and scooched the fabric above her elbow. His fingertips glided over her skin from the palm of her hand to the crease of her elbow. Gooseflesh rippled clear to her toes.

"Then add in a little bit of this," he whispered, kissing her jawline.

She closed her eyes, savoring each tender display of affection. "Then what?"

He removed her glasses and stuck them in his shirt pocket. "Then we'll finish the evening with a whole lot of this." He cupped her face in his palms, and his sultry kiss made her heart thrum as loud as any press machine in the print room. His lips softened, and he pulled her close.

"Thank you, Etta."

"For what?"

"For saving all your dances for me."

He tugged her closer. As they swayed together, his soft voice floated on the evening breeze.

"In the shade of the old apple tree,
Where the love in your eyes I could see,
When the voice that I heard, like the song of the bird,
Seemed to whisper sweet music to me."

A NOTE FROM THE AUTHOR

March 20, 2025, marked the 120th anniversary of the catastrophic steam-boiler explosion at the R. B. Grover & Company in Brockton, Massachusetts. At the time of the disaster, Brockton was home to more than ninety-one shoe manufacturing plants. These factories employed nearly ten thousand men, women, and children in 1905, earning Brockton the moniker "Shoe City."

While the disaster at the Grover plant is not widely known, I was first drawn to the calamity as the subject for my novel when I saw the side-by-side images of the massive factory before and after the explosion and subsequent fire—nothing remained but the smokestack. The image begged the question, how did anyone survive? (To view the image, visit https://www.pinterest.com/KellyGoshorn/the-undercover-heiress/)

Remarkably, of the 360 people estimated to be inside the building at the time of the explosion, as well as those in nearby homes and businesses, only 58 people perished. Truly a miracle, considering firefighters had only twelve minutes to assist those fleeing the wreckage before the fire spread too wide and the flames burned too hot, forcing the shift from a rescue operation to fire containment.

Located in the predominantly Swedish neighborhood of Campello, the factory produced the highly popular Emerson shoe, generally considered to be stylish and affordable. With business booming, Grover added a fourth floor to his large factory that covered half a city block on the corner of Main and Calmar Streets two years prior to the incident. At the time of the expansion, a new steam boiler was purchased to heat the factory and power the machinery.

However, on the day of the explosion, the older boiler was online while the newer one underwent routine maintenance following heavy use during the winter months. At 7:50 a.m., the boiler overheated, triggering a blast that thrust the massive tank through the roof and knocked out the factory's water tower, which collapsed onto the building. All four floors in the left rear corner of the plant pancaked, trapping employees.

Burning coals from the boiler soared over the factory, igniting severed gas lines. Flames feeding on wood flooring treated with linseed oil were fanned by the oxygen that flashed throughout the burning wreckage when the building's three hundred windows burst. Roughly ten minutes later, a second explosion occurred after a storage shed caught fire that housed a highly combustible solvent used in shoe polish.

In creating my fictional work surrounding these tragic events, I took a few small liberties with history. Located across the street from the Grover Factory, St. Margaret's church was a checkpoint where survivors could be accounted for. The church, however, was not a triage location as I portrayed in the story. Many of the small businesses and homeowners in the neighborhood, unaffected by the blast, opened their shops and residences to help the wounded.

I also moved the time of the city council meeting that declared Thursday, March 23 a city-wide day of mourning and established the Brockton Relief Fund from Tuesday evening to Tuesday afternoon to quicken the story's pace.

Although a handful of women worked in the newspaper industry by 1905, the majority of periodicals would only hire female reporters to write domestic columns. I would be remiss not to mention the accomplishments of Sallie Joy White, the first female staff writer for *The Boston Post* (1870). Sallie, along with five other women, formed the New England Women's Press Association in 1885 to enhance professionalism and further their careers in a male-dominated profession.

All scenes regarding the arson investigation were purely fictional. No such events occurred around the time of the Grover disaster, and arson was never considered as a possible cause of the factory fire. Nine days after the explosion, following a thorough inspection by the Hartford Steam Boiler Inspection and Insurance Company, Robbins Grover was cleared of any wrongdoing. The culprit was a crack in one of the boiler's riveted lap joints—something undetected in any of the boiler's routine maintenance inspections. Grover declared bankruptcy, and his remaining assets were distributed among his creditors. Despite financial ruin, Robbins Grover spent the remainder of his life raising money to aid the victims.

The Grover catastrophe remains the second-largest boiler disaster in American history, surpassed only by the explosion on the steamship *Sultana* in 1865, in which over one thousand returning Union soldiers were killed. In the aftermath of the horrific events in Brockton, and a similar tragedy in Lynn, Massachusetts, the following year, the state legislature passed An Act Relating to the Operation and Inspection of Steam Boilers in 1907. This legislation introduced the most stringent safety guidelines for the use of steam boilers in the nation and led to the passage of a national boiler safety code.

Recounted throughout this work are the stories of real people who put the welfare of others above their own. Among them is the priest from St. Margaret's who rushed into the burning factory and, in conjunction with other passersby, lifted heavy floor joists, freeing trapped workers, and then led them to safety. Father James O'Rourke returned to the inferno seven more times before receiving serious injuries himself. Workers from the nearby Churchill & Alden Shoe Company left their workstations and aided in the rescue of their fellow union members.

There is also the heroism of trapped employees. Most notably, George E. Smith, who, unable to free his pinned legs, selflessly worked to free three of his coworkers before he himself perished in the fire. Mr. Smith left behind a widow and three young daughters. The Smith children were three of the fifty-five dependents who lost a parent in the disaster. My fictional paper boy, Noah Desmond, does bear the surname of Timothy Desmond, who perished in the disaster, leaving a wife and four dependent children. It should also be noted here that Dora Clark, Ray Cole, Lilian Hurd, and Wallace Ambercrombie, all mentioned in the novel, were four of the fifty-eight souls lost that day.

Of all those who assisted in the rescue mission, none were more fearless than the men of the Campello fire station. Situated on the same block as the R. B. Grover factory, these firefighters were first on the scene. Without the benefit of modern firefighting respirators, these brave men charged into the flames and successfully guided dozens of disoriented and injured victims to safety. One firefighter, a man cited only by the name of Moore, dismantled an iron gate with nothing but an axe, saving three trapped employees from certain death. Fireman Moore's courage and dedication inspired my hero, Leo Eriksson.

The good residents of Brockton and the surrounding communities didn't forget the survivors or the families of those that perished. Within hours of the disaster, Mayor Keith received an unsolicited $1,000 donation from the United Shoe Machinery Company of Boston, to be directed toward aiding victims and their families. That gift would equal $35,864 today. Subscriptions to the fund came from shoe workers' unions both in and outside Massachusetts, shoe factory workers in Brockton and surrounding areas, and local newspapers, as well as individual donations from the citizens of Brockton. Even Mr. Andrew Carnegie, the Pittsburgh steel magnate known for his magnanimous philanthropy, donated $10,000. By the end, the Brockton Relief Fund distributed more than $105,000 in cash to aid the sufferers from the disaster and their dependents. Although that may seem like a pittance, its 2025 equivalent is a whopping $3,765,741—a true testament to the compassion and generosity of the donors.

Under the guidance of Mayor Keith and the city council, a citywide day of mourning occurred on March 23, 1905. Services were held throughout Brockton, followed by an extensive processional. Among the participants was the Liberty Band of Campello, playing a funeral dirge. A young boy preceded the band, carrying engineer David Rockwell's clarinet draped in black crepe. The cortege made its way through the packed streets of Brockton to Melrose Cemetery. Here the city would erect a memorial to those who died in the catastrophe, including all thirty-six unidentified dead who are interred in a circle at the foot of the monument.

The legacy of the Grover disaster was more than the adoption of stricter safety codes; it was the triumph of the human spirit, the countless acts of bravery, and the benevolence of strangers toward their neighbors. It's the story of a city that came together in great sorrow, despite class, religious, or political differences, to share in common grief, to heal their mutual wounds, and to provide for those in need of assistance.

"There was no creed, no color line, no hostility of capital and labor; the common strifes of men were forgotten, and all were brought closer together in the beautiful harmony of the universal brotherhood. Sorrow, the great leveler, the great arbiter, had done its work."
~*The Brockton Times,* March 24, 1905

Perhaps that is the greatest legacy of the Grover disaster: the choice of an entire community to focus on those things they shared in common rather than those things which divided them.

A lesson well-suited for today.

Thank you for reading Etta and Leo's story.

Blessings,
Kelly

ACKNOWLEDGMENTS

Only one name appears on the cover of a novel, but so many more people deserve recognition. For truly, without the names mentioned here, *The Undercover Heiress of Brockton* wouldn't have found its way to publication.

None more so than my heavenly Father, who graciously allows me to co-create with Him—a joy I never anticipated in this life.

To historical romance readers everywhere who stumble upon this novel. The gift of your time reading my story is a blessing I cannot repay. Thank you.

To my Darling sisters, C. Joy Allen, Debb Hackett, Lisa Kelley, Dani Pettrey, and Stephanne Smith, who were always willing to Zoom-write, troubleshoot, beta read, and brainstorm with me. Your prayers and encouragement helped get this project over the finish line. You are "my people," and I wouldn't want to be on this wild writing ride without any of you.

To Crystal Caudill, Tara Johnson, and Kimberly Duffy for reading and endorsing *The Undercover Heiress of Brockton*. Your support has blessed me beyond words.

Many thanks to my childhood friend, Francie Lehr Chiado, and to my first cousin once removed, Peggy Hartzell, for lending their names to two of my characters. I enjoyed spending time with you on the page.

Heartfelt gratitude to my friend and agent, Cynthia Ruchti, Books & Such Literary Agency, for your guidance and encouragement. I'm so thankful to have you in my corner. Your insights and suggestions are greatly appreciated.

My deepest gratitude to Rebecca Germany, Barbour Publishing, for acquiring this novel and for continuing to make my publishing dreams a reality. To Ellen Tarver, whose eagle eyes and keen insights have made Etta and Leo's story shine. I'm forever in your debt. And to all those at

Barbour who worked tirelessly to bring *The Undercover Heiress of Brockton* to print. I appreciate each of you.

And last but not least to my dear family, especially my husband and best friend, Mike, for always believing in me even when I don't believe in myself. Thank you for every grocery run, dog walk, and supper you made so that I could meet my deadline. I love you. And to my adult children, Madeline, Michael, and Noah, who tolerated me spending quite a bit of time at my computer over the Christmas holidays. And for their faithful response to every request to "feed the writer." I love you all so very much.

Kelly J. Goshorn weaves her affinity for history and her passion for God into uplifting stories of love, faith, and family set in nineteenth-century America. Her debut novel, *A Love Restored*, won the Director's Choice Award for Adult/YA fiction at the Blue Ridge Mountain Christian Writers Conference in 2019, and earned recognition as both a Selah Award finalist in the Historical Romance category and as a Maggie Award Finalist for Inspirational Fiction. When she is not writing, Kelly enjoys spending time with her young adult children, binge-watching BBC period dramas, board gaming with her husband, and spoiling her Welsh corgi, Biscuit.